HIGH PRAISE FOR MELANIE JACKSON!

"Melanie Jackson is an author to watch!"
—Compuserve Romance Reviews

TRAVELER

"Jackson often pushes the boundaries of paranormal romance, and this, the first of her Wildside series, is no exception."
—*Booklist*

"An exciting other world fantasy thriller."
—*Midwest Book Review*

THE SELKIE

"Part fantasy, part dream and wholly bewitching, *The Selkie* [blends] whimsy and folklore into a sensual tale of love and magic."
—*Romantic Times*

"A page-turning paranormal romance."
—*Booklist*

DOMINION

"An unusual romance for those with a yen for something different."
—*Romantic Times*

NIGHT VISITOR

"I recommend this as a very strong romance, with time travel, history and magic."
—*All About Romance*

AMARANTHA

"Intriguing . . . Ms. Jackson's descriptions of the Cornish countryside were downright seductive."
—*The Romance Reader*

MANON

"Melanie Jackson paints a well-defined picture of 18th-century England. . . . *Manon* is an intriguing and pleasant tale."
—*Romantic Times*

TWO HUNGRY FEYS

It would be prudent to take a little time to analyze this sudden attraction to this very unsuitable man. Falling for him was not something she could do. It was not something she knew how to do. She made a feeble attempt at pulling away, giving Roman a chance to come to his senses. "I'm hungry. And you must be starved. It's been hours since we've eaten."

"Ravenous," he agreed, but made no move toward the kitchen.

He smelled of shampoo, and Lyris found the scent comforting. But beneath was another perfume: the scent of naked flesh, of Roman himself. That smell was wild and did something other than comfort her. She brushed the ends of his hair with her fingers. It was thick and glossy and heavy.

"I wish I could wear you like aftershave," he murmured, showing that his thoughts were running parallel to her own—what few thoughts she was still having.

"Roman." It was a word that conjured, that was somehow vested with more longing than she intended. She wanted him. He wanted her. That desire was frightening.

Other books by Melanie Jackson:

OUTSIDERS
TRAVELER
THE SELKIE
DOMINION
BELLE
AMARANTHA
NIGHT VISITOR
MANON
IONA

THE COURIER

MELANIE JACKSON

LOVE SPELL

NEW YORK CITY

For everyone in WIH, but especially Christine Feehan and Douglas Clegg for knowing what to do with goblins.

LOVE SPELL®

March 2004

Published by

Dorchester Publishing Co., Inc.
200 Madison Avenue
New York, NY 10016

ISBN 0-505-52576-3

Printed in the United States of America.

The Courier

Prologue

Quede spent a lot of time in his conservatory. It quite pleasantly happened that an environment good for his orchids was also congenial to aging goblins. Especially since the greenhouse walls had been replaced with UV filters. It was a place where he could be alone—to think, to breed, to plan his botany lectures for the orchid society, to organize world takeovers.

He reached out with a delicate talon and caressed the luminescent flower before him. It would be the star attraction of the show. The family *Orchidaceae,* the epiphytic or terrestrial monocotyledonous, commonly called *dendrobium, phalaenopsis, oncidium,* or *catalaya,* were the oldest flowering plants in the world. There were twenty-five thousand species of orchids scattered across every continent on the globe. Many didn't even require soil to grow, but could suck what they needed right out of the air. Even with the world's forests being overrun by humans, they continued to evolve and flourish. Orchid hunters discovered an entirely new species at least once a decade, and new subspecies every year—why the hell couldn't his workers find just one?

Shaken by one of the sudden fits of anger that troubled him these days, Quede stepped back and stared broodingly at his collection. He had at least one of every species of orchid known to man, any and all illegal and endangered species included. But that wasn't enough anymore—not for personal satisfaction. His desire for discovery of a new orchid that would be named after him had reached the level of an addiction—of insanity, really.

Quede laughed once, an ugly metallic sound that no one liked to hear, not even Quede.

Turning away from the bank of luminescent *catalayas,* he began pacing the greenhouse aisles. It was strange, but sometimes he even forgot his original purpose in collecting orchids. That was dangerous. Especially now. But his chief rival—that braggart, Sir Harrington-Smythe—made it almost impossible for him to stay focused on any other plans.

No, it wasn't logical, but the need to be known as the best in the field would not be vanquished. And yet try as he might, spend what he might, Quede still couldn't find what he wanted. He'd sent his minions—hundreds of them—into every cloud forest left on the planet, but to no avail. The lutins in South America ended up shot by terrorists and drug dealers; the ones in the Philippines—an especially stupid lot from his earliest cloning efforts—had ended in the belly of an aggressive tiger.

The group in New Guinea, almost as dumb, had finished up in a cooking pot. They weren't actually eaten, of course. Or not much. Goblins didn't taste good to humans, but their heads were now small enough to fit on a doll's body. Quede kept them on the desk in his office, stacked in a fruit bowl, next to the blotter made of the skin of the other moron he had sent to find them. The stupid creature had brought back their shrunken heads, but not the orchids they'd gathered.

Was it worth it? Quede's human servant at the time had had the nerve to ask.

What a stupid question. Of course it was worth it. Orchids were clever, carnivorous, enduring. In a lot of ways they were like Quede himself. Or the way he used to be. They were sensual—not in any romantic way, but still appealing and extremely sexual. It was partially because their male and female reproductive organs were fused together.

And like Quede, orchids did not need the opposite sex to propagate.

They were sly, too, about drawing workers to labor for them. Foolish insects were lured into pseudocopulation with these glorious flowers, deceived by sight and scent into an act that served only the bloom—just like the foolish female lutins that were lured to Quede. Or the humans, too, for that matter.

But unlike females of either of those species, insects and flowers did not whine about betrayal. And Quede never had the urge to strangle them. Or bite them.

Well, perhaps he bit them a little. And the results had been interesting. It just went to prove that there was no such thing as the safe exchange of bodily fluids—at least, not with a vampire.

Quede turned abruptly and began pacing. The problem was, he was surrounded by unmotivated, unthinking idiots. But that was the nature of the beast he was breeding, and probably the lesser of evils in the long run.

All goblin colonies were run like insect hives. Of course, unlike in the realm of insects, goblins still had some individual personalities that sometimes led to unpredictable behavior. That was almost always inconvenient and had to be discouraged by hive masters. The smart, individualistic lutins were never good order-takers.

For Quede, the problem of inconvenient independence had been partially solved through genetic engineering. The new worker goblins he'd cloned were measurably more dronelike—and they were perfect carriers of *Goblinus vampirius*. Regrettably, however, they did not thrive or even function in situations that required spontaneous and original thought. Some were, in fact, too stupid to come in out of the sun. Or to find orchids.

Of course, circumstances that required these brighter characteristics were rare in a worker-goblin's life. They usually only arose when interacting with humans on the topside. Or hungry tigers.

Other goblin lords had chosen disparate ways of dealing with their subjects; terrorizing the masses, brainwashing, mind-control through magic, and highly addictive drugs had all been used with varying degrees of success. Quede had accidentally found a better way: the unholy union of vampirism and technology. Through the aid of a company he had invested in at the birth of the science of genetic engineering, he had arranged for the creation of a class of stupid goblin workers who were little more than vessels awaiting his instructions, and who were perfect for infecting with his virus. But perhaps it was a mistake to use them for everything. Maybe he needed another kind of goblin.

Quede turned the corner and began pacing up a new row of tables. His use of cloning was no secret among his subjects. They knew what they were. Well, sort of. The vampirism was still a surprise. None of them knew about that, at least not yet. His stupid clones had short life spans once infected, and they were just bright enough to perhaps care about that. He didn't need to deal with mass hysteria.

Of course, he also kept a few trusted servants of elevated intelligence whom he did not need to micromanage as they went about their daily tasks. They were made into fledglings, vampiric thralls. Quede found the system mostly satisfactory. These closest aides were thinking beings, but not independent. A master's control over his fledglings was nearly absolute if it needed to be, as long as those fledglings stayed physically close. Places such as Borneo were beyond Quede's reach. Once his thralls got over the horizon line, they started to regain their will, and then they usually did something stupid that got them killed.

Quede tried not to lose his caretaker servants too often. Finding and creating reliable minions was a painstaking process, because he couldn't simply bite them and handle it the old-fashioned way. They had to be mentally overshadowed; and then it took time to train them, to reshape their minds, and obliterate any traces of pesky independence or self-interested thought.

Of course, eventually they all grew beyond the fledgling stage even if they stayed near him. Then they tried exerting their will—or, worse, began to believe that because they still looked human they should also act human. Then they had to be gotten rid of. There was no retirement program for vampiric thralls. And no graduating to full vampires, though Quede never told them this. He didn't understand why—a curse was as good an explanation as any, he supposed—but nothing he bit reacted normally. They all mutated, and most died during the final change. It was annoying.

And now he had Schiem. Quede had been working on him for eighty years now and he was still not entirely what Quede wanted. The stupid, pathetic creature still mooned over his days as a silent film actor. There were days when his long face was so aggravating that Quede considered putting the final bite on him just because.

Quede stopped pacing and looked unhappily at a bank of wilted *catalayas* before him. Some of the workers had gotten confused again. They were supposed to tend to his miniature blood-orange trees by licking the fruit with their long tongues. Goblin saliva produced a strange phosphorus compound that sealed the miniature globes and made the delicate fruit resistant to both frost and insect pests. This was an excellent thing. For orange trees.

However, goblin saliva had the effect of napalm on orchids, and Quede's workers were forbidden to enter certain greenhouses—this one most particularly. Gimmel, the head gardener, was marginally brighter than the others and supposed to keep an eye out, but obviously he wasn't up to the task.

Sighing, Quede closed his eyes and sent a mental summons. Gimmel had just earned himself a trip to parasite-infested Borneo as a member of the next orchid-gathering team. It was bothersome losing his head gardener just now, but discipline had to be maintained and the idiot might as well do something potentially useful before he died.

Schiem would have to select another head gardener. Quede was too busy to waste any more time on such trivial, domestic matters. Let his melancholy servant deal with it—that's what thralls were for.

It just wasn't fair that good help was so hard to find. Not with what he paid to engineer it.

Chapter One

Lyris Damsel leaned closer to the screen and peered for the thousandth time at the piece of film that an anonymous source had somehow dropped into her private, security-screened e-mail. Everyone believed that the Zapruder tape was the only one that existed, and therefore was the only one to reference. Now, it looked like they were wrong. A much more detailed film of that day existed. A much, much more detailed film. It had been shot by someone—*an agent of H.U.G. or perhaps the F.B.I.?*—with what was then an experimental, heat-sensing camera. The deliverers of the film also had the ability to hide their electronic signature. Lyris's geek friend couldn't back-hack to the source and find out who had sent it to her. The movie had arrived without any server information.

With a sigh, Lyris clicked the mouse and ran the

digitized film again. She tried to ignore the auditory hallucination that had plagued her since she first watched, but in the back of her mind she could still hear the faint ticking of a clock—a stopwatch maybe—that seemed to be winding down toward some unforeseen disaster related to the Kennedy assassination.

Lyris focused on the screen. There was a lot of traffic outside of Love Field, but that was only to be expected when a president came to town. They hadn't been careful about crowd-control back then.

John Kennedy was in the second car of the motorcade with his wife, Jackie, and John and Nelly Connally. The heat patterns said that the driver was a goblin.

The film cut to a quick shot from a freeway overpass that showed the motorcade passing beneath, then switched to the limousine as it turned onto Elm off of Houston Street where the two very famous bullets changed history. The film showed clearly that the first hit the president in the shoulder. The second blew part of his head off. It was all just as the Zapruder tape suggested—except for one thing. That famous bit of standard film couldn't show that at least twenty goblins were standing in the crowd on Elm Street, watching intently as the president was assassinated.

Goblins in daylight? But how? This was presunscreen. Even with hats and sunglasses they would have been in agony.

The tape abruptly cut from the shooting of JFK to the day that Jack Ruby killed Lee Harvey Oswald. The heat signatures were interesting on that film, too. Ruby and Oswald were both glowing goblin green. And there was another green aura in the crowd as well, haloing the same lean face that had been in the throng lining Elm Street. It was—Lyris was certain—the infamous but seldom photographed Robert Schiem, retired silent film actor and now right-hand man to King Quede of New Orleans.

The film cut a third time. Lyris was now looking at a series of close-ups of Lyndon Johnson. In one clip taken from the presidential election campaign, Johnson's heat signature was the standard human blaze of orange. In another, taken after the assassination, he had turned a dark glowing green.

Lyris sat back.

The implication was clear. If this tape wasn't a hoax, then LBJ had been replaced sometime in the sixties. And that meant everyone had it all wrong. It wasn't Hoover or the Mafia who had taken out the president; it was the goblins.

Which raised all kinds of questions—like whether young Caitlin St. Barth, who had made many of the suspicious travel arrangements, was also involved. Or had she been yet another goblin victim? Unfortunately, there was no film to tell.

Lyris looked at her watch with bleary eyes. Two o'clock on . . . Saturday, right? It had to be the weekend. She could hear children outside. She should be out barbecuing or washing her car or shopping—whatever the hell it was people did on a fine fall weekend. Instead she was locked up in this dark bedroom, rehashing events from four decades ago, surrounded by an army of file cabinets and yellowing books with the shades down and the burglar alarm turned on.

She glanced at the drawn shades and wondered briefly if she was finally turning paranoid as well as obsessive. Suspicion was fine, if you domesticated it, used it as a tool to help keep you secure from danger. But experience had taught her that it was not safe to be prone to fears that could turn feral and overwhelm reason. Reason was Lyris's life jacket, her god. She couldn't afford to have her judgment impaired.

There was also the fact that thinking you were paranoid could make you paranoid.

"Damn. I can't worry about it right now," she muttered, and went back to thinking about her theory, testing it, tweaking it—realizing that she wasn't doing anything useful, that she was stuck in an infinite loop, like a computer program with a logic error.

She had a great hypothesis, tons of circumstantial evidence—enough for a crackpot conspiracy-of-the-week TV special probably. But that wasn't enough. She had to break the logic glitch. She needed something concrete she could take to her former editor. Doug needed to see that she wasn't off her rocker.

Then maybe she could take her theory to the police. She needed some building blocks for her case that were more solid than this supposition . . . and she wasn't going to get an exhumation order over the protests of LBJ's heirs to uncover his remains in his grave and test them for goblin DNA.

Tick, tick, tick.

All that was left was proving the other end of her theory. Everyone agreed that Quede of New Orleans had to be a goblin. After all, whatever he looked like these days—and though there were no photos, the rumors of his beauty were rampant—he was still that city's king. She needed to prove he was also a vampire. The theory of a vampire goblin king of the Big Easy sounded far-fetched when said aloud, but it worked so well with the evidence she had collected.

King Quede came from a long line of powerful goblins, but his longevity had surpassed by a century any of his ancestors, even Gofimbel, the founder of his line who had been known for drinking the dragon blood that was a sort of goblin fountain of youth. Quede also seemed to possess a certain gravitas—seriousness and focus—that was very ungoblinlike.

Most of the green humanoids had no self-discipline and relied on brute strength or sneakiness to take them to the top. But the 411 among those few willing to talk about the goblin king was that he was prepared to be ruthless about business, but only when necessary. He didn't glory in bloodshed the way some other goblin kings and queens had. His games were more mental. He liked psychological torture. And so expert was he at it that he didn't need troll enforcers to police his city. Nor had he gated New Orleans the way other goblin warlords had gated their cities. The lack of walls around the Big Easy was a tremendous show of power. Or arrogance. Probably both. That was definitely more of a vampire than a goblin trait: rule through terror.

It was also said that Quede used some super kind of mind control to direct his empire. The kind of mind control that could order goblins—lots of them—out into the sun at eleven A.M. on a sunny day; the kind that would make one of them remain passive and silent even during arrest and questioning about a presidential assassination when he surely knew that he was going to die. The only creature Lyris had ever heard of who could do something similar was a master vampire. . . .

It fit, *damn it!* She was 99 percent sure that she was right. Quede had to be a bloodsucker. Everyone said that all the vampires were dead—wiped out like the pure-blooded feys at the time of the Great Drought. But maybe they were wrong. Fey crossbreeds had survived—why not vampire crosses?

Lyris pushed back from her desk and began to pace the small space near the smaller table. A sense of urgency was growing in her, filling up her head with imagined ticking.

So, what next? Should she actually go to New Orleans? It made sense. That was where Kennedy's aide, Caitlin St. Barth, had disappeared after she began *dating* King Quede. Maybe there was something else to be learned from the angle even after all these years. No one else had ever really examined the situation, and Lyris had certain skills—gifts—that she could use to determine the truth.

Also, since Quede didn't travel, it was plain that she would have to take the mountain to Mohammed if she wanted to see him—and she thought she did, at least from a distance. How bad could it be? She only needed to see him for a moment and then she'd know. That was her gift: the ability to see someone and *know* them, see what they truly were. One glimpse of the king and she'd have her answers. Probably. She'd never met a vampire before, but she was fairly certain her power would work on one.

The question was how to approach him. Feys weren't welcome in New Orleans. And one didn't exactly telephone for an appointment with a king of goblins. Lyris would need to get into his city, attract Quede's attention and bring him to her some place public. The king was known to have two interests: exotic women and even more exotic orchids. Fortunately, Lyris knew all about one and could learn about the other if she needed.

It wouldn't be easy, though—or safe. She needed to interest Quede enough to get a meeting, but not to arouse his ire. Or his lust. Or betray the fact that she was part sylph. There were some truly nasty stories about his treatment of unwilling—and even willing—lovers. Especially among the fey. According to one of the few faeries who had escaped to talk about him—*once, and the fey had died shortly thereafter*—there wasn't a black deep enough to dye Quede in.

Lyris caught a glimpse of her reflection in the monitor: a triangular face, raptorlike eyes the green of polar ice, a lean body. And then there was her back—though the fused wings didn't show when she had clothes on. Of course, all she needed was a backless dress and then she'd have all the attention she wanted and then some. Oh, yes, she was plenty exotic.

Unhappy with that thought, Lyris spun away from her reflection and resumed pacing, trying to outrun the frantic ticking in her head.

Damn. It blew her mind. The goblins had killed Kennedy! This was important. It would change history. And she had been chosen as the courier to carry this news. But if she pursued it, would it be the story of her lifetime or the end of it?

"Paranoia," she muttered. But was it?

At first, her successful investigation had seemed the result of a string of happy coincidences rather than a sequence of orchestrated events and discoveries. If anyone asked, she would have said that if anything was guiding her, it was fate. But she was taking another look now, and it didn't seem to be fate's fingerprints that were all over her investigation. Someone clearly wanted her to find out about Quede—and to find out about him now. And that someone preferred to remain in the shadows, a puppet-master. Which just begged her to be suspicious.

What should she do? Take fate's—or whoever else's—dangerous dare? Or should she just forget the whole thing? She could do that, couldn't she—just let this cup pass her by? There was no law that said she had to put herself in danger, no higher power that she had to answer to if she chose to let this sleeping bloodsucker lie. So what if she had chased this story for years? Maybe it was time to let go, to stop brooding and start barbecuing.

Lyris looked back at her computer. The screen glowed an eerie green, accusing her, taunting her. *Tick, tick, tick.*

No—damn, damn, damn! She couldn't let it go. At times there was nothing to do except take the next step. And if you survived that one, you got to take another. As the saying went: Sometimes the only way *out* is *through*. Lyris was going to New Orleans.

But she wasn't dumb. She'd arrange for some insurance first. Time to call on the man with the answers and the useful friends in even more useful places. After all, this film was likely his challenge.

Lyris picked up the phone and punched in an unlisted number for the answering service of the mercenary goblin-hunter, Jack Frost.

Chapter Two

Roman looked impatiently into the hazy floodlights and figured, not for the first time, that he was probably short a few marbles. Certainly, his exasperated mother had insisted he was missing those aggies. But then his mother maintained that he favored his father—an irresponsible, heartless horse's ass. In other words, a pooka.

Roman really couldn't argue with her, because for many years it had been true—though he felt he had come a long ways in the days since his parents' deaths and shouldn't be judged so harshly when they appeared in his dreams. For instance, he used to have a hard time with those black-and-white moral choices his mother was always throwing at him as pop quizzes over meals. He had wanted to please her, but was innately honest. He also wasn't one for embracing categorical imperatives—especially if they were inconvenient and required a great deal of thought. And often when it *was* convenient enough to consider an idea, he'd look an issue right in the eye and find out that it was gray and fuzzy instead of clearly delineated the way his mother claimed.

It wasn't that he didn't want to be on the side of the angels; he just didn't know where the angels were most of the time. Often, what he found in the details were devils and more devils.

Of course, that was probably because he didn't really care about the *moral* issues that excited everyone else in his small Texas community. Or he hadn't, until the goblins. Until Quede. The goblin king of New Orleans was one barb that he couldn't pull out of hide.

His visit to New Orleans hadn't started as a holy pilgrimage or self-salvation. It was supposed to be a simple reconnaissance trip, a favor for a friend who was in a tough spot and needed a reliable set of eyes and ears to look into a couple of financial things. He was just going to do a quick taste test of the new and improved Big Easy, lift the Quede-produced urban entrée up out of its bed of freshly laundered greenbacks, and see how rotten its monetary underbelly was. He'd listen to a little zydeco, eat some gumbo, and then report back to Jack about the state of the unholy goblin union on the mighty Mississippi. It was a vacation really, a time to kick back and unwind after his stay in New York arranging for financing of a new off-Broadway musical.

And, oddly enough, this was the moment when he'd finally got his moral twenty-twenty vision. It was like the old saying went: There were no atheists in foxholes. And if there ever was a foxhole in a war zone, this town was it.

The other tourists didn't seem to sense it, but Roman knew from the moment he climbed out of Baby, his ancient Jag, that he was in some sort of spiritual battle zone. Instead of feeling wooed by temptation in the rich, magnolia-scented air, he felt watched by excited yet hostile eyes. The thing about having nearly always been on the wrong side of an issue was that you got good at knowing when you were being watched—and a wise man knew to pay attention when the hair on his nape started to rise.

So, rather than give in to the pleasures that he sensed were supposed to help tourists ripen for some sort of seduction, Roman found himself buckling up a figurative chastity belt and in other ways girding himself for battle with the unknown. It was a tectonic shift in attitude, a karmic kick to the head.

He'd e-mailed Jack on his second day there to tell him about his decision to stay in New Orleans and keep an eye on things instead of heading out to Cadalach—and the smug bastard hadn't even had the grace to pretend to be surprised. The death fey had suggested that Roman take his love of dancing and put it to use in a strip bar, because the tips were good and the gossip even better.

Roman had thought about suggesting Jack do something he was fairly certain was anatomically impossible, even for a death fey, but decided instead to surprise Jack and take the suggestion seriously. There *were* lots and lots of deals being made in the strip joints and bars. The next night, he applied for a work permit.

So that was how Roman Hautecoeur, theater financier, had become Romeo Hart, the stripper, resident pooka party boy of New Orleans's Quarter. And from that day onward he had been looking for a classic Sherlock Holmesian dog-in-the-night sort of lead, something that would scream Colonel Mustard with the candlestick in the library. But so far, he'd found nothing useful. The money laundering was complete, and everything was so clean it squeaked. Quede's wealth seemingly came from a financial version of the Immaculate Conception.

Roman didn't believe a column or row of it. And he had started to dream. He sometimes had a nightmare of his soul being trapped outside the city. The poor naked thing had been dissevered from his body and was out there, waiting for his return to the normal world. His dream self worried, if he died, whether his soul would know to move on. Or would it stay there forever, awaiting his reclamation until the final trumpet?

Roman pushed the thought away and faced the

audience he couldn't see that well—though he could certainly hear them—and began to grind to the music. Dancing at the Easy Off was kind of like being inside a tacky jukebox: It was bright, loud, and short on soothing, tasteful music. It also had strange magical acoustics that brought on a group phenomenon that the owners called a dry drunk, a state where no alcohol needed to be consumed, but where audience judgment became rather fuzzy and they felt a little high.

The other two performers who shared the stage were more or less with Roman on the routine. Quaalude, a former junkie who spent his pre-Quede-employment days with a spoon up his nose, was a little ahead of the music and, as usual, was more lewd than 'lude. Alcohol always made him sleazy, and he was double jointed. He'd taken to shaving his genitalia and painting himself with bright red lip gloss—the eight-hour no-smudge type—and then stuffing himself into fishnet stockings. Roman found the look vaguely alarming and wholly disgusting, but Quaalude insisted that he was starting a fashion trend. And the crowd did love him, of course. It was that sort of place.

The dancer on Roman's right was called Viagra. She had started out in the *Apocalicks Now* dance review, but had been chosen for solo work because of her "*assets*." She was a nice enough woman, but she looked like she had fallen out of the pages of one of the cheaper porn mags. Not that the audience minded her slutty packaging. They came to the Easy Off because they wanted to see physically "*gifted*" performers in breast- or ass-centric costumes strip down to their seventy-one-inch bionic boobs—or other supernatural features.

In Roman's, a.k.a Romeo Hart's, case, they came for his rather elongated body. He had elongated everything, thanks to a pooka ancestor who'd been half water horse. He had something else, too—another gift from his sire: While not being particularly immoral himself, something about him inspired the impulse for immorality in others. The management at the club found this both convenient and amusing, and had signed him on even though he was fey.

Roman had once been amused by his talent, too, but these days he found it made him feel like he was constantly playing a bit role in a poorly written, puerile sex comedy for animal fetishists. And somehow, he didn't think his act would make his mother proud, though surely she couldn't have argued with his reasons for being in New Orleans. She had detested the goblins.

Of course, he'd been stripping for a lot longer than he intended. It almost felt normal now. He'd honestly meant to be in and out of New Orleans in the space of a couple of weeks, a month at the most. But the floodlights weren't the only things that were blinding in this town. It was hard to see what was really going on, because everywhere he went he was surrounded by a jungle of greenbacks—and euros and yen too. And the closer Roman got to Quede, the denser the green became. All that money being planted around the city guaranteed that the king was seen as a public benefactor. Yeah, the goblin Good King Quede. Which meant the general public protected him with mindless loyalty.

It was bloody hard to argue against the creature, too, because unlike other goblin metropolises like Sin City or Detroit, new New Orleans was clean, crime-free, EPA-compliant, and FDA-approved. There were no troll thugs eating tourists, no goblin fruit pushers making addicts of teenagers, no experimental drugs being piped through the ventilation systems of the hotels. Quede even made regular contributions to the American Civil Liberties Union. There were no racial problems anymore. There weren't even any rapists or serial killers on the loose—or if there were, the stories never made it into the papers. Hell, even the strippers in the Quarter were drug-free. Quede's kingdom was open twenty-four/seven for inspection by anyone, because it was the safest place on earth. They even said that in their tourist brochures—*the Safest Place on Earth!*

Yet it was also evil, an utter abomination. It didn't matter how clean the city looked on the surface; the place was rotten. Roman felt it in the marrow of his elongated bones and knew it in the depths of his mind. His id was screaming that he should tell someone about what he sensed, or do something to stop Quede before it was too late.

But too late for what? Roman knew that he and Jack couldn't push the matter with the "authorities"—assuming that was what Jack wanted to do with any information they got. No, they couldn't go to the government. Well, not without rock-solid proof. And proof was hard to come by without taking huge risks. And considering taking those risks, Roman had learned you can only ask so much of your guardian angel—and his had been working overtime since his birth. He knew better than to request she work triple-time watching his naked, dancing butt as he tried to take on this goblin king single-handedly.

A younger Roman would have walked away from the frustration of this task, but he had discovered a new, inconvenient, and unpleasant sense of responsibility lurking at his core. His life before this had always been low-drag. He moved around without disturbing the environment, breezing through everything like a well-designed airfoil. He had ruthlessly pared down his relationships and responsibilities to those that demanded nothing of him spiritually and supplied him with no emotional baggage. But those carefree days were over—at least for now. He was committed to finding out the truth about Quede however long it took.

And his patience was about to be rewarded. Maybe. It seemed that he might finally have a chance to get something concrete that he and Jack could use on Quede. Jack had e-mailed him with some strange news. A reporter—a conspiracy theorist with some idea about Quede knowing who bumped off Kennedy—was in town and coming to the club tonight. Roman didn't see how she was going to help—or how he could assist her—but he was willing to give it a go, if it would in any way upset Quede. Too bad that just naming the king in the crackpot press wouldn't do lasting harm. Brief public concern—and maybe a governmental investigation—seemed an insufficiently unpleasant fate for the goblin who had cleaned up New Orleans.

Unless the investigation involved the IRS, of course. Roman would just have to hope that this investigator could prove that Quede had been evading taxes.

Roman felt something shift in the atmosphere of the club—someone female had entered and her presence sent a shiver down his spine. He squinted into the lights . . . Ah! He had her now. For just a moment she was caught in a passing beam of white light and seemed something not of the earth, a creature of heaven that came from no mortal place or time. People near her turned their heads and stared, probably thinking that they had never seen such a woman—and they probably hadn't. Certainly, Roman hadn't. She was one of a kind.

Then she stepped out of the light, lowered her eyes, and returned to being just a woman.

But still a damn fine one. Jack had described her well enough, but left out a few important parts. Like the fact that though she wasn't any bigger than a minute, and as Roman's granddaddy used to say, she was the best-looking minute he'd ever seen. What a shape! Of course, she probably kept her contours by avoiding the high-calorie potables and edibles in places like the Easy Off. And that was a shame because Roman loved to eat and liked women who shared his appetites. Ah, well, he'd forgive her as long as she didn't try to make him eat a Lean Cuisine diet with her.

Roman wound up his lasso and began to dance her way. Jack had called her a little buttoned up, kind of prim and proper. But she couldn't be all that orthodox and afraid of originality or she wouldn't be in New Orleans. And teasing her into letting her guard down might be fun. It was best to find out now if she had a sense of humor. He wouldn't stand a prayer's chance of working with a real Marion-the-librarian type.

Suddenly, as though feeling his scrutiny, the woman looked up at him—and then *into* him. Her bright gaze locked on Roman like some tracking device and then went right through the skin and down to the bone. And when she didn't find what she wanted there among his kidneys and pancreas, she started looking for his thoughts and soul, fine-combing his nerve endings as she went.

Roman shivered—half in pleasure, half in alarm—

and shut her out immediately, not caring if his ejection was rude. *Magic.* She had some kind of mojo that she could turn on at will. Jack hadn't mentioned it, either.

Roman didn't like spooky women—witch, faerie, psychic, or angel. Those kinds were nothin' but trouble. He knew because he was one and had had a mother who was neither an angel, nor a psychic, nor a fey. It didn't matter how pretty they were, something about them provoked a defensive antagonism in him.

But . . . look at the way she moved! Like a gazelle. That wasn't a human walk—that was sin on the hoof, a sauntering mantrap. Who would even try to resist her? There ought to be a law!

Roman blinked and ordered his body to stand down from red alert status while he thought things through. He didn't think of himself as being predatory, but he certainly felt like jumping this girl's delicate bones and finding out what she was really made of. Marion the librarian? *Ha!* Yep, she was pretty as peaches piled high with whipped cream—petite, delicate, temptation in heels—just exactly what he liked in a woman. She probably sensed it, too, since he hadn't been hiding anything when she turned those scary peepers on him.

But, damn!

Well, he just had to be sensible and forget those long legs and think about those X-ray eyes! They were the kind that could always spot the black and white through the fuzzy gray. They could sober up an amorous man faster than a right cross to the chops, or a bath in snowmelt. They were dire news for his kind. Eventually, a guy started feeling resentful that he had no secrets. Before the poor schmuck knew it, he found himself going around on tippytoes trying to gain never-to-be-had female approval.

Frowning, and feeling oddly cheated, he looked at the woman again. *Still lovely*. Too bad, but he just couldn't fall for her. Couldn't allow her to get close at all. It just wouldn't do. That way lay misery and madness.

Beautiful, though. Just perfect. Damn.

Of course, though he'd never get really close to the little witch, it didn't mean that he couldn't have a little fun with her from a distance. If he was reasonably cautious, he added encouragingly when his wiser self protested.

Distracted and annoyed by the young waiter leaning over to look down *his* girl's blouse as she was seated at the table, Roman completely forgot that he didn't actually know how to be cautious around women and rushed like a moth toward the flame. Renewing his hip tosses, he began working his way toward her.

Chapter Three

The Easy Off was the sort of joint you'd find only in the third circle of Jazz Hell. Or in the old Bourbon Street. In the *new* New Orleans, it seemed a little anachronistic and contrived—and sleazy. Pretty much everything else in town was so clean it squeaked.

The atmosphere was authentic dive, though, and the oxygen could have stood some refreshing—a lot of refreshing. The music was far too loud, the decor painfully garish and soul-eroding, and everything that a strip joint ought to be. All in all, it wasn't Lyris's usual home away from home. Still, this story had taken her to many places just as sordid. In fact, a lot more sordid. She could endure it for a while. Lyris was growing inured to such things. Anyway, it blotted out the sound of the stopwatch in her head. For that alone, she would endure it for a time.

Her mercenary friend, Jack Frost, had been especially helpful about getting material on Quede and feeding it to her at regular intervals. Unfortunately, that info nearly always took her to unpleasant places. She wasn't anxious for anyone to know what she was doing in New Orleans, but she trusted Jack; if he said this Romeo Hart could help her, she'd give the guy the benefit of the doubt—whatever his profession.

The Easy Off shill gave his rehearsed spiel and the spotlights came up. Out walked three very unusual people who began dancing more or less in time with the music. Lyris watched them carefully from the back of the club.

The woman she dismissed immediately, obviously being of the wrong gender, but it took a moment to decide which of the men was Romeo Hart. She figured it out when he started throwing winks and kisses—and the occasional groin toss—her way. Only a being with inhumanly keen eyes could have seen her through the gloom.

Going along with their agreed cover of a casual pickup, she tried to answer with winks and smiles, but elected to remain a safe distance away from the stage—even when the other women began screaming and throwing their undies at the platform and calling out lewd suggestions. Lyris was pretty sure that Romeo's groin tosses were a lot more polished than her own might be, and she didn't see any need to embarrass herself with childish competition. Or to put herself in the way of flying panties.

A waiter came to seat her. A quick look into his mind showed that he was no threat. Not wanting to be too obvious about her keen eyesight, she allowed him to lead her by the arm to a nearby table, dutifully ordered a beer, all the while trying for full eye contact with Mr. Hart. She didn't get much of it. He seemed to be avoiding her gaze.

The dance number went on far too long, but Lyris remained outwardly patient and smiling. This life undercover didn't suit her innate honesty. Still, she was learning. She had known before coming that she would be in New Orleans for nefarious purposes, but she still felt guilty and uncomfortable deceiving people about both her species and the purpose of her visit. And she was deceiving everyone—from her former editor and onetime lover, to the nice goblin taking her visa info, to the helpful lutin bellman at the hotel. They'd all been lied to and not just by omission. Her usual crusading style was to name the devil and shame him. She didn't like lying. But truth wasn't even an option in new New Orleans.

Worse, there was something extra sinister in the air tonight. She'd had to give herself a pep talk before venturing out to meet up with Romeo Hart. She felt observed. Her impulse was to skulk in the shadows and spy anonymously, using her natural abilities to avoid human sight. Only the thought of what kind of attention that might bring from Quede's spies had kept Lyris from actually trying it. Acting guilty, or displaying any fey traits, was a sure way to get caught. She was deep down in the heart of Quede country now—so deep she might fall right out the bottom and disappear if she wasn't real careful.

Romeo's dance finally came to an end with him showing off: dropping his lasso over Lyris's head and then whipping it right back off again without the rope ever actually touching her. Lyris forced a broad smile of welcome as he sauntered down off the stage and strolled to her table. He dropped his hat almost on top of her beer, pulled out a chair, spun it about, and thrust it between his legs before sitting. Lyris concluded that any man who could do that wearing chaps and little else was really *not* self-conscious about his anatomical differences. Still, she kept her eyes firmly on his face.

"Howdy, cowboy." She knew she sounded stiff and tried to relax the tightness in her throat. It was a problem she'd been having all day. Her lungs were reluctant to breathe in the goblin-tainted air.

"I'm Romeo Hart." He leaned closer to her, invading her space with his eerie gold eyes and the musky smell of his perspiration. He added in a soft voice that had slight shadings of Texas: "I'm also Roman Hautecoeur. Jack told me you were coming."

Something warm and invisible brushed over her

skin, making her nerves spark. She nodded. "I'm Lyris Damsel," she responded reluctantly.

"No way." He grinned at her. His smile flashed like Jack hopping out of his musical box, and was just as startling in such close quarters. "So, when you get into trouble, I'll have a chance to rescue a real Damsel in distress?"

"Ha, ha. I've heard it before, so spare me, okay? Anyway, I'm not going to need rescuing. I'm just doing research. It's perfectly safe." Lyris pulled back a little, hoping distance would calm her nerves, but no such luck. The invisible something in the air continued to stroke her. She tried to glare, but it wasn't easy. She could almost hear "Pop Goes the Weasel" plinking away behind Roman's shiny teeth and it made her want to smile and relax. And at least he hadn't made any jokes about damselflies. Given the markings on her back, she found those even less amusing.

"Uh-huh. Research. I hear you're in town because you have a thing for *the king*." Roman leaned even closer, pressing lips to her ear so they wouldn't be overheard. His whispers made her shiver. "I've kind of got a hard-on for the big man myself."

Lyris felt herself color and made an effort not to see if he meant it literally. With a pooka, you never knew. And she was fairly certain now that this man really was one of those mischievous animal spirits—probably a river horse.

"Should we be talking about this here?" she

asked, turning her head so that her lips were against his right earlobe and her voice would not carry.

Roman turned his head back to Lyris's ear. It was almost like doing a seated tango. "Sure, as long as we keep it to sweet nothings. There are lip readers around sometimes, but I don't see anyone from Quede's organization tonight. Yet."

"Lip readers?" Lyris asked, startled.

"Sure, too much noise for bugs, and Quede likes to keep on top of things. No fan of laissez-faire management is our goblin king."

"Oh . . . so, you actually know something personal about—*the king?*"

"Bits and pieces, his routines, the general gossip . . . but not any of his really dark secrets. Those got buried long ago. Buried in graves so deep God Himself couldn't dig them up—or so I'm told."

"But you know where those graves are?" She closed her eyes, trying to shut out the strobes that had suddenly begun throbbing onstage. They made her feel dizzy. Or something did. Maybe it was Roman himself. She could only soak up so much degenerate atmosphere and then she started feeling like her brain was getting soggy. That wasn't something she could afford to let happen.

"Maybe I do. You know what's in them?" he asked back.

"Maybe."

"And you think you're going to dig something up. Did you come armed with some protective juju for raising the dead? 'Cause I promise you, anything Quede's buried is going to have some bad stuff around it," Roman added. He ran a hand over his arm, and she noticed the fine hairs there were raised in a mild case of gooseflesh. She looked at her own arms. They were much the same. There was definitely something in the air between them.

"No," Lyris answered seriously, raising her voice slightly. Another dance team had taken the stage and the music was rising in a frenetic tide. "Jack seemed to think that you were guardian enough for this venture. Will I need something more?"

"Probably not—as long as you stay close." The man shifted in his seat, and the muscles in his body rippled. Again his fine, animal scent washed over her. Lyris found it distracting.

"So, you . . . have some magic?" she asked. She wasn't sure if she wanted an answer to the question, or if she would believe his answer anyway. Humans lied all the time about having magical gifts. And feys lied about not having them. Obviously Roman wasn't all human, but it remained to be seen if he was truly part fey. He didn't have to be pooka. Or only pooka. He might be modified troll or goblin. These days, it was hard to tell without a thermal scan. Some of those creatures came with a sort of inborn power that had nothing to do with learned spells.

Without thinking, she spoke aloud, her eyes assessing him from head to toe. "You certainly don't look human. You are too long. You look like someone grabbed you at both ends and stretched you. You *must* be part fey—pooka, at a guess." She didn't add: or troll. She really didn't want him to be part troll. He was too attractive. "I'm amazed you got a work visa."

"Stretched? Why, thank you. I try to live up to my billing as the longest thing in the West," Roman answered, eyebrows ascending. "But I can't help feeling that a truly good girl would not admit to noticing something like that. Your mother would be shocked to know you've been checking me out. But then, maybe I read you wrong. Maybe you aren't a good girl after all." He flicked a finger at the top button of her blouse. It had come undone.

Lyris was annoyed when she felt herself blush. "That wasn't what I meant! Though, given your attire—"

"*What* wasn't what you meant?" he teased, clearly at home with his odd body and highly amused by her reaction. She should have been annoyed, but he seemed without malice.

And maybe he couldn't help it, if he was a pooka. They were notorious for being both mischievous and oversexed. They were what they were. There was no avoiding it. The thought relaxed her slightly.

"Can you really be a pooka?" Lyris asked curiously. "I've never met one. I didn't know any were left."

"Well, isn't it sweet of you to ask! Most girls just

take a look and draw their own conclusions." His eyes danced, the gold irises glittering. "Ask nice, and I might give you a ride during the next full moon. That would end all your doubts."

Lyris had a ridiculously strong urge to smile, but she suppressed it firmly. It wouldn't do to encourage him. She knew from experience that sexual banter got tiring after a while, and it made one careless.

Lyris gathered her straying thoughts, making a note to have a few words with Jack about sending her to meet this creature without warning about his natural charm. She'd never encountered anything this potent.

"So, about your *magical* gifts?" she asked firmly.

"Well, there is more to me than meets the eye. Of course, being an animal fey, I've never really mastered my inborn magic the way others might. I have, however, learned to maneuver it a little." He grinned at her again, and again Lyris had an urge to smile back. Probably it was some sort of fey charisma she hadn't encountered before. Maybe all pookas had it. Something about pookas lured women into trouble.

"How do you mean?" She did not mention what she thought of his *maneuvers*. Those *gifts,* she assured herself, were of no interest to her. She was a woman on a mission, trying hard to be omniscient about the past, if not the future.

"Well, for instance, I can use other people's latent psychokinetic abilities. Watch!" He leaned back and raised his voice slightly. "Everyone who believes in goblin mind control, raise my right hand."

Lyris glared at him as his right hand floated into the air as though pulled by invisible strings. She leaned into Roman's space and said a bit sharply: "You may laugh, but I know that other goblin hives have been using mind control on human visitors. And Quede has, too—I'm sure of it. It's just that no one has caught him at it yet."

Roman sobered and leaned into her. "I know about mind control. I was in Detroit and have been in New York. The hives are all different, but they're all the same. Even here. Especially here."

Lyris nodded, absentmindedly rubbing her face in Roman's thick mane of hair as she searched for his ear. She whispered: "I know what you mean. This place looks so wholesome compared with other goblin towns. But it's still . . . *off*. There's a smell, a feel—"

"Yeah. People can get fooled by all the open encouragement to lawful living. At least at first."

"Not me," she said firmly. "I've learned Quede's dirty scent, and he can wash the surface with as much soap as he wants. It'll still smell rotten. He's been a bad man for a very long time and it rubs off on everything he touches."

"He'll tell you he's reformed—a nonsmoking, nondrinking, nonaggressive goblin. He is all about clean and peaceful living these days."

Lyris snorted. "And I also know all this clean living won't do anything to improve his character. He may live longer, but he'll always be evil."

"Well, there's a lot to be said for dying healthy, I guess." Roman sounded thoughtful, and Lyris wished she could see his eyes. "He *has* lived for a very long time—even for a goblin king."

"Too long," Lyris agreed. Unless he was a vampire. She added in a tired voice: "Too damned long. And I've been chasing him for too long, too. This has got to end. I'm going to get black lung from hanging out in places like this."

"I agree—with all of it. And while I adore your ear, I'd kind of like to see your face while we talk. So, let's get out of here. I know a place where you can refresh your inner woman with some spicy gumbo. We can also speak as plainly as we like because there are no green ears pricking in the smoky air."

"Yeah? And where might this place be?" she asked with barely masked suspicion. She could practically feel the pickup line coming, and was disappointed he'd use one.

"My apartment." He waited a beat, and threw her off. "Or your hotel, the Palais du Monde."

"Of course. But how do you know that my hotel has good gumbo?" Lyris asked, wondering if Jack had told Roman where she was staying, and not being terribly happy about it. But she wasn't all that unhappy either. If he had mentioned it, then Jack really trusted this man.

"All the hotels here have good gumbo. It is the first of Quede's Ten Commandments: Feed the tourists good gumbo. And pecan praline pie. It makes them fat and content."

"Ah."

"But *my* gumbo is way better than anything you'll get in a hotel. It's hot, spicy—almost as good as an orgasm. Almost." He gave her a pointed look.

"I'm sure it is," she said politely. "Yet, I think I'll pass on that tonight. I'm not quite up for anything that . . . might keep me awake this evening. I'm feeling jet-lagged."

"Is that your final answer?" he asked. He looked neither disappointed nor discouraged by her refusal—while she was suddenly feeling both.

She fought off the feeling. "It'll have to be. My brain is tired of thinking and my ears are tired of noise. Can we meet tomorrow during the day?"

"Of course. You know the Riverwalk bandstand?"

"Yes."

"How do you feel about a noon rendezvous? Another place that has really good gumbo. Not orgasmic gumbo, but you probably wouldn't want that in public anyway."

Lyris began to smile. She couldn't help it. There was nothing else to do in the face of such relentless cheer.

She said, "No, I *wouldn't* want that—in public or anywhere else on such short acquaintance." She checked for her handbag, relieved that it had not been stolen as she'd forgotten all about it. "Okay, noon it is. But I think I should tell you now . . ."

"Yes?"

"I don't really like gumbo. This will have to be something out of the ordinary."

"Woman!" Roman gasped and sat back, slapping a hand over his heart. The resultant noise was loud enough to hear even above the music because he wore no shirt. He looked over her shoulder, his expression hardening though he went on easily enough. "That's heresy. That's treason. In fact, it's enough to bring out the G-men! You better run for it before they find out what you've been saying."

Lyris glanced over her shoulder where Roman was staring. A group of five goblins in conservative business suits had come into the club. Their dark sunglasses made them look like members of the goblin Mafia. Their Hollywood-caricature bad-guy look should have made her laugh, but it didn't. In spite of the costuming, the goblins' inexpressive faces were genuinely scary.

"What's the deal with Quede's bush-league muscle?" she asked, trying to remove the wave of nervousness that rolled over her. "Are they any good?"

"They have a good tailor. You can hardly see their guns. Also for goblins, they scrub up fairly nice. You know, some of them have actually married humans. I haven't been able to make up my mind if they are socially ambitious, or just not too particular."

The topic was an interesting one, and Lyris had to give Roman credit for looking at things from the goblins' perspective. Most men were narrower in their thinking, and would have demanded to know what was up with such tasteless humans. But she was simply too tired to pursue it this evening.

"I don't think I'll actually run along since I'm in heels, but it is definitely time for me to be going," she said, pitching her voice just loud enough to be heard by Roman and maybe the nearby table. She stood up. "This place gives me a headache. It's the smoke. And the lights. And the music. It's too much on top of jet lag."

"Well, just so long as it isn't *me*." Roman also stood. He was lean and wiry but a good deal taller than she was. He also displayed his superior strength by reaching down and lifting her at the waist until their eyes were level. That left her feet dangling about twelve inches off the floor. His eyes danced, and he smiled and said outrageously: "Bye now, sweetheart. You come back soon, hear?"

Before she could answer, Roman pulled her close and kissed her. Then he turned his head and whispered a last message in her ear. "Smile pretty for the curious goblins. Remember before you kick me somewhere painful that they all work for King Quede and will be wondering what you are doing with me."

Lyris found herself back on the floor before she could decide if she liked the experience of a rough-

and-ready kiss or not—or whether Roman deserved kicking.

Shaken, and not trusting herself to speak again, Lyris waved a hand at Roman and started for the door. Her skin crawled as she strolled by Quede's tidy goblins, but she made herself keep a slow pace and a slight smile until she was back out in the thick but clean night air.

Though her lungs appreciated the escape from the smoke, and her ears rejoiced in the comparative silence, it didn't take long for her head to fill back up with the sound of ticking. The clock in her head was again running rapidly down toward some dark fate, and that didn't make her happy.

Lyris wished that she had some sleeping pills, but she never used drugs and very rarely drank. She and chemicals were a bad match, and she had figured out long ago that, in her case, enough would never be quite enough. She had to get by without such help.

She sighed.

Chapter Four

She stood for a moment on the balcony outside the club and looked out at the river. Thanks to Quede's removal of the old transmission towers, thickets of phone lines and cables and ugly satellite dishes, Lyris had an excellent view of the night as it packed up its mantle of moon and scattered stars, getting ready to hide out from the storm they said was galloping in at dawn. So far, all that was riding her way was a stiffening wind and a cold smell that drifted in off the water. But she knew that soon there would be a spiderweb of silver mist creeping up over the banks and webbing the narrow streets. The fog, along with painfully clean streets, was a feature of the *new* New Orleans. No one else seemed to notice that this phenomenon had only begun after goblins took over the city, and that it happened no matter how hot the night.

But then much of *new* New Orleans was like a trip through the looking glass. The city had not been built to terrify or humble visitors in the way of the capital, but something about this city seemed to do both. It was difficult to explain how. The visual trappings hadn't changed that much from the days when men had built it. It looked the same in postcards as it always had, but something—the optics; the smell, certainly—was different. And unnerving.

Lyris walked quickly down the stairs on her less-than-moderate heels, trying to clear her head of its mental congestion and her lungs of smoke. It was difficult, because everywhere she went, she detected the faint odor of goblin and it kept her nerves firing with small trills of alarm. The enemy was omnipresent.

And then there was her contact at the Easy Off to think about. He disturbed her, too—and on many levels. Damn! She didn't know what to make of this Roman Hautecoeur. He wasn't all pooka, obviously. *But*, said a long-stifled reactionary part of her, *even a little can be more than enough*. How much could he be trusted? Jack had complete faith in him, apparently, but Lyris knew that pookas were notorious for their playfulness and their inability to stay focused on any task unrelated to mischief. Their morals—what few they had—were repositional, and they had all the loyalty and adherence of an aging sticky-note.

The thought was no sooner formed than she was

scolding herself. Hadn't she given up on this sort of judgmental thinking? It wasn't fair to make generalizations based on species. After all, she was part sylph and part siren, and she'd never hunted anyone. Except Quede. And she wasn't using tooth and claw on him—*ugh!* No, she wasn't touching him at all. All she wanted was information—proof of what he was—and then she was out of there. It would be someone else's job to act on what she uncovered. Hers was not a vigilante's heart.

"Excuse me," she said to a group of exceptionally tall teens who were standing three abreast on the sidewalk and blocking the way as they stared over the heads of a gathered crowd. At her repeated words, they finally turned their heads in her direction and looked at her blankly. It was a long five count before they began shuffling aside, and she had to wonder if she had used the wrong language with them. Or maybe it was the wrong sentiment. Perhaps she should have just said "Move." A lot of people that lived in Quede's orbit seemed to need explicit instructions. Was it possible that he sucked IQs along with blood? It would be about par for the course if Quede's fountain of youth turned out to be everyone else's fountain of stupid.

Feeling vaguely nervous, Lyris looked about quickly, constantly scanning the crowd for familiar or hostile faces. The crowds were thickening rapidly as midnight approached, congregating near Bourbon Street as if waiting for the party to begin. She had the feeling that they were headed toward some emotional critical mass, and spontaneous activity would soon begin breaking out. The crowds would swarm. Swarms could be violent.

She began feeling both wary and curious as she pushed through the glassy-eyed horde ringing a tourist shop called Headlines. Slowing like the others to watch the mixed crowd inside, she noticed something disturbing. It was a photo shop where they would take your picture and then paste your head on top of a porn bunny, or the pope, or some freakish muscle man, and then slap a famous magazine banner along the bottom. They would also just take your picture riding—or whatever—a giant stuffed bull. Such places were common on boardwalks and at fairs, especially with fetishists, and it wouldn't usually have attracted her attention. But a number of the photos in the window were of people pretending to be King Quede.

It was crazy, but no one seemed to care that nobody knew what King Quede actually looked like. He hadn't been photographed since the days of the tintypes—hence the sepia-tone photos. Yet, people still wanted to have their head pasted on the body of a lean man in royal robes. What was especially interesting was that Quede didn't have four arms in the new photos—the original had plainly shown him with both sets.

It really was the perfect visual metaphor for what was going on in New Orleans, she thought, walking on after a moment, pushing through the congealing masses on the sidewalk. No one knew who was in charge—and no one cared so long as their immediate needs were met and things looked neat on the surface. And once again the tourists were inadvertently contributing to the con job being perpetrated upon them. That last part was classic goblin M.O.

Tired of the mobs and suddenly very aware of her aching feet, Lyris broke away from the gaping crowd and cut down a dark alley that headed directly for her hotel. She steered to the right side of the street to avoid the drainage channel cut in the middle of the cobblestones.

She saw at a glance that it was the sort of street that a prudent person would avoid. It was too silent—no tourists. For a moment she paused, listening. The quiet somehow suggested stealth. But that was just her nerves again. Or maybe it was a trick of the acoustics that dimmed the sound of traffic and crowds. She couldn't hear anything; there wasn't so much as a mouse breathing in the deserted gutter.

And it was possible that there was some odd refraction of light that made the shadows seem darker than they should be. Her eyesight was keen and it told her that the alley was empty. By definition, an empty alley had to be a safe one, didn't it?

She went on, walking carefully under an iron arch where some wakeful, but strangely blank eyed pigeons congregated, still unasleep even at that hour.

Had even the birds somehow altered and become nocturnal?

There was no warning of danger, except a soft hiss from a dark doorway and a whiff of rotting meat. But that was enough to prepare her intuitively for the four clawed hands that shot out of the night to grab at her arms and legs.

The silent thing that attacked her looked like a goblin, and as such, she didn't expect it to smell like Chanel No. 5. Still, she didn't expect to smell something so vile that she choked. More than anything, it was the odor that told her she was in terrible danger. Death had come calling.

"Come . . ." it seemed to breathe at her, though the word was far from distinct and might not have been true speech at all. It felt like a voice in her head.

"No!" Drawing on instinct and years of training, Lyris leaned into her assailant and immediately brought a knee up hard between its legs. She shoved a stiff palm at her attacker's ugly yet inexpressive face, thrusting with all her inhuman might.

Nothing happened. At least nothing happened to the goblin. Though her sylph body packed more power per pound than any goblin or human could, the thing didn't react. It continued to hold her in a tight grip, continued to slowly reel her in toward its enormous body and suffocating smell. And its teeth. Long pointy teeth.

New data started pouring in, cutting through what

she now realized had been some sort of perceptual amnesia, a supernatural blanket thrown over her senses either by this creature or some third party. It was telling her frightening things about this unwanted intimacy with her attacker. Impossibly, the knee and hand didn't seem to have done anything to her assailant. She had felt the pain in her palm as she delivered the blow to his nose, and she heard that curved beak break. The goblin's head snapped back, just as it should. But he didn't let go. He didn't even cry out.

Lyris was stunned. That blow should have killed him—*it*. Given her unnatural strength, it was a cranium crusher. The horny protuberance of the goblin's nose should have been rammed up into its brain, giving it a crude lobotomy. At the very least, the monster should have been laid out cold while its brain filled up with blood. Instead, it was like she had struck a robot.

It wheezed some word again, and she realized that it only seemed to inhale when it wanted to speak. A greasy hand fumbled toward her throat and she gasped, taking in a lungful of bad air. *Death!* It reeked of it. She gagged and another wave of adrenaline flooded her body. Unable to any longer contain her true nature, she put on an obvious burst of inhuman strength as she tore away from her attacker. Nails scraped her skin but didn't penetrate. It got a handful of her skirt near the hip, but

Lyris managed to pull free with only minor damage to the cloth as a pocket and seam tore loose.

Her back slammed against a wall as she skidded on the wet cobbles, trying to regain her balance. She looked around quickly and righted herself, ignoring the sudden ache in her bruised wings. Seeing another goblin enter at the end of the alley, she spun about on her heels and began running back the way she came. One on one, she might have stayed to fight. Surely a broken nose would slow the creature! But she couldn't take on two goblins—or whatever the hell they were. Especially not if one of them was able to manipulate her thoughts.

Her self-defense instructor had told her there was danger in pulling away from an assailant and turning your back to run away. He could kick out with his feet if he had martial arts training. He could throw a knife or use a gun. And since you couldn't see what he was doing, there was no way to defend yourself.

But her instructor hadn't been talking about a combat situation with a goblin. Goblins were strong and they liked to strangle, and for that they needed to be close. Getting far away was a very, very good idea if you liked your neck unwrung. And since running backward wasn't an option, she had little choice but to do a one-eighty and flee.

There was another reason for breaking away from her attacker and trying to get away, if avoiding strangulation wasn't enough. She had betrayed herself as being inhuman. It was rare, but some goblins were into supplementary abuse of fey females: torture, rape—none of it was fun. Some of their games were unquestionably *worse than death,* especially for feys, who didn't die easily or quickly. And *worse than death* was a real possibility if this wasn't just a mugger goblin, and she was being gathered up for Quede. Some people thought vampires were sexy, but to Lyris they were just disease-bearing parasites.

Of course, chances were a hundred to one that whatever Quede was, he would prefer her dead to enslaved and she was probably panicking for the wrong reason. But the one-in-a-hundred possibility was enough to make her put on another burst of species-betraying speed. She ran for the crowds in the street. Fear made her back ache as her phantom wings tried their best to unfold and aid her in her flight.

Impossibly, footsteps pounded close behind her as the wounded goblin somehow gained. Stupid! She had been stupid—trusting to the fact that there would be no overt move made on her in public even if her identity was discovered. She had been thinking in terms of normal, civilized cities where a police force would simply expel her. But crowd proximity wouldn't stop Quede if he really wanted Lyris dead or captured. He'd just blank out the tourists' minds after he did whatever he wanted.

But did Quede want her? Why would he? Could

he have somehow discovered what she was investigating and sent someone to capture her? She'd been so careful, so cautious! She hadn't told a soul what she really suspected, and no sane person would imagine such a possibility on his own. No one except Jack—or Roman, though she dismissed him as quickly as his name occurred to her—knew even half of what she had discovered, and she was certain Jack hadn't betrayed her. If anyone knew how to keep his mouth shut, it was Jack Frost.

But someone had sent her those film clips. She had assumed it was Jack, but maybe it wasn't. Assuming things was stupid. She should have delayed her trip until she had heard back from him about the film. She needed to wise up about things, and fast. Her investigation had just turned lethal. Someone was trying to kill her and she didn't know who or why.

Okay, so think! Quede might have good reason to want her for questioning. On the other hand, one thing that Quede didn't want was any scandal or whiff of crime among the tourists in the Quarter. And his stooges had probably been ordered to keep a low profile.

Knowing it was a risk, since it might bring the police who could very well be in Quede's pay, Lyris nevertheless opened her mouth and screamed as she erupted back onto the crowded street.

"Filthy beast!" she yelled, spinning around to shout into the startled goblin's sunglassed face.

Then, to the few other pedestrians near them: "He pinched me! Right on the butt. I'm gonna be black and blue!"

To prove her point to the shocked onlookers, she pointed to the tear in the seam of her skirt. There was a nice slimy handprint that wrapped around her thigh. "Oohhhh! And this is a new skirt, too!"

Around her, the growing crowd began to laugh. A few voices jeered and made lewd suggestions. Mostly they were relieved, those couples and families with children. No real crime was being committed. It was just like the travel agent had promised. They were completely safe in New Orleans. It was just a goblin boy getting a little fresh with a girl. These things happened when girls dated green men. One shouldn't have interspecies relationships. It wasn't natural or God-fearing.

The giant goblin stood there with his broken but unbloodied nose, clearly undecided about what to do next. Or perhaps that wasn't correct. He seemed more to be debating what he should do, opposing wishes doing battle to see which would triumph. Lyris watched, horrified and yet fascinated, as he twitched and shuddered.

His head was cocked as though listening. As Lyris waited, a second goblin came up behind him but remained in the alley's shadow. The second one's hidden face irritated her. They weren't being sporting, double-teaming her this way. Safe in the crowd,

Lyris had half an urge to snatch the first creature's glasses away and look into the eyes of her attacker.

If he has eyes. The sudden image of facing empty eye sockets made her skin chill and killed her impulse cold. She suddenly just wanted to get rid of the creatures before she was unmasked as a sylph. All he'd have to do was tear her blouse and her wings would be exposed. And if they discovered that she was fey and had entered the city without a visa, at the very least she would be deported. At worst, she'd be taken to Quede.

"Nasty brute! Go away! I never want to see you again!" she shouted, and then, putting hands over her face, she began to loudly sob. Even as she cried, she noticed the strange clothes the creature was wearing. He was covered in dirt and bits of broken glass. It was a warm evening. If a villain was going to be out running foul of King Quede's rules and committing various acts of physical violence, he should be doing it in something lightweight. After all, goblins had special problems with heat and sweat. But this creature looked like he had broken the window of a vintage clothing store to get dressed. Maybe that was what smelled so rotten. Could wool rot?

Could that be grave dirt? a voice in her head asked. *Think what that would mean.*

Lyris stiffened and looked hard at the second goblin. It was hard to see details in the gloom, but the second goblin was definitely smaller. And his glowing eyes were uncovered beneath his hood. And Lyris had the sense that this one was a *he* and not an *it,* though she was quite certain that he, too, was no ordinary goblin. He couldn't be if he was speaking in her head.

Come with us. I just want to talk with you.

Lyris slammed all her extrasensory portals shut and dropped braces against them. The dry whisper made her feel slimy and shaken. She had a sort of inborn, neurological wall that had always kept out unwanted magical eavesdroppers, but somehow this creature had slipped over it while she was distracted.

"Shall I beat him up for you?" asked a familiar, and much more pleasant, voice. A warm arm settled around her. A long finger wiggled through the tear in her seam and caressed her shaking thigh.

The familiar invisible touch stroked over her skin, stimulating the nerve endings. Her burgeoning hysteria immediately died, along with her shivering. Not entirely for effect, Lyris leaned into Roman's warmth, hiding her face but also crushing his busy fingers between their bodies. She noticed as she snuggled into his linen shirt that he had changed clothes but hadn't showered. Obviously he'd wasted little time in following her from the club.

"Yes, please. He scared me and was being mean. And he ruined my skirt." She added in a voice softer than breath: "Look at the second goblin in the alley. He's some kind of psychic."

"The brute!" Roman's voice was light, but the expression he turned on the goblins was not. There was a great deal of speculation in his gaze, frankly more curiosity than anger. And not nearly enough fear. He whispered to Lyris: "Cool it with the crying. You're overacting."

Well, what had she expected? Gallantry? He was part pooka. They didn't make the best white knights. They barely made adequate white knights' horses since they had a bad habit of giving in to temptation and dumping their riders into streams.

Frustrated by Roman's appearance, and with at least one of the team being unwilling to make an even bigger scene, the larger goblin hissed something that might have been a curse—and then again might not have been—and then disappeared back down the dark alley in the wake of his smaller companion.

Lyris couldn't explain it, but she had the sense that she had surely just escaped something *worse than death*.

But maybe that was just nerves talking.

As the crowd laughed at her opponent's ignoble retreat, Lyris again turned her face into Roman's neck. She asked quietly: "Were those Quede's creatures?"

"I don't know. I haven't seen them before," he replied as he combed back her hair. He studied her dry eyes for a moment and then added in a louder voice: "Someone cue the fat lady—things are all over. Come along, sweetheart. I know just what you need to settle those shaken nerves."

"Let me guess. Some gumbo?" Lyris sniffed and pretended to wipe her eyes. She hoped no one else noticed that no tears had touched her face. Sylphs couldn't cry like normal people. When she wept, it would be over her dead mate, and they would be tears of blood.

"Exactly—gumbo, opiate of the tourist classes—and maybe a shot of rum. I've been thinking over what you said earlier, and I can only conclude that you don't like gumbo because you've never had *mine*. Once you've had authentic Romeo Hart on the tongue, you'll never settle for anything less." Roman spun her about, managing to keep his arm in place as he hustled her down the crowded sidewalk. He kept up the flirtatious patter. "You are in for a treat tonight."

"Am I?" She didn't ask where they were going. Suddenly, she wasn't certain she wanted to go back to her hotel room. She certainly didn't want to go there alone.

"You are indeed. Now, no more crying. The next time one of those G-men gets fresh with you, you just give him a shot in the balls. It works the same as it does for normal guys."

"I already did that," Lyris answered. Her expression was serious and her voice hushed as they worked their way down a quieter side street. Still nervous, eyes darting from doorway to doorway, she added: "But I don't think the big one had any balls."

"Was it a female?" Roman glanced behind them. "It couldn't be. It was too big and ugly. Even for a male goblin, it was large. Besides, it looked like a praying mantis with a hair helmet. No female—not even a goblin—would go around looking like that. Well, except Lilith. I hear she was Queen of Ugly Green Things."

"I don't think it was anything," Lyris answered, ignoring his comment. Sin City's goblin queen was dead. "I mean, I don't think it had a gender. It might be one of Quede's experiments."

"Experiments?" Roman's eerie gold eyes shifted from the sparse crowd to her face. His gaze wasn't as lighthearted as his patter.

Lyris nodded. Deciding that Roman had earned a degree of trust for coming to her aid—however ungallantly—she dropped her voice still further and confided: "If the rumors are true, Quede is breeding a new kind of worker goblin. One that can be either male or female. All he has to do is give it the right drug, and it can turn into either sex. I heard they were small though. That thing was almost seven feet tall."

"But why the heck would he do that?" Roman asked. He didn't say he disbelieved her, a fact Lyris found encouraging. "And why would he dress one in a wardrobe older than *Australopithecus* and send it out on the town to smell up the air with its rancid

B.O.? All the goblins around here have had their scent glands out and bathe in aftershave."

"That is something I would very much like to know." Lyris looked down at her hands. The right one hurt. A bruise was forming in her palm where the creature's horny beak had landed. At least it hadn't broken the skin. The risk of contagion was lower. Come to think of it, Lyris's feet were throbbing too. Her shoes were pretty, but not meant for athletic endeavors like running for her life. She hoped Roman's place wasn't deep in the Quarter. "You know what else was weird?"

"Aside from the bad wool suit from *Angels With Dirty Faces*?" Roman asked. "Or wearing dark sunglasses in the middle of the night? The dirt dabbed behind the ears? The smell? The public attack when Quede will have its head for making a scene in front of tourists?"

"No . . . well, that was all weird too. But I meant that it didn't bleed. I broke its nose, but there wasn't a drop of blood. Not one. An embalmed corpse would have bled more." She shuddered as she said the words.

"You did that number on its face?" Roman whistled softly. "Remind me not to piss you off. I wouldn't want to get whapped with your ugly stick."

"I will remind you. Probably repeatedly," she muttered, aggravated at his apparent inability to focus on the salient points of their conversation. "Did you understand me? The thing didn't bleed when it should have. That isn't normal. It isn't natural."

"Sure. Hey, you know what?" Roman asked, pausing outside a wrought-iron gate that opened onto a small courtyard. He pulled a set of keys from his pocket and selected one. Lyris could feel him taking down invisible wards even as he opened the physical lock.

"What?"

"You were wrong. I *did* get to save a damsel in distress. I just love it when I'm right!"

"Roman?"

"What?" The gate snapped open.

"Try and focus here. I have a problem. And since you've been seen with me, you may have a problem too."

"Sure, I'm fully focused and tuned in." He gestured her inside. "I was just saying—"

"Well, don't." She knew she sounded cross, but couldn't help it. Her feet and hand really hurt.

"Okay," he answered good-naturedly. Then: "I've been thinking."

"I'll believe that when I see it."

"No, really." He gestured again, urging her up a narrow staircase. It was suspended from the overhanging roof by chains, and swayed alarmingly as she stepped onto it. Maybe goblins with their extra set of arms found it charming, but it made Lyris feel as if she were spelunking. Still, it was the only way to reach the ledge of a balcony that ran along the second story of the old building. She sighed and caught a firmer hold on the chains, favoring her right hand.

"So, I heard a rumor that the goblins were out excavating in the desert near Nevada—this was before that whole dragon thing happened," Roman went on. "Anyhow, they supposedly dug up some old desiccated remains that weren't actually as dead as remains usually are. The thing was in some kind of coma or hibernation, and it had a name like Rawbones or Rawhide. It sounded kind of like a hobgoblin and supposedly smelled to high heaven. I thought it was just gossip, or urban-legend stuff, but I wonder if that might not be what our strange friend is."

Lyris glanced at him. When she spoke, she felt how unsteady her voice was.

"Not *Rawbones*. Raw-Head and Bloody-Bones. And it's a bogeyman—a particular kind of hobgoblin. First written reference to him was in *Wyll of the Deuyll* in the sixteenth century. But he is supposed to be an entirely fictional creation. There hasn't been an actual hobgoblin sighting in over seven centuries. . . . Damn it. Was it Quede who went looking for the hobgoblin?" she asked worriedly, wondering what else she might have missed in her apparently less than thorough research.

"I don't know. I don't think so. I heard it was some nutcase minister—it's the first door on the right," he added as she reached the top of the swaying stairs. "It's just a hole in the wall, but it does have a view. And I was lucky to find anything in the Quarter."

"A *goblin* minister? Of what? A voodoo sect?" she asked, standing aside so Roman could unlock his door. She forgave him for rubbing up against her because the balcony was narrow. And because she was still feeling a bit cold and frightened and had to admit she enjoyed the frisson that passed through her every time they touched.

"Hey, this is New Orleans. Anything is possible. But I heard he was a Christian minister."

"A Christian goblin minister. You know, that is a truly terrifying thought. A goblin with a religious mission."

"Ain't it just? And by the way, you're welcome." Lyris turned and blinked up at him. She felt herself color as he went on: "I had to give my last set of dances to Stormy Feathers so I could come after you. I won't mention what I gave up in tips. That was a hot crowd. I've never seen so many crotchless panties."

"Stormy Feathers?" she asked, taking her turn at ignoring the main point of the conversation. Saying thank you now would trivialize her genuine, if belated, gratitude.

"Yeah, that bird blows up a storm." Roman grinned. "But she is one of those things that you probably don't want to hear about before dinner."

"Or ever," Lyris muttered.

"You know, we're alone now. And I'm attracted. You can turn down the sex mojo you're using on me."

Lyris stared at him. "You think I'm using attraction magic on you? In your dreams. I don't know what this is, but I'm not the one doing it."

"No? Well, that's very damned interesting." He turned away. "Let's eat."

Chapter Five

A very nervous goblin presented Quede with a bottle of the '88 Clos du Mesnil Blanc de Blanc, which meant that they were again out of the Cristal Rose. Quede did not actually care for champagne, but he made a point of drinking it when he entertained and he had specifically ordered the Cristal for tonight.

Quede briefly considered doing something nasty to the little creature as an early warning to the kitchen staff about his displeasure. Wede, was that this worker's name?—certainly expected something bad to happen. But Quede decided against a bloody display in front of his guests. With these transgendered worker goblins now being bred, it was difficult to threaten them with colorful old punishments like castration. The act just didn't carry the same weight—for either the victim or the audience. To deprive already sexless goblins of their reproductive organs wasn't a threat, not unless their normally nonfunctional bits had been activated hormonally by the hive's master.

Also, Quede hated messing up his carpets. The Persian rug they were sitting on was almost as old as he was. It deserved better than to have phosphorescent goblin guts spilled all over it while he hunted for shriveled testes or useless ovaries in a twitching body. Wede might have either. Or both.

Anyway, it was the wine steward who deserved gutting. Occasionally, it amused Quede not to be capricious and unjust.

And it was all right not to punish the goblin, because his guests had no idea that anything was wrong. They were still completely enthralled.

Before Quede could say anything, Schiem slipped into the room and ghosted up to his chair. The minion leaned over and whispered his news about what had happened in the Quarter that night.

Quede inhaled, taking in the scent around Schiem. *Aaahhhh! A sylph*. He inhaled a second time, drinking deeply of her invisible portrait, which Schiem had unwittingly captured on his clothes and skin. He hadn't smelled this scent in ages but recognized it instantly. A faint scent clung to sylph skin and the air around them, patchouli that spoke to him of joyous times and purer love. He remembered with delight the sylphs he had known. They were the minks of the fey world—eager and uninhibited. At one time he had considered trying to manufacture a sylph oil to wear as an aphrodisiac, but it hadn't been commercially viable.

But in that moment, quite oddly, he didn't think of her perfume as the product made of scent glands ripped from animals or pressed flowers being drained of their oils, but only of soft laughter and softer sighs. It made this unknown creature as lovely as any of his flowers.

He thought, with rare sentimentality, that it was a pity he'd have to crush her if his intelligence was accurate and she really was investigating him and his connection to the Kennedy assassination.

Perhaps he would have her essence distilled so he could wear her when she was gone.

Schiem interrupted his reverie to share another bit of disturbing news—and this tidbit did not make Quede feel sentimental at all. Who would *dare* bring a hobgoblin into his city?

Obviously not the little sylph, since the thing had attacked her.

Find the thing, Quede ordered Schiem, using his mind rather than his voice to speak to his half-human servant. *And keep an eye on the reporter. Don't do anything to her just yet. She may be useful in luring out of hiding whoever has control of the hobgoblin.*

"Why don't you take a shower while I get our dinner?" Roman suggested, flipping on a light. "Not to be offensive or anything, but the apartment is kind of small—"

"And I reek of hobgoblin," Lyris finished, looking about the place. Roman knew it had a minimalist, temporary look that the jungle of houseplants could only partly disguise. "So, where's the bathroom?"

Roman pointed at a bead curtain half obscured by a luxuriant ficus and got the expected *get-real* look. He was tempted to make a funny remark but canned it. Humor worked like a magic charm with a lot of women, but he had the feeling that he was going to have to throw out the *Cliff's Notes* for Seduction 101 and try something else with this one. Lyris Damsel wouldn't fall for the usual charming shtick.

"Hey, the decor is not of my choosing. It came this way. If you're shy, just don't turn on the light. The red beads are fairly opaque unless you use a light on your side. Anyway, I'll be busy cooking."

Lyris looked them over again and then turned to study his face. Even with her shallow breathing, her nose stayed slightly wrinkled. He made an effort to appear innocent. He was winning with the aid of the hobgoblin's stench, but one grin and the deal was probably off.

"Come on," he urged. "My gumbo deserves a clean palette."

"Oh, goddess, you're right!" she said, letting slip her probable affiliation with fey culture by her choice of divinity to call upon. "I won't be able to eat anything until I'm clean. This smell is nauseating. Why didn't someone tell me that hobgoblins smelled so foul?"

"Their smell is a new one on me. I'd rather be roasted over a slow fire than go around smelling like that. I have a robe in there"—which he kept for visiting girls—"and there's some nice soap"—left by another. "Go ahead and rinse your clothes out, and they can dry while we eat. I have a clothesline." That had been rigged up by a different girl—whom hopefully Lyris wouldn't smell. "If you need anything, just call. I'll be right here at the stove."

Lyris hesitated for another moment and then nodded. She disappeared behind the bead curtain with a loud rattle. Her head reappeared almost immediately.

"Roman? There's an imp in your bathroom." A pause as she looked back over her shoulder. "I think he's stuck."

Roman walked over and poked his head through the beads. "Darn. I've been trying to teach him not to drink out of the toilet. Don't worry. He isn't stuck. It's just a game he plays. He'll leave when he's done with his bath."

"Oh. Okay." Her voice was dubious, but Lyris didn't argue or clutch his arm with girlish fear, so Roman tactfully retreated.

"So tell me, do you like your job?" Lyris called. He listened but could find no sarcasm in her question. "I don't know why, but I just can't picture a fey wanting to work in a nightclub where the air is so smoky."

"Well, it's rather a crime. It pays well and the hours are flexible—and I have the added bonus of knowing that my family wouldn't approve," he answered candidly. Then: "You doing okay? The imp isn't scaring you?"

"I'm fine. The imp left through the air duct. He seems to use the loose grill like a doggy door."

Roman knew that she'd have no trouble finding everything in the dark. Feys were good that way. Of course, what Lyris had forgotten was that he was also fey and would have no trouble seeing her in the dark either. The thought made him want to smile, but he again repressed the urge. It wouldn't do to get caught now with a grin on his face if she stuck her head through the curtain again.

He set up a screen of innocent noises, opening the fridge and banging some plates around until he heard the water in the shower turn on. Using the shiny surface of the toaster, he took his first peek of his guest, making sure that her back was to him before he turned around.

And it was. The sight of what graced her back and shoulders almost made him drop the pan he was holding. She was a sylph! He could see her dragonfly wings—or what should have been wings, lying like a ridged tattoo from shoulder blades to the small of her back and wrapped around her sides in delicate scallops. They were beautiful, like a golden net, and they shimmered brilliantly even in the gloom.

Well, that explained the rather modest outfit she was wearing. Bikinis and backless dresses were obviously out for her this visit—unless she wanted to be *outed* as a fey, he thought, watching as she stepped into the shower. A sylph! Who'd have guessed it? They were howlingly rare. And raptor sylphs were the rarest of all. Even before all the pure-blooded feys had died they were almost legendary beings. What were the odds that he had found her?

Of course, he hadn't found her. Jack had. That rather reduced all the mystical significance of their meeting. After all, Jack was on a mission to gather up the last of the feys and organize them into some sort of society.

Then another thought occurred to Roman. Never mind her rarity; she was an animal fey. Like him. That meant whatever the prim and proper packaging said, she was capable of the same lusts that moved him, if sufficiently aroused. She wouldn't be a creature of air or light, too delicate to touch without the greatest care. She would be strong, red-blooded—*hot* blooded.

The idea left him so dizzy that he had to sit down. An animal fey! That explained the attraction between them: that whatever it was that shimmered in the air and made his hair stand on end.

"Have you seen Quede's latest advertisement?"

Lyris's voice asked above the shower's roar. A strong scent of violets and something else wonderful filled the air. " '*Quede Enterprises—redefining the relationship with mankind*.' And no one seems worried about this. Like goblin redefinition is nothing to be concerned about."

Roman cleared his throat and forced himself to think of an intelligent answer. It was difficult because his head was still swimming with carnal possibilities and his thoughts were a long way off from the shores of casual conversation.

"What's to worry about? Don't you read the papers? Quede is very busy winning orchid shows with his new neon green *dendrobiums*." Roman's hearing was as good as his eyesight, which was only slightly less acute than his sense of smell. He had no trouble hearing Lyris snort her derision even with the water pounding.

"No, really," he reassured her. "He is manic about orchids. I accidentally got copied on some mass mailing to all goblin employees. '*Pick up your environmental bags. Remember, spores need a contained environment for incubation.*' "

"I don't doubt he is involved with his orchids," Lyris answered. "As they say, 'Alexander wept when he had no more worlds to conquer.' I'm sure goblins need to keep busy, too. But this isn't all about peace, love, and petal power. Hitler loved dogs and small children. It didn't mean he was so short of time that he couldn't try and take over the world." She paused. "Anyway, I doubt Quede was talking about *orchid* spores in that e-mail. He was probably talking about goblin fruit. They are all growing their little victory gardens."

Roman forced himself to his feet. He had to start fixing something for dinner. She'd be out of the shower in another minute and likely to guess that he'd been peeking at her instead of cooking. Their relationship wasn't yet so cozy that she would look happily upon the notion of being spied upon. And this was not something he wanted to mess up.

"So, I've been thinking," he called as he turned back to the stove and tried to remember what he was doing.

"Uh-huh?"

"If you don't like gumbo, how about if I fix a hero sandwich instead? The secret to a really superb hero is the horseradish sauce. You've got to shave the root so it's fresh." He had an assortment of meats and cheese in the fridge and some fresh rolls from the boulangerie.

"A horseradish hero sandwich? As in, only a brave man should eat one?"

She'd made a joke. It was a small one and not very funny, but Roman found himself smiling. "No. As in, '*you will crown my brow with laurels and proclaim me Caesar—*' "

"Not *Miles Gloriosus*?"

"No. Caesar," he said. "I will settle for nothing less." The shower shut off and Roman hurried to the small fridge, trying to ignore the rustling of the towel and then the sound of silk as Lyris slipped on the robe.

"Well, I don't think I can call you Caesar—"

"You could in the right moment," he answered. Then, making his voice high and breathy: "Oh, God! Oh, Caesar! OOOhhh, yeeees!"

Lyris chuckled, shocking Roman. The deep sound was close to a lion's chuff. He watched her sniff at the cuff of his robe and was very glad he'd had it cleaned last week and it had no scent of woman remaining. "A sandwich would be fine, but I guess I really will have to try your gumbo someday if you are that great an epicure."

"I am! I am!"

"Uh-huh. But I have a feeling you are something else as well." She paused. "If I had to guess, I would say that you come from a long line of court jesters. Maybe they were also good chefs, too."

"Good guess," Roman answered as she pushed through the strands of beads and out of the bathroom. "Mom used to work for King Richard."

"Which one?" Lyris asked, suddenly sounding serious.

"The Third." He turned, unable to resist having a look at her in a sheer silk gown. He'd wanted to feast his eyes on her body, but found himself snagged by her sober gaze and then by her flushed lips.

"I can never tell when you're kidding. It's a little

disconcerting," she told him. He watched her lips move as she spoke, finding that the sight of them made his heart speed up. "Usually I know the truth when I hear it. That's sort of a gift of mine."

"Part of my charm—" he answered, finally turning away. *Slow down!* he scolded himself. "—is that I keep people guessing."

"Was your mother really a jester?" she asked, persisting.

"No," he answered. Then he added, with rare truthfulness that annoyingly showed the lingering pain and bitterness he felt: "My mother never jested about anything with me. But why would she? It couldn't have been easy to look at me and be reminded daily of the night she was raped."

He heard Lyris catch her breath, but he didn't turn around. His color was too high and he was feeling the sting of embarrassment for letting the thought slip out. He'd have to watch it around her. Something about Lyris compelled him to speak the truth—and the truth was very unattractive when it sounded like *oh, pity me*.

"She called it rape, but it wasn't as if it was anything violent," he went on after a moment, slicing through several rolls. "Pookas needn't be physically coercive. They simply trick or charm people into giving them what they want."

"I've heard that," Lyris said. Her voice was carefully neutral; she clearly sensed that he didn't want to hear any expressions of sympathy. He was glad of that because he already felt like he should be wearing a long cap and bells while he capered around the room. His stupefying attraction to her both excited and annoyed him.

"Unfortunately, not all women make that distinction. And she needed someone to blame for what happened, for her fall from grace and her loss of power."

"And your father wasn't around to take the heat?"

"No, he wasn't. Which was probably a good thing."

"Well, sure. After all, it's taught you to be a stand-up guy."

At that, Roman did turn around. "Why the hell would you think that?" he demanded, revolted by the suggestion. "I'm nothing of the sort."

"You're not?" Lyris's voice was still neutral, but those eerie, all-seeing eyes were not. As though sensing his discomfort as well as his attraction, she swiftly lowered them. "Okay, you're not. Are the sandwiches done?"

Roman glared at her, wanting to enumerate his many examples of healthy male depravity, but decided it might sound like he was protesting too much. Anyway, his prowess among females wouldn't impress her, which was his long-term goal. He needed to stay focused. The sudden surge of emotion was derailing him.

"Yes, here." He slid her sandwich onto a plate

and passed it to her. He asked stiffly: "Would you like some wine?"

"No, thanks. I don't drink. Funny things happen when I get near booze."

"Yeah?" Roman pulled out a chair at the tiny table and sat down. He asked interestedly: "What kind of things?"

"Oh, just things," she said airily. Taking a bite of her sandwich, she suddenly rolled her eyes back in her head and moaned ecstatically. Swallowing, she began to chant: "Oh, God! Oh, Caesar! Oh, yeeees! Yeeees!"

The last of Roman's discomfort died away. "Wait till you try the gumbo."

Lyris smiled at him, and he decided that maybe her eyes weren't so spooky after all. They might see a lot, but they didn't seem to judge too harshly. And if she was a witch, she was a good one.

"So," he asked, "where do you want to sleep tonight?"

She blinked at him.

"The sofa is pretty comfortable," he said. "But I'll share the bed if you want."

"What about my desperately picturesque hotel room? I actually paid a small fortune for it."

"You don't really want to try and sleep alone, do you? That place won't have any wards on it. Who knows what might come creeping in while you sleep."

Lyris stared at him in tired consternation. "Put

that way, no, I don't want to sleep alone—at the hotel, I mean." She took another bite of her sandwich, rolling her eyes in pleasure but not moaning. She swallowed and added: "I'll take the sofa."

Chapter Six

Roman couldn't honestly wish that females were made less attractive to the senses; life would hardly be worth living, if they were. It would be simpler, of course, and certainly less costly—but dull, dull, dull. He supposed that he might wish that he found women more easy to resist, but once again, what would be the point of living? Being attracted to a girl was more fun than almost anything. Besides, it was futile to even think this way. He was what he was—which was a fey male without any inclination to mend his erring ways.

He got up and paced to the hotel window, pulling back the sheers and looking down at the teeming street. He was grumpy after his night of poor slumber. Knowing Lyris was near, smelling and hearing her, had kept him awake until the very early hours.

Knowing that there were rules to the games of

courtship, he was prepared for a certain amount of requisite boredom while he politely wooed the latest object of his fierce—if fleeting—attention. But so far, Lyris hadn't done anything either girlish or boring or expected. The only thing even vaguely close to standard female behavior was her insistence on stopping at the hotel to change clothes, and he couldn't really fault her for that because the hobgoblin reek hadn't completely left her outfit of the night before.

Roman had always found female behavior to be largely incalculable and at times frustrating, but Lyris Damsel was something altogether new and intriguing. And yet, still annoying because she *was* different. There was no waiting around in her hotel room for her to dress while she dithered indecisively about what to wear. She hadn't wanted to meander about and visit gift shops they passed. She didn't even want to stop and dance to the zydeco playing on the Square. Heck, she didn't even want to dawdle over their early lunch of delicious boiled crawfish he'd insisted they have since it had been three hours since breakfast. It was almost unnatural for her to be so focused on goals.

Actually, in the light of day, he couldn't explain why he was still so attracted to her. She wasn't pretty so much as exotic, and not at all his usual thing in the personality department. And then there was her hair. He only liked mussed hair if it was his fingers that had done the mussing, and her hair plainly had a mind of its own—and that mind was fractured with multiple personalities all pointing off in separate directions, none of which seemed headed his way.

He didn't understand her. She was a woman of paradoxes, oddities, and strange contradictions. She seemed able to look inside people and weigh their souls, but she apparently didn't judge what she found there. She had great sexual appeal—what was called animal magnetism—but she didn't use it. In fact, she buried it. She was a woman of exotic physical gifts and strengths, but she didn't employ them either—though he could understand that more, given that they were in a war zone, and any suspicion that she was anything other than a human tourist could get her in a lot of trouble. Still, he was willing to bet that in her normal life, whatever that was, she didn't make use of these talents either. That was unnatural in her gender. Most women were peacocks. But not Lyris.

He'd watched her walk by a moment ago, shoes in hand, and been shocked at the change. Gone was the feminine creature of last night. Today, she wore dull, sensible clothing—so uncompromisingly sensible that he found himself almost aesthetically offended. Especially since she had worn such wonderfully frivolous, if prim, clothing the night before. It was as though after spending the night with him, she wanted to disavow her femininity.

Normally he approved of jeans, but hers contributed nothing to her figure. They had been bought in a hardware store and sprouted numerous, deep cargo pockets—all packed with bulgy objects, and they came with a hemp utility belt that jangled like a heavy charm bracelet with assorted strange tools. The hideous insult to her femininity was topped off with a vest that had to have been made from a wrestling mat, or maybe a bumper from a truck. She'd taken her sensuality and buried it in mothballs. He wasn't even sure he could flirt with this woman.

Her conversation had also turned spiky as her thoughts veered inward. Only a fool would rush in this instant and impale himself on her tongue. And yet, hadn't he been a fool for lesser reasons than assuaging his curiosity?

"Can I ask you something without pissing you off?" he inquired as she stepped out of her bathroom, sensible, lace-up boots in place on her feet.

"I don't know. Is it something I can answer without *getting* pissed off?"

"Well, it's about your vest. Is that thing a floatation device? Or maybe some kind of Kevlar that stops speeding bullets? I'm pretty sure it isn't being featured in *Vogue* this season."

Lyris shook her head at what she no doubt thought was his facetiousness. "Stop kidding around. A photographer's vest is the best way to hold everything we need. And it's waterproof. That's always handy in the swamps."

"Oh. I see." He paused. "No, I don't see. Why

do we need to hold anything in a swamp? Especially a camera?"

"Because today we are going sight-seeing. And to test a theory I have."

"And that theory would be . . . ? If it is that swamps are wet and unpleasant, I can save us a trip."

"I'll explain all this later," she said evasively. Turning to her purse, which Roman was stunned to find that she apparently needed on top of all her pockets and utility belt, she draped it over her chest like an ammo belt. "We just need to fill in some history before I decide what to do."

"Swell. Why do I have the feeling that this is going to be about as much fun as a Borgia wine-tasting party?"

"It's probably safer. If you don't drink anything." She smiled a little.

"Do I at least get to know which swamp I'm gracing?" he asked, pulling sunglasses out of his shirt pocket. He only had one pocket on his shirt, and a camera would not fit in it. "Some are less fashionable than others, and I'd like to leave word where my body can be retrieved. If the gators haven't eaten it."

"Certainly. We are going to visit some abandoned plantations, among them King Quede's country getaway, Toujours Perdrix, a nifty little mansion a few miles outside of town. And it isn't exactly in a swamp, it's just rather damp and a little watery around there. The building itself is up on a hill."

"Ah, I do see. Only it's abandoned, you know. He hasn't used it in years. He doesn't even have guards out there anymore." He cocked a brow at her. "And it is so in a swamp. The fact that there are trees and a hill shouldn't mislead you. The place is a mosquito-infested marsh."

"I think maybe it haunts him," Lyris said grimly, doing an inelegant squat and testing the tightness of her laces. She didn't deign to argue about the terrain or what infested it. "I'd like to think it does. It would mean he has some conscience."

Roman snorted. "Don't hold your breath. Well, I guess we better stop and get sandwiches at the deli. We're bound to be in the swamp for a while."

"I know that Quede is never out during the day, and all goblins avoid the sun. But I still felt watched," Roman complained as they stepped out of the rental car and onto the spongy ground of the parking lot. It had been gravel once, but damp earth had swallowed most of the small stones.

"Goblins can go out in the daytime if they wear the right clothing and sunscreen," Lyris answered. "But I'm not worried about goblins just now."

"Then it's as I suspected. You *are* nuts. You don't think any goblin spies that are about today are going to fail to report our visit here? It isn't like we're just two among hundreds of tourists." Roman patted his only full pocket, making certain his handgun was still there. He'd added it after hearing their destination.

"Let them report it. This house is listed in the official guidebooks of historical New Orleans and environs. Tourists must come here all the time." Lyris opened her purse and pulled out a battered paperback. She handed it to him. "We shall display this prominently and consult it often as we walk. And if you want, we can go visit another historic home that is only a couple of miles from here and play tourist there, too."

"No, thanks."

Next came an odd-looking digital camera disgorged from her front hip pocket. "We are also going to take lots of pictures today."

"What brand of camera is that? I've never seen one like it."

"You wouldn't have. It's specialized. It takes thermal pictures. Ghost hunters use them."

"So, we're here in Quede country looking for ghosts." Roman sounded increasingly skeptical. "Gee, you really know how to have a good time."

"Ghosts aren't the only thing that leave strange heat signatures. Goblins and other beasties do, too—and at even longer ranges. I'd just like to assure myself that we're alone before we go inside. Let's start in the graveyard."

"So, do you think we *will* see goblins?" Roman asked as they turned toward the old cemetery. His skin rippled with gooseflesh as he took in the abandoned mausoleums that were being swallowed in vegetation and the miasmic heat waiting to come swooping down upon them. He wasn't afraid of ghosts, but there was something about this place—a desolation that went beyond the unpleasantness of mere physical death. The shadows seemed to breathe, weren't just shades of other things substantial and real, but maintained their own thinking presence. And their dark thoughts pressed close in a subtle threat the deeper into the swamp Lyris and Roman went.

"I don't know what we'll see." Lyris sighed and tried to explain. "Roman, this is a hunch I am playing. I can't give you a good reason for doing any of it, except that I have learned to follow my intuition. It has led me to information that I would never have discovered if I had been guided only by logic. It brought me to Quede and to New Orleans. All I can do is follow the trail and hope I see the next clue and hope I don't get swatted down on the way."

"I know about hunches," he admitted, not mentioning that he was having one that very instant, a bad one. The only thing that kept him from bringing it up was that he'd look like a coward when she was so calm.

"Haven't you ever asked yourself why no one ever comments on the fact that there isn't a single homeless person in New Orleans?" she asked. "How poverty—or at least the poor—disappeared overnight? The druggies, too. I look at the people, the residents, everywhere I go and they have changed. They're homogenized, pasteurized—like pod people. The individuality is being drained out the population by something or someone. It's like a cosmic parasite is sucking them dry. Or controlling their minds."

Roman looked at Lyris. "You're trying to tell me something, aren't you?"

"Yes." They stopped at the spiked gate that blocked the entrance to the cemetery. Lyris picked up her camera and shot a couple of pictures of the half-buried graves. "But I'd like you to figure it out on your own. That way I won't feel like I've infected you with some kind of paranoia. And you can be my reality check."

"Too late. Your bug has already crawled up my ass. I'm paranoid as hell."

"So long as it's my bug and not something from the swamp grass . . ." Lyris's lips twitched. "Maybe you had better open the guidebook and start reading about these historically significant mausoleums."

Roman sighed but obligingly read while. Lyris snapped pictures. When the short paragraphs were exhausted, they turned and started uphill for the rotting mansion. Here the book waxed slightly more poetic, going so far as to call Toujours Perdrix an architectural treasure. The building had been constructed of oversized brick fired on-site in 1726 on top of an existing mound, the guidebook said, and had the unusual feature of having no windows on the ground floor. It rose for three stories into the trees, without having any visible external form of support, making it unique for buildings of this era.

No mention was made of Quede or the fact that he had been the owner for the span of a few human lifetimes, or that he'd openly become the Goblin King of New Orleans some decades ago.

"You know this is probably some ancient Indian burial mound. They don't have naturally occurring hills out here," Roman pointed out.

"It wouldn't surprise me," Lyris answered. "If it had any sort of power, he'd use it."

"Does Quede have kids?" Roman asked.

"No. Or, I would be very surprised if he did."

"Why? You don't think he'd like raising another blot on the family escutcheon?"

"I don't know his feeling on blots. And I don't think that they're relevant," she answered absently. As they slogged through the soggy drifts of piled leaves, Lyris was thinking that having no windows made the building pretty damned unique for *any* era—and went a long way toward confirming what she suspected.

Roman stopped reading when they reached the stoop and they both stared at the crumbling hulk before them. Damp had turned the red bricks the color of dried blood. The only bright point around them was a stray beam of sun that found its way between the tree branches and blazed off the wet slate roof. Obviously this house stood outside the pattern of normal human architecture. Yet it was not wholly goblin, either. Lyris couldn't believe that tourists had been coming here for forty years and not noticed how bizarre the place was.

"Well, shall we go inside?" she asked, her tone less than enthusiastic, even though this had been her idea.

"I had a feeling you'd want to. You do know that we'll have to break and enter? And I'm pretty sure that's illegal even with an abandoned building."

"No, we won't break anything." Lyris slipped something long and slender out of her rear pocket and stepped up to the door. "I think we'll find that someone has carelessly left the door unlocked."

Roman watched in admiration as she forced the latch without any effort at all.

"That was pretty slick, Uber-sleuth," he complimented. "I thought you'd have to fiddle around for a second or two, but you—"

"It wasn't locked," she interrupted, then said again slowly: "The door really wasn't locked."

"Still want to go in?" Roman looked up at the sky. Little of it was visible through the thick trees overhead, but what he could see was growing dark and ominous. "If we leave now, we can miss the storm."

"Of course we have to go in." Lyris put her wedge away and pushed open the door. She hovered cautiously on the threshold, looking about with nervous eyes. Seeing Roman's concern, she explained: "I hate spiders. I'm just checking the ceiling."

There was nothing to see on the first floor. There had been some fine paneling, but a colony of parasitic vines had gotten a foothold inside the house and were rapidly consuming the decomposing wood beneath the gray-green mat. The floor itself was spongy and required caution while stepping between the house's sagging joists. Roman and Lyris spent most of their time looking down as they fought their way through the shaggy jungle.

Roman was not anxious to explore the probably flooded basements, knowing it was possible that water moccasins and even alligators might have taken up residence there, but was surprised when Lyris also declined to venture down into the dank darkness. After all, if the goblins had a hive entrance in the area, it would likely be through the basement. It should have been something she was keen to see.

"Let's start upstairs. The third floor, the first bedroom on the right," she said softly, being careful that her voice didn't disturb any of the sleeping spiders she feared. "Stay away from those hanging vines. They look carnivorous."

"So, what are we looking for here? A goblin love nest?" Roman stepped around the thorny vine.

"No, nothing so romantic. A prison. I believe that this is where Caitlin St. Barth, Kennedy's mysteriously disappeared aid, was kept until she died. A gardener who worked here back then claimed that he sometimes saw her in that window."

The upstairs was in as bad repair as the downstairs had been, and smelled even mustier because some of the furniture remained and it was rotting. There was a paucity of any homey touches, the only art being the statue of a gryphon—its face sneering in ungodly disdain as Roman and Lyris approached. The house was filled with a silence that only came in buildings when walls were two feet thick and the floors were laid with massive beams. It was the silence of a tomb.

Lyris forced herself to walk up to the old warped door and open it. In the corner of the small bedroom, a carved throne sat in dusty isolation. The floor was covered in an alligator skin rug that for some reason Lyris was reluctant to actually walk on.

Roman might have been nervous, too, but he didn't allow himself to show any fear. He strolled over to the old iron bedstead and pointed out the iron shackles there. They were not mink-lined sex toys, and the rusting metal conveyed a meaning that could not possibly be misunderstood. Worse still, an old iron flail lay on the bedside table. A beating from that would have left deep scars—assuming one didn't die before one had the chance to scar over.

Scars were something Roman knew about. He had the chronicles of past violence and accidents written into his own skin, especially his legs. The chaps he wore while dancing didn't completely cover them.

Lyris turned her back on the shackles and walked over to a dusty mirror. Seeing something beneath the detritus accumulated on the glass, she read aloud the clumsy circle of letters smudged in the dirt on the mirror.

S D
R I
E A
P

"What do they mean?" She started with the D and read clockwise: *"Diapers?"*

"That doesn't seem like the sort of message a prisoner would write."

"But what else could it be? This isn't a nursery. Maybe it's an anagram for something else?"

"Hm, maybe. I'm good at this. Let's see . . . *I parsed? Or ears dip? Rapes id? Oh! Aspired? Or praised,*" he guessed.

"Or is it *despair?*" She frowned. Had the rumors been correct after all? Had Kennedy's young aide not run off with Quede, as the tabloids reported, and spent the rest of her life living some Cinderella story of cross-species love? Had she instead been driven insane by her long captivity in Quede's home? Lyris shivered at the thought. Her theory was coming alive, growing teeth and long claws.

She walked slowly around the room, snapping photos, and found other messages traced in the dust of an end table.

A-G-T-A-O-M-I-H-S.

"*A Gotham is? A Magi I Host?*" Roman suggested.

Lyris stared a moment, watching as the letters arranged themselves in her mind, and then addressed the chilling air in a whisper. " '*Am I a ghost?*' Is that what you were asking? Well, poor soul, I bet you are one now. At least, I hope you are."

"What do you mean?"

"Just that it is probably best that she's dead."

"Do you have any doubts?"

Lyris shrugged, and Roman stopped smiling. He felt it too now, the atmosphere of forlorn hopelessness that filled the place. Whether Caitlin St. Barth's spirit was there or not, the place was definitely haunted by her despair.

"Here's another. E-M-E-C-U-R-E-S. I doubt it's *crème Sue*—though with goblins around, you never know," Roman added, making an effort to fight off the gloom.

"No." Lyris's slight chill grew deeper. She said with conviction: "It's *rescue me*. Poor woman. She didn't even feel safe asking these questions and requests plainly. She must have been terrified of him. No, this wasn't a love nest. It was a cage. And he probably kept her in it until she died."

Roman nodded. He stopped pretending that they were just playing a game. What Lyris was suggesting was that Quede had committed kidnapping and the cold-blooded murder of a human woman. That shouldn't have surprised him, but somehow it did. Quede had gone to great lengths to present a squeaky-clean image to the world. This was blatantly goblin behavior.

"So, what now? Do we go to the police? The evidence seems a little thin, but maybe they'd reopen the investigation of her disappearance if we both raised a fuss and threaten to go to the press." Roman's eyes were on Lyris's face. His posture looked relaxed, but she was coming to know him.

"What do you think?" she asked carefully, her own stance as careless as his but probably as unconvincing.

"You know, I am normally a law-abiding citizen, I really am. And under other circumstance I would urge you to place this information in law enforcement's capable hands—even if it is far too late to help this girl. But the hands around here seem to be all thumbs. And I've noticed that the people they are holding in protective custody end up dead as often as not, the result of some highly unlikely sounding accidents."

"The goblins own the parish, of course."

"Don't think so small. Evidence and witnesses disappear all too often when Quede is involved—and not just in New Orleans. In fact, no one has ever lived to testify against him about anything. Personally, I don't much like the odds if we go to the police."

She nodded in agreement. "And anyway, you have another agenda. So, first things first."

"Yes," he said, surprising her with his first unequivocal answer. "I do have an agenda. And so do you, so don't point fingers. Isn't it time we talked—played a little of *I'll show you mine if you show me yours?*"

"Maybe." Lyris thought about how everyone near Kennedy had mysteriously died. And then how the people who asked questions had died, too. Talking to anyone else really wasn't safe—for her or them. And yet . . .

She said softly: "I don't suppose that you would like to be a gentleman and *show* me yours first?"

"I would actually, but not here. And not until you say pretty please with sugar on top. I have some standards. I like to be wooed even if we are doing tit for tat." The words were teasing, his expression was not.

"I see." She turned toward the window. There was nothing to see beyond the bars but grime and the remains of a spider's ancient dinner. Even if the glass were clear, she couldn't have seen much. The storm had worsened while they were inside. Nature—or Quede—was wielding the wind like a whip, and the trees outside howled while it battered them.

They'd have to leave soon. Before nightfall. Goblin . . . vampire . . . *he* would come out at night. "And what would I need to do to get some straight answers from you—without showing all of mine right away?" she asked.

"You could begin with a small gesture of trust. Like explaining to me what you are hiding under that sweater. On your back. It looks like wings from here. Don't you think it's time you admitted what you are, since you know what I am?"

Lyris stiffened. She didn't have wings now, only a slight tracery of scars in the elongated pattern of a dragonfly's wings, and they couldn't possibly be seen under her blouse—even if it was wet. So how the hell could he know about them? Unless he'd peeked while she was changing in his apartment last night?

Lyris spun about, and for the first time displayed a temper. "You bastard peeping pooka! You watched me shower, didn't you?"

"It was the toaster's fault," he said, throwing up his hands. "I keep my appliances shiny clean. It was just like a mirror. And your wings kind of glitter, honey." Actually, he had a sometimes girlfriend who kept things clean, but he saw no need to bring Monique into the conversation.

Lyris continued to glare at him, but she didn't call him any more names as she pondered his words and their truthfulness.

Roman did his best to keep his thoughts pure and

righteous. "Does Jack know that you're a sylph?" he asked, trying to distract her.

Lyris blinked and exhaled slowly. "I don't think so. We've never discussed it."

"I bet he does know. Jack knows everything. It's probably why he's helping you. You should ask him next time you talk. Though you'd probably do as well to ask how many angels can dance on the head of a pin. His answers and motivations can be a little hard to figure out," Roman added.

"They can, huh? Well, maybe we don't need Jack right now. Let's see if we can do some figuring on our own. Are they fat cherubim-type angels, or thin pre-Victorian ones?" she asked, deadpan. "And is this a quilting pin?"

"Now who isn't focusing?" he scolded, but he was glad she had relaxed. He had hoped to avoid, but half expected, a huge temper tantrum. "You've got to learn about timing. It's the key to successful comedy."

"Sorry. I didn't mean to yell. It's just that I thought I had things well hidden. You caught me by surprise, that's all." Lyris ducked her head for a moment and rearranged her poker face. "I don't like surprises."

"Honey," Roman said kindly, "I don't know how to break it to you, but anyone who knows anything about feys will be able to tell who and what you are. It's those spooky eyes. You might pass among the human tourists as being magic-null, but the goblins and other green nasties have obviously figured out what you are. And that means they have probably figured out what you are doing. So how about letting me in on it too, since it's my ass on the line right along with yours?"

Lyris nodded jerkily and then glanced at the darkening window. "Okay. But we need to get out of here. I don't want to be anywhere near this place when dark falls, and there is somewhere else I want to go."

Roman nodded in return. "I don't think Quede is around here. I could take one old goblin if it came to a fight, but Quede would never travel alone. More than three goblins could be a problem—unless you're feeling feisty too."

"Feisty isn't the word. And no, he probably wouldn't travel alone." Lyris looked up, her face pale as she said earnestly: "But, Roman, you mustn't think that you could beat Quede in a fight even one on one. He is worlds stronger than you can imagine. If he ever comes at you, just do your best to get away. I promise you, it's what I'll be doing."

He stared at her. "You are really beginning to creep me out."

"Good. It's safer for both of us if you feel that way."

Chapter Seven

The battered sign announced GOBLIN CHRISTIAN COMMUNITY CENTER—*We live for God's words*.

"God probably doesn't speak much, though, because words fail Him," Roman muttered, eyeing the dilapidated building. It was painted with a crucifix adorned not only with a bleeding body but also a cheery rainbow that served as a loincloth. The decor was less than appealing in the dirty rain, though it wasn't the sort of place that would have appealed to either Roman or Lyris even on a sunny day. "This can't be the lot who were financing archaeological expeditions. They don't look like they have a dime to spare."

" '*Jesus lives here*,' " Lyris read aloud, still incredulous. She wiped dark water from her forehead. It stung slightly.

"But does He like it?" Roman asked irrepressibly. The water didn't bother him.

"I should think it is no worse than any other place He has been," answered a paper-thin voice. "And here we really do believe in the resurrection."

Lyris and Roman spun to face a heavily cowled figure who had ghosted up behind them. It was difficult to see his features clearly in the deep shadow of his hood, except for the two long wisps of mustache that hung down like catfish whiskers, but it was apparent from his stature that he was a goblin. He also seemed vaguely familiar.

" '*And it shall come to pass when I bring a cloud over the earth that the bow shall be seen in clouds . . . and the water shall no more become a flood to destroy the earth.*' I am Father Lobineau." The thin lips smiled. The weary and doleful voice went on: "You shouldn't be too surprised. Grace operates where it may. Any living repository will do. And Christianity appeals to the humble feelings in a person's nature. It is a natural choice for these modified goblins of Quede's. They are credulous as children, inclined by their breeding to submit and obey. The Carpenter's religion offers discipline, forgiveness, and simplicity of ritual. The soil is fertile. The Word has been well received."

"And Quede allows it?" Lyris asked before she could stop herself.

"Oh, yes. Not because he is filled with the Holy Spirit himself, of course." The old goblin's thin smile grew and sharp teeth began to show as tiny glints of light. He waved a badly scarred hand that looked like a glove that had been charred on a barbecue. "For him it is just one more tool to keep everyone obedient, and he believes me, Father Lobineau, the right sort of person to wield this tool for him."

"If it's a tool for Quede, what is it for you?" Roman asked pointedly, his body alert.

"A sword, of course. A lovely, shining sword of retribution that shall lop off the goblin king's beautiful, arrogant head." The goblin priest turned away, adding softly: "Won't you come inside? I know that you want to see me, or rather, someone like me. And I believe we have some important things to discuss."

"Like what?" Roman asked, still not trusting this silent-stepped stranger who moved like a ghost.

"Well, for starters, I was in Dallas the day Kennedy died." The goblin turned back toward them, but looked only at Lyris. "You see my hands? The rest of me is as scarred. It happened while I stood for hours in that blazing sun waiting for the president's arrival."

"And Quede made you do it," Lyris said softly, not looking at Roman though she plainly felt his gaze when it shifted toward her.

"Oh, yes. Our goblin king most definitely made us do it."

"But how?" Roman asked, believing but unable to understand. "How could he *make* you stand in the sun and burn? No goblin has that much control over his people. They don't have that kind of power. That's why they keep trying to use goblin fruit, and drugs, and brainwashing."

"Quede does have that much control," Lyris said. She spoke with a confident and depressing certainty. "And he doesn't need drugs, or goblin fruit, or brainwashing to do it, does he?"

"No, he doesn't," the old goblin agreed, again turning away and heading for the warped side door in the south wall of the building. He added without looking back: "His power has grown beyond all bounds ever imagined by either of our species. But it isn't because he's a goblin. Or merely a goblin."

Roman looked at Lyris. "Okay, so just what is he, Super Goblin? *Goblinus prime?*"

"Sort of." She hesitated for a moment and then sighed. "He's a vampire. He is, in fact, the master vampire of New Orleans. Haven't you noticed that all of New Orleans's famous vampires are gone?"

"Of course they're gone. Vampires are dead. They died with the feys when the sun flared."

"I know that's the conventional wisdom. But they were gone before then. Anyway, crossbreed feys survived," Lyris said softly. "Why not crossbreed vampires?"

Roman stared at her for a minute, but didn't argue. "All right. Maybe. But do we have to use the term *master vampire?* That implies that there are more of them."

Lyris nodded. "That may or may not follow. I'm sure he's tried making fledglings, but they may have died. Many crossbreeds are sterile. And a failure to reproduce that way would explain some of what he's doing."

"Let us hope they're dead." Roman mused, "So, because he has turned vampire, Quede is now firing blanks? He won't ever hear the soft pitter-patter of little green feet?"

"That's the idea," Lyris agreed.

Father Lobineau's voice floated out at them, around the corner of the building, and carried on the rising wind: "In the beginning of our migration, we wandered the shores near rivers and oceans, passing always from wet climate to drier climate, then from dry climates to wastelands."

Roman abandoned the discussion of Quede's infertility, and he and Lyris started walking toward the disembodied voice that was offering a history lesson.

"Always we were pushed to the margins, the places that humans didn't want. And we went—without war, without even protesting. We watched the humans, those heartless murderers who killed their own kind in ways and numbers that no goblin would ever dream of doing. We didn't have the numbers or weapons to fight back." Lobineau looked down and said softly as Roman and Lyris joined him under the modest overhang that sheltered the warped door; "And what the humans didn't take from us, Quede did. I had a wife then. Damiana was her name. He took her too. And when he was done playing with her, he killed her—without effort, without thought, without regret. Later, after his change, he killed the vampires and gave us New Orleans as a consolation prize. But it wasn't enough, because you can never make restitution to the dead. And nothing will ever be enough while we live under this monster's bloodied boot." His voice changed. "Go down to the next door and I'll unlock it for you. Don't come in here. The supply room is filthy and dark."

Roman waited until Father Lobineau disappeared inside the dark structure and closed the door before he muttered, "That guy looks like a goblin Fu Manchu and talks like a bad version of Ben-Hur."

"Fu Manchu? I had some of that once. It's not bad with oyster sauce."

Roman stared at Lyris, not quite perfectly amused. His look stopped short of complete admiration. "I already mentioned the timing thing. You need to work on that."

Lyris smiled tightly. "Sorry, it's nerves. One thing I am not joking about is being away from here before nightfall. I don't care how interesting this conversation gets. We are still way too close to Quede's plantation, and I don't feel safe."

"And I don't like the smell," Roman agreed.

They started walking for the second shadowy doorway, their footsteps splashing in the dirty puddles of the cracked parking lot that ran right up to the weathering walls.

"I've always wondered, is it true that pookas are summoned when humans dream of running with animals?" Father Lobineau's voice was normal as he opened the second door and then flipped on a bank of dreary florescent lights. He gestured Lyris and Roman toward a battered worktable and chairs. If there was any anger left in him, it did not manifest itself in his tone.

"Personally, I think that if you want me, it might be wisest to use the phone. I'm in the book," Roman said untruthfully. His nose wrinkled as he took in the musty air.

"Perhaps. Did you know that I knew your father?" the priest asked, taking a seat at the battered table. The chair creaked under him, suggesting he was heavier than he looked. "He came from Carrig-a-Phooka at the Pollaphuc. Later, he settled near New Orleans. Like my kind, he needed to be near water. And away from humans."

If this bit of familial trivia was meant to soften Roman's attitude, it had no effect. "Then you know more about him than I do." He pulled out a chair, spun it about, and thrust it between his long legs. He folded his arms and rested them along the chair's rough rail and glanced at the door they had come through as though expecting company.

Lyris seated herself in a more conventional manner, but she also elected to face the doorway. She wasn't exactly anticipating that someone else would be arriving soon, but a feeling of unease was growing in her. She felt observed. She was also—finally—doing some math about who was who and what motivated them, and she was coming up with answers that made her nervous. The truth would be known again, just with a disconcerting lag time.

"Your father had no chance to say good-bye to you before he died? That must have been a cause for sorrow," Father Lobineau said sympathetically. The seemingly benevolent questions began to annoy Lyris. All feys had had tremendous losses. They never spoke of them. Such was a cultural taboo. Lobineau had to know this.

"Pookas never say good-bye." Roman's voice was flat. "And like I said, I didn't know the guy."

"That's right. I had forgotten that about pookas. Well, then, what do the other feys say? '*Merry we meet. Merry we part. Merry we meet again.*' Perhaps we could use that when we part."

"Whatever turns your crank." Roman sounded unusually surly. "Now, if you don't mind, we need to talk and be out of here before nightfall."

"Very wise. Quede would not come here himself, but . . ."

"But he has servants."

"Yes. Many, many servants. And most of us are obedient to his wishes." Father Lobineau folded his hands. The goblin's long, scarred fingers were bent and stained nicotine brown, except on the tips where they were ashen gray. They looked as if someone had smoked them and then stubbed them out in an ashtray.

Which didn't mean that they weren't still strong enough to break a person's neck. Roman looked at his own long hands and experimented with making a fist. Satisfied with its solidity, he looked back at the goblin priest's shadowed face. He knew that he should feel compassion for this creature, after the story he'd told. But he didn't. Couldn't. Something about him forbade any soft emotions. Lyris was also looking very nervy.

"May I offer you some tea? It is the universal restorative."

The gesture was conventional, hospitable, but somehow breaking bread with this creature seemed, at the least, a morally ambiguous gesture. With a human, Roman wouldn't worry, but goblins sometimes trucked in symbolic magic. And poison.

"I think that's brandy, not tea, that's the universal restorative. Unfortunately, we don't have time for either." He spoke before Lyris could and hoped that she would follow his lead.

Lobineau looked pained by Roman's barely concealed suspicion. He turned to Lyris. "Then may I ask of you, my dear, what you intend by your investigations?"

Assuming correctly that the "*my dear*" was directed at her rather than at Roman, Lyris answered vaguely: "What I do will rather be determined by what I find. And how much proof I have to lay before the world as justification for any actions."

"A sensible answer—and gathering the facts is certainly a meretricious goal. Accusations of this nature—unsupported by facts—would be actionable, assuming Quede bothered with formal law when he wished to remove a problem." Lobineau cocked his head. "I can see that you have already thought of this. So, tell me truthfully, given this suspicion of Quede's nature, and the fact that you have no normal, legal recourse available to you, were you not perhaps considering slaying Quede yourself? If he is proven guilty to your satisfaction, of course."

Lyris appeared to think for a moment and then said mildly, "It is not in my immediate plans, but the day is still young."

Roman didn't blink, but he was surprised by her answer. Truthfully, he suspected that she was surprised too. She had never mentioned any intention of attempting to kill Quede. The very notion of trying was suicidal.

Nevertheless, he thought he understood what was happening to her, because it was also happening with him. The feeling was growing that they and the goblin king were locked onto a course that would surely lead to their eventual collision. Wreckage and disintegration would be the fate for at least one of them if they ever met. So, if this was destined, it seemed best that it be Quede who died.

"Please tell me about Dallas," Lyris urged,

clearly doing her best to shake off her preoccupation. Roman followed suit. One problem at a time, that was the only way to take these things.

Lyris went on, "Why did he do it? Not for the money surely. And why did he make a film of the event?"

"No, of course it wasn't about money. It was about power. It's always about power. Quede finally had a chance to put one of his minions in the White House and he did it." Lobineau's lips smiled thinly. "He didn't reckon on losing control of his creature though. Or that bit of film ever being turned against him."

Lyris was suddenly positive that Lobineau had been the one to hold the camera that day. She looked aghast at Lobineau's hands and then over at Roman.

"What film?" Roman asked.

"A film of the assassination taken with a heat-sensitive camera. It shows who in the crowd was goblin and who was human," Lyris answered.

"Quede really arranged for the murder of a president? And filmed it?" Roman asked.

"Yes. It wasn't the first one, of course," the priest answered.

"Not the first film?"

"First assassination," Lobineau answered impatiently.

"Who else?"

Lyris didn't add to Roman's short question, but

she was just as startled by Lobineau's announcement.

"Quede arranged for Harding to die, too. He controlled the wife." Lobineau spread his hands and shrugged slightly. "The president was pursuing certain social programs that would have been detrimental to Quede's power base here in the South. Harding would not be deterred by other means; therefore he had to die. That assassination was less spectacular of course. People still think that it was a heart attack or pneumonia."

"Just to be thorough—Oswald and Ruby were also goblins?" Lyris finally asked when the appalled silence had spun out to an uncomfortable length.

"Of course—and they were no more volunteers than I was. But Quede felt it necessary, on many levels, to make an example of the killings. Both for humans and for goblins."

"For humans?"

"Yes, humans. Humans!" He added in annoyance, "Unfortunately, they must always be taken into account."

"Unfortunately." Roman's tone was filled with irony, but Lobineau didn't seem to notice.

"Most unfortunately. They live in a world of sheer illusion. Americans especially do not perceive that there is any opposition to them in the world. Even natural disasters cannot deter them. They see their prosperity as a right to exist, as Truth received from some divine source. Their faith in this is unshakable. Look how they rebuild in flood zones and in the path of tornadoes. And just try to budge them from this view—they only get angry. Certainly they know there are bad men out there, but they believe those are freaks, loners, individuals acting independently. Or insane countries." Lobineau's voice roughened and he again showed signs of agitation. "They take no responsibility for their pollution, which kills all other species, or the wars that devastate the land. They were and are irresponsible, destructive children who want to be taken care of by their government. And Quede knows this well. Of course, lessons have to be taught slowly to these self-absorbed creatures. He intended LBJ to do that. But he had to give them someone for their lost president, a sacrificial goat to keep them calm while the change of power was made."

"Oswald?"

"Yes, Oswald." Lobineau snorted. "And the blind public was satisfied with their John the Baptist once his head was on a platter. Quede had meant to reveal LBJ later, to show the smug human world that a goblin president was a good thing—but the creature went insane from sun exposure, and Quede never did appear to the world as the *éminence grise* he is."

"So what did you goblins get from this killing—aside from an insane president that was one of your own?" Lyris asked.

"We got nothing so gentle as the humans received,

be sure of that. We were given a salutary lesson in just how powerful Quede is," Lobineau answered bitterly. "Our scarred bodies and those two martyrs are a reminder that opposition—even in thought—will not be tolerated. It worked, too. For both goblins and humans in the know. No one has ever taken on Quede. No one has ever even questioned him. Until now. That makes you two very brave—pioneers, in fact."

"Never mind the past and pioneers. Do you think Quede will ever plot such evil again?" Roman's voice was low but harsh. "Would he assassinate another president? Is he going to kill this one?"

Father Lobineau hesitated, and Lyris wondered if he was considering lying. She watched him carefully, wondering if she could read his lies as easily as a human's. "I don't believe so. Not because he has reformed, but because Quede has found power far greater than any achievable by political means. Far greater and far more evil. At least, evil for anyone near him."

The father's words were shocking—and truthful, as far as Lyris could tell. He meant what he was saying. But it seemed to her that there was a lie being told also; perhaps by omission. It took some effort for Lyris to ask, "And that power would be?"

"Complete control of the masses, of course." Father Lobineau added gently, "It's always about control and power. He began with goblins—breeding out our individuality, making us sexless so that he could control our population levels until the time is right for propagating an army. That's our only use to him anymore. We are apparently not very good food."

Lyris and Roman stared at him, not wanting to believe in Quede's vampiric evil, but not daring to disbelieve either.

"And when might that time be?"

"Soon, I think. He started experimenting with the drifters. We have the usual floating human population of scum in this city that live through nefarious means, feeding like parasites off the societal body. The difference is, here Quede puts them to better use. In *new* New Orleans, even leeches have their place." Lobineau reined in his sarcasm. "However, he has been experimenting on healthy human tourists recently, determining how many he can control with his mind. How many he can infect with a virus containing buried instructions of behavior. His will is prodigious, and he has been very successful, but he can't subjugate everyone.

"His preference would always be to work by stealth," Lobineau explained, "and take over this state and then the nation a little bit at a time—because he has time, an eternity in which to work. But he won't be able to do it that way. There are simply too many people, too many politicians, too many self-centered parasites. And he loses his ability to influence his victims the farther away they get away from him. He'll give up soon, and then he'll turn to war to get what he wants. What he needs."

"What he needs?" Roman echoed. "And that is?"

"Safety, of course. He knows what humans are—how they fear vampires. He has already lived longer than he should. How long before people begin to suspect the truth? He can't feed off of goblins, you know. Or, at least, he can't feed on us alone. He must have humans." Lobineau turned to Roman and added with a purely goblin hiss: "And when the humans are gone, he'll turn on the feys—if not before. They are an even richer feast."

"Feys may have something to say about that," Roman answered. Lobineau just shook his head.

"What is he doing to the tourists?" Lyris asked. It seemed to her that there was a new, sour smell floating on the air, mingling with the odor of rotting building. In spite of the moist breeze swirling into the room through the open door, her mouth was dry, a dusty, desiccated cavity with a tongue that was growing stiff and furred. She began to feel both nauseated and sleepy. It might have been the conversation, but she suspected it was something else—something more dangerous and unnatural. If they had had anything to drink, she would be worrying about being drugged.

"Nothing, for now. I think he is reserving the ones he has infected as stock—a breeding, willing food supply." The priest turned his head back her way. His neck seemed stiff and he wasn't quite able to hide his contempt as added: "You'll want to save them, of course, if you can—those tourists."

"Don't you?" Long sleeves hid her arms, but Lyris could feel the gooseflesh rising as Lobineau stared at her. His small red eyes seemed suddenly brighter. Flames of fanaticism lit them. She wondered if Roman could see it.

"Of course," Father Lobineau agreed. But even without Lyris scanning him for the truth, both she and Roman knew he was lying. Disciple of Christ or not, Lobineau didn't care about humans. He went on, "But of course the welfare of my flock must come first. I must plan for their survival. After all, they are saved, washed in the blood of the Lamb. Who knows about these humans who come here for sin and vice?"

Lyris felt ill. She did not know how to answer, even if her tongue were able to shape itself into speech. "The good of *my* people"—it was the hallowed, ancient excuse for all forms of atrocity. She hoped that she was mistaken in Lobineau's intent.

"Well, it's been a blast, but we really have to go now." Roman stood up, radiating menace and aversion. He hadn't liked Lobineau's answer either.

"Of course," Father Lobineau replied, also rising. Not wanting to be left sitting at the table if things got violent, Lyris also stood. The air seemed cleaner higher up, and almost instantly she began to feel better. "I'm quite certain that we'll meet again. Soon. Fate shall bring you to me. After all, you have some decisions to make. And I can help you make the right one."

Roman started to ask if those words were a threat, but Lyris's soft touch on his arm stopped him.

"What is the saying—'*Man proposes; God disposes*'?" she asked politely.

Lobineau inclined his head, making his whiskers sway to and fro. "Of course, we are not *men*."

His words were gentle. And terrible. *Of course, we are not men*. The phrase seemed to renounce humanity, to suggest that Lobineau, his people, and even the half-feys of the world were beyond all moral consideration. To a goblin, they probably were.

The priest held out a hand. "So, until then—merry we meet, merry we part, merry we meet again."

"You'll have to excuse me if I don't echo the sentiment," Roman answered. "But you know how it is with us pookas. We never say good-bye."

Chapter Eight

"Do you think Lobineau was telling the truth?"

"As in *the truth, the whole truth, and nothing but the truth?*" Lyris asked. "No. But he wasn't lying either. Not exactly."

"Too bad. The dire news just piles up—and the pile is getting high enough to be unstable."

Lyris nodded in agreement, then walked around a pair of imps rooting through a discarded brown bag in the optimistic but apparently futile hope of a tasty snack.

Roman continued in amazement, "And knowing that Quede was an impotent psycho vampire, you still came here. Alone."

"I suspected he was a vampire, yes. And I'd heard about his genderless goblins—but there was no proof that it was true. And there was also no explanation of *why*. And whom should I have taken this sketchy information to, anyway? Who could I trust? Not the F.B.I.'s Genetic Crimes Unit. As you pointed out, going to law enforcement about goblins is a tricky business these days. Heck, maybe always if what we've heard is true." Lyris looked at Roman, really looked, not bothering to hide what she was or that she was seeking answers. "Is that where you come in, Roman? Are you the person I should trust?"

The question, whether intended to or not, stung.

"You better hope so, darlin'," he answered shortly, pulling a flyer out from under his Jaguar's windshield wiper. It said *Radiation Without Representation* and had the standard red circle with a slash through it laid over the top. He held it up so Lyris could see. "Because excepting our new goblin friend—and the odd lutin nuclear protester—I don't think there is anyone else around here who cares about you, Quede, or anything else—and I'm wondering what will keep us alive past sunset."

She nodded, breaking eye contact with him while she thought. "The trouble is, I don't think Lobineau is a friend. At best we are only temporary allies. Did you notice that he forgot to bless us? Given what we are facing, he should have been calling out regiments of saints and angels to watch over us innocent wooly lambs—even if we belong to the goddess. He's only for his own kind. I would bet his morals are so elastic, his definitions of Christianity so flexible, he doesn't even count feys as worth saving." Lyris pulled open the door of the car and looked toward the west. The sky was too cloudy to pinpoint the sun's position, but it was definitely getting dark. "Well, I've 'shown you mine' now. How about you show me a bit of yours? Who are you, Roman? Why are you here?"

"You don't think I'm just a freak, making a living in New Orleans because I could get a work permit and feel welcome here?" he asked.

Lyris climbed into the car, suddenly smiling. "Not for a minute. I may not be able to see into you completely, but this much I am certain about: You're more than a freak. You're good."

Once again, Roman felt both flattered and aggravated. How could she hold such a high opinion of his morals and motivations? He didn't think much of himself; it was a bother that she did.

"It isn't fate that brought us together, you know," he warned her.

"No, I think it was Jack," she said seriously. "I am also beginning to suspect that Jack isn't just some mercenary with a thing for Quede, is he? Jack Frost is someone—something—much more important. A sort of éminence grise just like Quede. He is probably the one who tipped Lobineau that he should send me that film."

"Maybe. Jack does move in mysterious ways his miracles to perform. But I bet this news about LBJ comes as a shock to him. Goblins just weren't that advanced in the sixties. I didn't know that they had thermal cameras back then."

"But it wasn't just a goblin who masterminded the assassination and replacement. It was Quede—a *vampire* goblin. Besides, goblins have been trying lots of new things lately—like building bombs in Sin City. The little green guys have finally gone high-tech. Very scary." She smiled a little. "But that is all a bit beside the point. You're avoiding answering my question about Jack."

Roman shut his door and put the keys in the ignition. He patted the Jag's dashboard. It was ritual. He had explained that he kept the temperamental car because, though he was from Texas and as macho as the next man, he preferred to drive sophisticated *on*-road vehicles. Lyris hadn't pointed out that bright red jags were neither ubiquitous nor discreet, and therefore the choice might not be the best one for those wishing to keep a low profile; suggesting Roman abandon his car would have been a pointless activity. Anyway, if they needed to make a fast getaway, this car could do it.

"No. No, I'm not and no, he's not just a mercenary." Roman reached a decision. It was an impulsive decision, the sort of thing that almost always got him into trouble and so he rarely gave in to anymore. Still, he found himself saying: "Jack Frost is the best hope for the survival of the fey. He is also the best hope for the survival of mankind. And the goblins know it now. He is Wanted Fey Number

One in the goblin world. He is also a sneaky, conniving bastard who will do anything he thinks best for his people. Do you know he is forming a parliament of feys?"

"Which makes him a very dangerous man to know."

Roman nodded. "He's dangerous all right. But he's also very charismatic. Have you noticed that? It clouds your judgment when you talk to him."

"Yes. We've never met, but I feel it even on the phone."

"I'll tell you something else. I'm normally a very clear-headed guy, not blinded by either machismo or turn tail and run fear, but I'm damned if somehow I'm not feeling both things right now. I hate it. The conflict makes me want to punch someone—mainly Jack. Or Lobineau."

"Yes, I noticed that impulse. Thank you for controlling yourself." Lyris knit her brow. "You know, I sometimes have the feeling that it is *all* Jack's—or someone's—doing that I ended up in New Orleans. It couldn't have been my own idea. But I've been following this story, the Kennedy assassination, for so long—years—because the clues keep getting laid before me at opportune moments. Could Jack really be behind it all? Or is it something bigger going on?"

Roman nodded again. He said with feeling, "I know that feeling well. You've been conned, but you're just not sure *how*. I do hope it's Jack doing the conning, though. I don't like the idea of something bigger taking a hand in our affairs."

Lyris sighed. Thinking of the magic—the attraction—between them, she added: "It feels like fate sometimes. That we are being guided. But I hate sounding mystical or paranoid." She shook her head. "We'd better go. The rain is getting worse."

"Shall we stop and eat? I saw a little roadhouse back toward town." Roman's tone was again cheerful.

"You want to eat *again?*"

"What? You're going to tell me you never snack between meals?"

"No, but there has to be some 'between meals' for one to snack in. You eat constantly."

"It's my metabolism. I never gain weight, either," he bragged.

"Selfish creep. You can just keep that fact to yourself. Do you know how much I have to exercise?"

"Not as much as a human, I'm betting." He grinned and turned the key in the ignition. The starter ground but the engine didn't catch. He tried a second time. Then a third. He turned to look at Lyris. "Damn."

"You have a cell phone?"

"Of course. But I bet you anything you like that we can't get a signal out here."

"That would be some bad luck."

"I don't think luck has anything to do with it."

They turned their heads in unison, looking with suspicion at the Goblin Christian Community Center.

"I don't see any phone lines, do you?"

Sylph—the invisible veil of perfume that cloaked her left a gorgeous, subtle wake in the still, dark room, marking the path she had walked. The scent of her reawoke Quede's imagination, recalled sweet moods and lost hours with dead lovers. And he hated that—especially here in this house, the scene of his greatest defeat.

Yet, even as he resented the fey for reawakening his memory, he inhaled again, deeply, absorbing her aura of painful blue skies, golden sun, and the emerald beauty of late spring.

He had to have her. Have her, or kill her. But not yet. How inconvenient that he should have to leave her alone for the time being! How annoying! But he was an old goblin, crafty, and had learned impulse-control since the days when he had taken Caitlin St. Barth and made her a prisoner here. He'd been too rough then, too hasty. When he found out that she was a member of H.U.G. and not just Kennedy's aide he'd lashed out in anger, broken her mind as well as her spirit. And, of course, he'd lost her. She was little more than a ghost now, a reproachful memory.

Quede went to the mirror and looked at his reflection in the spotted glass. Emotion had made the black of his eyes bleed and overrun the whites until it was like looking at spilled pools of ink. He reached for his sylph with his mind and whispered softly: "Come, O come, whoever you are, and tell me of your dreams. Do you lust? Do you worship? What do you seek? The balm of Gilead? Life everlasting? Or is it my destruction you desire, lovely fey?"

It seemed for a moment that the room trembled, but there came no answer. Her mind was hidden from him.

Turning away from the glass, he reached out with his thoughts a second time and located his half-human servant.

Where is she now?

She and the pooka are at the Goblin Christian Community Center. There was a pause. The handsome Schiem was preparing to deliver unpleasant news. Quede was amused to note that his minion had begun to wonder about his sanity and to weigh every word. *They have been talking to Father Lobineau.*

Have they? How very, very interesting. Tell the priest that I want a meeting. And get out your raincoat. A storm is coming.

Quede felt Schiem sigh.

Lyris and Roman climbed out of the car. They were already wet enough that a little more rain didn't matter.

The wind picked up suddenly, and the imps, who

had been squabbling over the remains of a peanut butter sandwich, froze abruptly. With a fearful look in the direction of the encroaching swamp, they scampered for a crack in the building's foundation.

"What—"

"Look at them!" The twin imps had recoiled from their chosen crevasse and were now scurrying for the dark beneath the Dumpster. They cowered there, tiny jaws chattering. "They sure smelled something they didn't like down there, and I doubt it's the Holy Spirit."

"I don't like this either," Roman said flatly. "Let's go."

Lyris didn't raise an objection. There was something in the air—she couldn't smell or taste it, but it was there all the same, and it raised the small hairs of her nape.

Danger. Magic. Run.

"Good idea. Let's go!" she answered before she realized that the voice of warning wasn't physical.

Though it was indiscreet, the two of them broke into an inhumanly fast dash and began sprinting up the road through the soot-colored rain. They had a good mile to travel before reaching the last building they'd seen, a fifty-year-old gas station with an attached diner. They were going to set the land speed record getting there, and at that, they knew they might not be fast enough.

* * *

Quede took a seat on his old throne and closed his eyes. It wasn't necessary that he be in darkness to communicate with his half-human servant, but before true nightfall he found it helpful when he wished to actually see out of Schiem's eyes.

Perhaps he had been wrong to avoid this place, he thought, settling into his familiar seat. The memories here were not all bad, and he sometimes liked to be away from the city. It wasn't a good sign, because it suggested mental if not physical aging, but on occasion he found himself longing for quieter days and simpler times. Those could be had here without sacrificing his ability to touch the many strands of his empiric web, or risking control of his minions.

Quede took another deep breath, savoring the tastes and smells on his palette. There was an ancient bit of Caitlin still in the air, and of course the sylph. He didn't care for the smell of pooka, but that could be ignored when the pleasure of the other two female scents was so great.

Never let it be said that he did not value women, because he adored them. They were his second favorite recreation. They might have been his first, but he had found that after the first thrill of discovery, they rather lacked diversity. Unlike his lovely orchids, women seemed to come in only a few varieties.

There were many ugly ones and stupid ones, of

course, but these he discounted, not deeming them worthy of inclusion on his list of exotics.

First among favored female types were the innocents, the ones who had power in their loveliness but did not know how to wield it. It was his pleasurable experience that a pretty woman who was not aware of her charms was apt to easily fall victim to her own beauty. And he loved these ingénues—he *truly* did! They weren't like the shrinking but homely violets, always running away from men because they had been teased. No, these sweetly unenlightened creatures would flutter close like little golden butterflies after the nectar of male praise and attention. And when they were close enough, he'd spin a glittering web of subtle flattery and let them climb in of their own accord. Foolish, lovely creatures—like Caitlin St. Barth.

Quede shook his head at the memory of the flawed child, slightly wrinkling his granite brow and almost smiling. She hadn't been stupid, just naive. Seducing her had been one part science and three parts poetry. Or so it had seemed. Later, when he found out that she had been approached by H.U.G., he had had momentary doubts about her innocence. He'd actually felt betrayed and had reacted badly. He should have just broken her neck and been done with her. Quede pushed the painful memory away.

Of course, of late, he'd seen few of these types. Women these days, like those horrid, commercially produced orchids bred for the masses, were apt to be aware of their assets. They worshipped at their mirrors, anointing themselves with unguents and powders, preserving their youth and beauty until they finally convinced themselves that they deserved to be elevated to the ranks of goddesses and worshipped for this conservation of youth alone. These types took more effort to seduce—not because of greater intelligence, but simply because preserving themselves from everything foreign had become ingrained habit. Nothing was as important to them as they were to themselves.

Quede sighed and relaxed his brow. These women were so rarely worth the extra effort. Perhaps it was all in his mind, but their oh-so-healthy, vitamin-fortified blood seemed to lack the sweetness of the pure and innocent. These women never looked up with wide eyes—he supposed that wide eyes were difficult to make when your cheeks were shot up with Botox—and whispered their consent to be ruined with shy voices and fluttering hearts. When they participated in their demise, it was with feigned innocence—yet cold hearts and an eye to increasing their power. The only fun came when they realized that they had been cheated, that they were going to die, that there would be no eternal life for them and all their cosmetic preservations wouldn't save them.

However, every now and again, while he hunted among the potion-prepared beauties, Quede would find someone truly twisted. These women were born predators, and were self-aware enough to recognize themselves as such. And these mantraps . . . *Ah!* There was a piquancy, a spice to them! It made Quede want to drain every last ounce of blood from their glorious, surgically created bodies. And he did! Every last drop. . . . After all, he knew it was true that you are what you eat—so he liked to dine on other predators. Devouring one's enemy for their strength was a time-honored tradition.

The question he asked himself now was, what sort of female was this delicious-smelling sylph? Was she a predator? Might she be something entirely new? And could he turn her without destroying her body, without infecting her with his viral ugliness? It would be a wondrous miracle if he could.

The really nice thing about pookas, Lyris decided, was that they seemed to have no capacity for lasting worry or unhappiness. There she and Roman were—wet, cold, running through a swamp in the dark, probably with some hound of hell on their heels—and Roman's spirits just seemed to fly right over the damp, the dark, and the sore feet. It was very strange, but his absurd happiness beat the hell out of listening to him whine about hunger all the way back to civilization and a pay phone. It also kept Lyris's own fears at bay.

"What are you staring at?" Roman asked as they ran toward the far-off lights of the gas station. Their fleet feet made only the softest patters as they went. "I can feel you drilling me with those ice-green eyes of yours."

"Sorry, I was looking at those Herculean sinews professional strippers all seem to have." Actually, she had been looking at his butt. She wouldn't admit aloud to appreciating any part of him, but fact was fact. He had a nice ass. He could probably crack walnuts with those buns.

"Well, I'm a bit long in the limb for Hercules—and possessed of a neck besides—but I can run like a racehorse."

"You certainly can." Lyris had been able to keep up, but she was beginning to feel the strain of the extended sprint. Her kind were better at short bursts of intense speed than marathons. "I don't feel watched anymore, but I suppose that it would be crazy to double back and try to catch whoever was spying on us."

Roman turned his head and stared at her. "Are you delirious? That is one bad impulse."

"I know it sounds nuts, but I would give a lot to know what frightened those imps—both in the swamp and in Lobineau's rotting building," she explained. "However, chances are that we could never sneak up on it and take it unawares. Whatever it is. Any guesses about that? Was it human? I couldn't tell."

"Information. That's the coin of the realm here. Unfortunately, my pockets are empty. I get as far as suspecting Quede and then go broke. It can't have been Quede that scared the imps out of the basement, though. It was still light out. A goblin *vampire* wouldn't go out in the sun."

"Empty pockets? With all your tips at the Easy Off?" His sense of humor was rubbing off on her. Lyris wasn't certain that it was a good thing, especially as she seemed to lack the ability to deliver her lines in a humorous manner, but oh, well.

"Honey, they stuff tips in my jock, not my pockets. Anyway, as curious as I now am, I'd rather hoped your pockets were empty too—that you've told me everything. If there's anything else I should know about Quede, I'd appreciate it if you told me." He paused. "That you can even think of going back is kind of alarming me."

"No, my pockets are empty too," she assured him. "All I have is intuition—and that intuition suspects Quede of being in the swamp. I know it wasn't full dark when we left Lobineau's, but I am still certain that somehow Quede was eyeballing us. It was almost like he was trying to influence me."

"Yeah, I felt that too. And that makes me very nervous. If Quede can use his servants or animals to do remote viewing—"

"It makes me unhappy. The good news is, I didn't feel anything while we were in the house. I don't think he was spying on us there, so he couldn't have heard what we were talking about."

"No." Roman slowed to a human jog as they

came close to the gas station, and his muscles settled back into familiar lines. "But I would bet almost anything that somehow he knows we were there."

"I wouldn't take that wager," Lyris answered. She also slowed. "Because somehow I think you're right. Who knows what sort of hyperacute perception he may have? Maybe he can sense us by some other means—smell or heat traces."

"Never mind his perceptions. If he knows we were there, that means we're probably in trouble."

"Potentially," she agreed. They trotted up to the gas station's old office, whose red paint was peeling away in hundreds of small curls. "Shall we pray for a tow truck? One with solid seats and no bad fish odors?"

"Save your breath and prayers for something more urgent. I saw a truck parked around back." Roman glanced at Lyris. "The thing is, I don't care about the seats or smells. We aren't going to ride back for my car."

"No?"

"No. Baby will just have to travel without me. I'll have her towed back and fixed." Roman paused and then said gently: "Maybe I'm way off base, but given Quede's history, it might be best if you stayed far away from him from here on out. Don't forget, he's a sexual predator on top of everything else. And he's very, very old. You don't become an old goblin unless you're a really, really mean one."

Lyris shivered. But she knew Roman was right.

* * *

Quede was annoyed but not surprised when he lost sight of his quarry. His half-human servant could not possibly run as fast as a pooka or a sylph, and it was of course understandable that they would sense Schiem's clumsy presence and flee. They were both part animal after all, and Schiem was not even a vampire—as much as he wanted to be.

Quede relented on the fury of the storm once they were outside the grounds and allowed the rain to taper off. The wind and lightning had only been conjured to delay and frighten them a bit—and that hadn't worked particularly well. Obviously, they were not given to nerves and moodiness based on the weather.

Amusing as it was to watch a lost Schiem stumble through the dark, he called his servant back from the chase and ordered him to go to Lyris's hotel while the two trespassers were busy arranging things with their car. He wasn't to touch anything in her room, but Quede wanted to see where she was staying, to drink in her air. Schiem's eyes and nose were not as keen as Quede's own, but Schiem would absorb some of the air into his skin and Quede would know more about the sylph when the servant returned.

In the meanwhile, he needed to go back to the city and dress for the evening. The governor was coming to dinner. It was election time again, and that meant the politicians were calling with monotonous regularity in hopes of refilling their perennially empty coffers. Human parasites! But Quede needed them for just a while longer.

He reached up and touched the small medallion he wore. He didn't worship Shiva, but he liked the image because the god looked like a goblin.

Sighing, Quede rose from his throne and headed for the basement. He'd take the boat back to the city. The less time he spent aboveground, the better. Goblins hadn't died out the way the pure-blooded feys and vampires had at the time of the sun flares, but the solar pollution was unquestionably hard on them. More than one goblin had been driven insane from staying aboveground too long during daylight hours. So far, he had not been able to breed total resistance to this defect. Goblins were proving trickier to hybridize than orchids—and far less fun.

Quede pushed open an old iron gate and descended the rotting stairs. The mansion's basement served as an informal ossuary. Perhaps the bony catacombs should have bothered him, but they did not. There were no ghosts there, no evocative odors, no memories, no resonance of any kind from the skeletons of those he'd killed. There was nothing down there but his own fragile silhouette and he noticed that it grew paler and smaller every year. Once it had been monstrous; now it was all but gone. The vampirism was taking him over.

Quede trod lightly over the skeletal jumbles, distantly admiring the earth-colored pelvic bones that looked a bit like giant, stiff orchids growing in his private subterranean garden. He didn't feel the smaller bones shattering beneath his leathery soles, and the sound simply reminded him of walking through drifts of crisp fall leaves. Autumn was his favorite time of year.

Chapter Nine

Outwardly, the world appeared peaceful and serene. The storm that had nearly drowned Roman and Lyris had turned out to be a localized event centered on Quede's plantation. In the city, all was calm. A golden moon, only a night from being full, was riding gently through a benign sky. The air that wafted through the streets of the Quarter was soft with the dreamy scent of magnolia blossoms and distant music.

The interior of Lyris's temporary domicile was less peaceful. Serenity, had she ever been present, was now fled. The artificial light of the room was harsh yet not at all illuminating, and the odor that floated on the air was something a far cry from creamy magnolia. Fear and repugnance, which were now all too familiar, rose in Lyris's breast.

Her eyes searched, carefully trying to identify

where danger might lurk. The hotel bed was pristine—a virginal bower without dented pillows or wrinkles in the snow-white sheets. The towels hung with military precision. Her closet doors were closed tight, her clothes behind them were tidy. There wasn't one speck of evidence to show that someone had invaded her room—but she knew someone had.

"Roman?" she said softly.

"Yeah, I can feel it. Smell it." He turned to her. "Pack your bags, honey. You're coming to stay with me for good."

"But—"

"Look, you know it's the only sensible thing to do. We need to get back to my place and run some of this info by Jack, and I want you there to fill in the details if he has questions. Besides, maybe he knows something we don't. What was that proverb? '*By wise counsel you shall make your war.*' "

Lyris stared at him, for once uncertain what to do or say. Roman seemed rather blithe about their situation—both about having the vampiric goblin king of New Orleans spying on them and about having a stranger move into his place without notice. But then, perhaps he didn't feel the same worries and attractions that she did. Or perhaps, if he did feel them, he was not unnerved by what might happen. She had always shied away from magical attractions. They were worse than any drug. Those who became infected became ravenous, slaves to their desires. Some were very happy this way, but she would never choose to surrender her will.

Not waiting for her to make up her mind, Roman took her suitcase out of the closet and unzipped it. Lyris watched, frozen by a mixture of amazement at his impertinence and also a large measure of gratitude for taking her in when she knew he was still somewhat shocked and suprised by her reasons for being in New Orleans. But when he started pulling her clothes off the hangers and wadding them indiscriminately into the case, she finally uttered a protest and took over packing herself.

That business with Kennedy would not go away—books, movies, endless conspiracy theories resurrected every year on the anniversary of his death. And now this sylph! To think that he could be tripped up by the petty matter of that puppet LBJ after all these years.

Of course, it had been an equally petty matter of taxes that finally got Al Capone, Quede reflected as he poured himself some bloodroot tea. What a loss that had been. Capone was one of the first to organize the goblins.

And now, loss had become a recurrent theme in lutin affairs. Glashtin, Horroban, Lilith—all gone. Quede didn't mourn their passing—Why would he? They weren't hive-mates—but the news that they were murdered was distressing.

Murder was not uncommon among goblin leaders. Indeed, they rarely died anything other than violent deaths. But it seemed a sort of bad omen that they should die so close together and by either fey or human agency.

Of course, where Horroban had gone wrong was trying to take the White House personally. A good general never entered the field of battle; he always sent pawns. Had Horroban asked, Quede could have told him that it was a useless ambition. Goblins had taken the Oval Office twice before, with LBJ and Harding. And both times the situation had become untenable. Direct political control was not the answer everyone fancied it to be. One had to be like Archimedes, but also had to use the *right* lever to move the world.

And Lilith . . . she should never have gotten involved with Fornix. The Pentagon had more leaks than a sieve. Even Quede had heard about their plans for Yucca Mountain. Obviously H.U.G. had gotten wind of their plans as well, and had had time to mount a devastating counteroffensive. No real estate was worth such risk, not even the beachfront in California.

Of course, Quede had done little better when he was younger and more foolish. It had been a mistake not closely monitoring the replicant LBJ and seeing that he remained discreet—and sane. At the time it had been highly amusing to watch him throw his weight around the Kennedy White House. His first words to staff had been: "Just remember this—

there're only two kinds at this White House. There're elephants and pissants. And I'm the *only* elephant."

His second defining moment had been when he looked over at a new secretary, a pretty thing, just married, and asked loudly: "Will she shuck her britches?"

His third act—and certainly the most important, though less entertaining—was the ousting of Kennedy's key people. Some were promoted out, some just fired, but in a matter of weeks they were all gone. And that was key—the entire point of the exercise. Kennedy had discovered far too much about Quede and his enterprises, and had started getting in his way. If they were to keep the war in Vietnam, Kennedy had to go.

And how could Quede have known that prolonged sun exposure would drive Polwygle—the new Johnson—mad? It was a long-term effect of solar pollution that had not been understood back then. He was not to be blamed for this calamity of the disappearing ozone layer.

It was just bloody unfortunate that this solar miscalculation had tipped off some of the brighter humans about the lutin empire and caused them to form Humans Under Ground.

Quede slurped his tea and brooded.

Lyris stood in the deepest shadows on the hanging balcony and watched as the goblins swarmed out of the ground at midnight: a green river of leathery flesh flowing through the narrow streets of the Quarter in search of booze and good times along with the hapless tourists. She was still a little shaken from the small squabble she and Roman had had on their way back to his apartment. She had caught him eyeing a young blonde in a very short skirt, and before she had been able to reflect on the wisdom of it, she had said something sharp to him.

Being Roman, he had just laughed it off: "*Men only stop looking when they're dead, darlin'. Being Pooka has nothing to do with it.*" She'd answered back, but he'd wisely refused to be drawn into a fight. However, his last observation about her reaction to his looking at another woman had wedged in her mind. He had called her a little prude and suggested she go ahead and take a swing at him, because all that repressed anger and pent-up sexual attraction was going to give her an ulcer.

Was she repressed? Angry inside?

No, of course not.

"It's the graveyard shift stopping off for a beer before going home to the wife and kids—or whatever it is that goblins do after work," she said about the sight below. "Do you know, even after all my research, I am still not sure just what it is that goblins do here. They might as well live in the Forbidden City."

Roman joined her at the narrow window, standing close enough that their bodies touched at chest and shoulder. Her heart acknowledged him by jarring sharply against her ribs.

"Never mind the goblins. There're scarier things out tonight. Look at the tourists down by the river. Look at them," he repeated more softly. "They think they're going for a ride on the *Good Ship Lollypop*. They don't seem to see that their dock jock and all the crew are goblins."

"Or worse. I think Father Lobineau was right." Lyris shifted her keen eyes toward the river and watched the laughing crowd with a mixture of frustration and pity. "I'll bet anything you want that when they come back, they will be as blank-faced as those zombies over there." She gestured toward a group of silent tourists sitting under the brightly colored umbrellas at the sidewalk café. The strands of green lights that bathed them in garish luminescence made their flesh appear sterile, unnatural, almost inorganic.

"Technically speaking, I'm not sure those are zombies, since they aren't dead yet."

"They don't look alive though, do they?" She sighed. "If we ever want to find Quede and talk face-to-face, I bet all we'd have to do is book a river ride. I know he can't actually be feeding off the tourists—at least, I don't think he can—but somehow he is doing something to them."

Roman looked again. The tourists looked like goblin changelings. Half-dead ones. Or maybe she meant goblin vampires. No fairy changling had ever looked so inanimate. So dead.

Roman nodded. He said abruptly: "I've been thinking more about Quede, and there are some things that puzzle me. Everyone who has seen him says that he can pass for human—that he's beautiful even. How does he manage that, being both vampire and goblin? I can see how plastic surgery and dentistry could make goblins appear more or less human in shape. But how do they get rid of the rough green skin? And the smell—even without scent glands they still smell *different*. And none of them has ever been beautiful. Their skulls are shaped wrong."

"There are surgical procedures to deal with all cosmetic problems," Lyris explained. "They extract the scent glands, as you know. They've been able to do that for years. We can smell the difference in their skin—because they don't sweat like we do—but most humans don't have such keen scent discrimination. And the skin bleaching and softening is easy—almost all cosmetic companies offer some line of products for goblins now, though I suspect that most goblins may be using harsher chemicals." She paused. "From what I've been able to gather, they become poster children for sunscreen after such processes, and they still age rapidly when out in the daylight. And even with protective eyewear, they develop cataracts at an unusually high rate."

"But bleached goblins would look like ghosts, wouldn't they?" Roman guessed. "Not human."

"Many people in the North are very pale. And if bleached goblins live somewhere like California and need more color to pass for human, they take Canthaxanthin. It's the food dye that bodybuilders use to look tan. It stains the layer of fat beneath the skin. You can tell when someone is taking it because their palms and the soles of their feet will appear a sort of orange-bronze color." She looked up at him, intentionally not stepping away though his presence was making her bruised heart beat erratically. She was glad for the collar on her blouse, because perhaps it hid her thrumming pulse. "I hear that Quede often wears gloves."

"Yeah. I always thought it was to keep from leaving fingerprints on his victims. Once upon a time, there were probably some forensic experts who went after him."

"It might be that, too . . . or maybe the answer's simpler. Maybe he hasn't been changed that much by the passage of time. Maybe he uses some kind of glamour on people—you know, covers himself in illusion so people think he's beautiful."

"Could he do that? I thought only certain feys had that power."

"In theory, he could. Vampires have a form of glamour that is similar to feys'."

"Swell. So we might not recognize him if we saw him," Roman complained good-naturedly.

"We'd know him. At least, I would. I think any fey would. He has power that can't be hidden. And that is probably part of the reason he doesn't go into public or allow his picture to be taken." Lyris half smiled. "It can't be superstitious fear about someone stealing his soul with a camera."

"I hope you're right. About knowing him, I mean. I'd like a little warning if we ended up sharing an elevator with the bloodsucker." Roman glanced toward the bed where his portable computer lay.

"Did you finish the report for Jack? Did the pictures upload?" she asked, turning the subject and her body. She was not used to feeling such tenuity. Always her body was strong, obedient. She wasn't sure if she liked being made weak—even by desire. Long ago, she had learned how to step outside herself and observe her actions as a third party might so that she could assess her vulnerabilities. Sometimes she wanted to cry at what she saw—or laugh. This time she wanted to swear. Her susceptibility to Roman was showing and she knew he saw it. He knew that she wanted him.

Relationships were both easy and hard for her. Like Roman, she had no trouble attracting people. But also like him, her own early moral ambivalence about who and what she was had left her somewhat insecure with taking these easily attracted people as lovers. They tended to get obsessed and things ended messily. She preferred relationships that were not emotionally challenging. There was less ethical responsibility that way, and it made moving on easier.

It was all bothersome, but it wasn't hard to see why she had become the way she was, and her textbook reactions annoyed her with their unoriginality. Freud could explain her in three paragraphs. She was an example of classic adolescent rebellion and overreaction.

She had been good at everything as a child, but unlike Roman, she was a joy to her parents—when they remembered her. That wasn't terribly often as both her father and mother craved the limelight and applause. Lyris had been left to her grandmother.

She did well in school. However, success in the human world wasn't enough to keep her happy for long. Even as a child she had longed for . . . *something*. Something greater than what the human world could offer her. Yet, every time she came home, she suffered a sort of cultural whiplash, and it became harder for her to move between the societies.

It was worse in her teen years. She hadn't been able to find a set of rules, or even consistencies, with which to run her double life. She was a fey in a human world—and therefore slightly feared by her classmates and neighbors—and more than a little human in the fey realm where she was also closely watched. Apart from that, the two societal moralities were very different, and Lyris had no parental guidance to help her navigate the rough waters that flowed between the worlds. She learned by watching and evaluating, and trying to sort out the cultural contradictions.

Human indoctrination was stronger and more easily understood. It had the upper hand.

Lyris's critical evaluation of morality and herself had begun at home. Just like the younger Roman, her mother had seemed unable to make the sorts of situational judgments that other people—humans—did. The woman had been a completely free spirit—loving, but by most standards immoral. Fidelity was a foreign concept to her, and she was not discreet with her lovers. She chose humans as her partners, often married men who lived near them. She didn't work any actual Love-talker magic on them, but her natural charm was almost irresistible. She certainly saw no harm in using human men when she was in town.

The collective female enmity in the neighborhood was a terrible burden for the adulteress's shy daughter. For a long while, societal disapproval haunted Lyris on her mother's behalf. Within her small family, she did not feel shame at being Anhedda's daughter; outside of the home was another matter. And Lyris was away from home more than not because home was rather lonely with no one in it. Her grandmother had been dead by then—one of the first to succumb to the solar poisoning of the Drought.

Soon, Lyris had started living her life by a long

list of strict procedures and rituals designed to demonstrate her human morality to the censorious world. Though she loved her mother, there had been no room in her life for the sort of moral improvising Anhedda enjoyed. Lyris was, in fact, nearly anhedonic. When the time came, she chose her father's magic over her mother's.

The rapid transformation of her daughter had shocked Anhedda. It did not seem possible that she could have given birth to a child who did not desire the same things she herself did. She had feared for her daughter's happiness and even sanity.

In the same way, Lyris had not understood her mother's dismay. She had explained herself in simple, even human, terms. Not everyone had a talent or desire—or the basic capacity—to indulge in a stream of love affairs. Some people didn't have the capacity for indulging in even one.

Anhedda had begun to fade after that, and she'd asked her daughter to come home. Lyris had put aside her human life and returned, but she'd told her mother expectations of behavior. Anhedda had promised to try.

Lyris soon realized the foolishness of the attempt. Expectations had to be based on reality to have any chance of fulfillment. It was an especially futile and frustrating activity when one wasn't basing one's hopes on nature's laws, but rather on foreign societal expectations. Her mother was what she was, and had only been behaving in characteristic Love-talker fashion. She wasn't truly sociopathic, just had no ability to understand why her actions could be deeply hurtful to her mixed-fey daughter. To her dying day, Anhedda had tried to please her daughter, yet had persisted in believing that Lyris did not know how to love and would someday discover her inner calling.

That sounds like someone is repressed, doesn't it? A voice inside asked. As the years went by, strange situations and circumstances kept arising in Lyris's life, and she'd found that she had to offer up her biology as mitigation for erring from the path she had set herself. Though she had disavowed her inherited fey mystique and lived as a human, eventually she erred more than she adhered to normal human life. She saw the truth and the truth would not be denied. The only way to avoid demonstrating her awakening nature and supernatural knowledge was to have no meaningful interactions with anyone, human and fey alike.

Also, she soon tired of a joyless life that by its definition proclaimed her disapproval of her ever-shrinking family, which in addition left her so isolated that she began to dream in black and white, bleak dreams from which she awoke, crying out alone in the dark.

One day she simply exhausted herself, used every last ounce of her emotional resources on a resistance to her gifts that was proving futile. Her nature triumphed. It was a case of ceasing the constant moral evaluations that kept her from all people or literally dying of loneliness. On that bleak day, she had made the decision in favor of life and simply stopped disapproving of others. The truth of the world's immorality could not be denied, but Lyris put up a wall in her brain that separated her judgmental and functional minds. It left her feeling alienated, but the old saying had been proved wrong: A house divided *could* stand. And life slowly got better. She learned to live with the segregation. Truth did not always bring judgment. And quite oddly, it was when she stopped striving for human approval and fighting her nature that she was finally able to forget she was fey.

Once her parents and grandparents were dead, there had been no reason to remember her mixed blood. She'd developed selective amnesia about her past and moved back entirely into the human world. Had she not her father's legacy fused to her back, she might have forgotten her roots altogether.

She wasn't sure why she was thinking about all this at that particular moment, except that Roman somehow touched a part of her that she had kept buried for a long time. It wasn't precisely soul calling to soul. More like fey calling fey. But whatever strange emotions he evoked, they moved her magic to life and acceptance.

Lyris's attention snapped back to the present as Roman began speaking about his report to Jack:

"Yeah, it's winging its way through cyberspace to

wherever he is now. I just hope that Thomas's encryption is as good as he thinks it is. I was fairly plain about what we've been doing and thinking. I've also asked Thomas to have another look at the hospital computers here in New Orleans. He hacked into them about a month ago but didn't find anything unusual."

"Thomas?" Lyris was feeling a bit disoriented and tried to focus on the conversation. It was difficult because her senses were being teased by many things. There was a salt smell from the gulf washing up over the land. The scent reminded her of tears, especially when it was carried in on the soft sobs of the rising wind. Counter to that was Roman—earthy, warm, and passionate about life.

"Thomas Marrowbone. He's Jack's hacker and main finance man. He isn't bad with explosives, either. He's spent a lot of time living undercover in goblin cities. In fact, he was the one who took out Sin City."

"I thought that was Humans Under Ground."

"Jack lets everyone think that, but it wasn't the humans who got the hive. It was Thomas and his wife, Cyra Delphin. She's part selkie and a kloka. I guess the goblins there were trying to use her in some mind-control experiment and it pissed Thomas off."

Lyris shook her head slowly. "It seems so odd. I never knew there was actually any sort of formal fey organization here in the states. Of course, I knew there had to be other survivors of the Drought, but I just figured that everyone was like me—living quietly and doing their best to pass as human."

"A lot probably are. I don't know that much about Cadalach—where Jack is—except that it was part of Ianna Fe's old strongholds. That's where the feys are gathering. It's our capital, our kingdom, our country—whatever."

Our capital. Our kingdom. The fragile cobweb of words settled on Lyris gently. Gooseflesh rose on her arms. Yes, something was calling to her—calling her home. Calling her to Roman.

"You've seen it?"

Roman shook his head. "I've never been there. Actually, it was only recently that I chose to get really involved in the fey underground or trying to stop goblins."

"Yeah, me too—with the goblins, I mean. And it wasn't by choice exactly. I didn't plan on getting involved with lutins."

"Jack?" Roman asked.

"Jack," she agreed. "Somehow or another I know this is his doing."

Roman nodded and then smiled. He didn't mean for it to be wicked, but the curl of lips called up naughty thoughts for Lyris. She thought about telling him so, but she had learned to be careful about what she said. Roman was apt to answer entirely too directly—even sexually—and then leave her to pick up the bones of social nicety out of the exploded conversation.

"So, is tonight the night you try my gumbo? You look like you need some," Roman said, watching first her eyes and then her mouth. His gaze was almost a caress, a touch as soft as a fall of moonlight. Somehow, it didn't sound like he was talking about needing a meal.

"I need something. Maybe. Orgasmic gumbo might be a bit much." Lyris cleared her throat, hoping color hadn't bloomed in her cheeks. Assuming innuendo where there was none would be embarrassing. Roman might only be teasing. He liked doing that. *Men only stop lookin' when they're dead, darlin'.*

She also knew that it would be prudent to take a little time to analyze this sudden attraction to this very unsuitable man. Falling for him was not something she could do. It was not something she knew how to do. She made one feeble attempt at pulling away, giving him a chance to come to his senses or be clear about what he wanted. "I am hungry. And you must be starved. It's been hours since we've eaten."

"Ravenous," he agreed, but made no move toward the kitchen. He inclined his head and his brown mane fell forward in a curtain. She was only dimly aware of the stuttering light from a passing bus whose headlight beams were broken by the iron railing outside on the balcony.

Lyris's sigh was as quiet as the silken whisper of his hair. He smelled of shampoo, and she found the scent comforting. But beneath that was another perfume: the scent of naked flesh, of Roman himself. That smell was wild and did something other than comfort her. She brushed the ends of his hair with her fingers. It was thick and glossy and heavy.

"I wish I could wear you like aftershave," he murmured, showing that his thoughts were running parallel to her own—what few thoughts she was still having.

"Roman." It was a word that conjured, that was somehow vested with more longing than she intended. Seeing his pupils suddenly contract, Lyris started to pull away. She wanted him. He wanted her. That desire was frightening.

"You think too much," he muttered, reaching out a staying hand.

Lyris didn't evade it. She told herself that this was simply lust, nothing to fear. Nothing dreadful would happen, after all, if she gave in. Neither she nor Roman had the right personality for a tragedy—however odd and dangerous the situation.

"I know. And I'll stop thinking now," she agreed. "If you're sure you want me to," she answered, surprising herself with the sudden capitulation.

She could see that she had surprised Roman, too. He'd obviously thought she would pull back from his banter as she had all the other times.

She couldn't explain why she didn't, except that thinking had made her brain tired. There'd probably be hell to pay later, but she sighed and gave in to temptation. She was very glad that she had chosen something a little more exotic than plain cotton panties after her shower.

When Lyris stepped back from him, averting her face, Roman wondered for a moment if he had read her wrong. But then she reached up and, undoing the button that held her top together, she pushed her blouse off of her shoulder and let it fall to the floor in a soft pool.

Unlike many men, Roman was tactile and *scentual* rather than visual. But looking at Lyris as she stripped off her clothing was not something to be missed. It called up heady instincts in the reptilian part of the brain. Or, in his case, the equine brain. It stirred something wild and uncontrolled that would be alarming if not solely and exclusively related to Lyris. He could—almost—understand his father's satyriasis. And he had a feeling that he, like others who suffered from hypersexuality, was not going to be satisfied with a single coupling. No one night, one month, one year—one life—would be enough to truly sate this craving he had for Lyris. He needed more from her than what the mere joining of their bodies could ever give. He'd never considered his future. His present was not the sort of thing you built foundations on, so he didn't waste time on pointless dreams of the future. But Lyris . . .

It all was alarming, and part of him protested. He shouldn't be having relations with curiosity's chief cat. Already she had led him into probably lethal trouble. And he didn't like smart women—not in bed, not in relationships. They were every bit as manipulative as the dumb ones.

It wasn't their fault, really. This had been a man's world ever since the first day that some fey had clubbed the first faerie over the head with a spell and dragged her back to the cave by her wings. You couldn't really blame women for being sneaky and manipulative, since countless generations of cave-men and wizards and even other fey had trained them to be that way, but—

"Roman," Lyris said softly. "You're staring aw-fully hard, and probably thinking hard, too . . . and I'm getting embarrassed. Shall I put my clothes back on while you continue your inner monologue?"

"Don't do that," he said hastily. She was right. He'd been staring. And thinking. Usually, reflection was good, but he'd worry about her motives in sleeping with him and the potential satyriasis prob-lem later. For now, the joining of bodies was enough. Indeed, he suddenly couldn't seem to think of much anything else. Something supernatural had a hold of him. It felt like magic, and yet like no magic he had ever known. He felt a little high with it.

He looked at Lyris, trying to understand what she was, and what she did to him, but he couldn't see that thing that drew him forward. Whatever was compelling him, it wasn't coming from Lyris.

She reached for his waist. Her hands were delicate but deft. They undressed him.

"I don't . . ." His words trailed off as he noticed for the first time that while she had very pronounced cheek and pelvic bones, she was not as thin as he expected. In the mirror, from the back, she looked more lush.

Weird magic, something outside them, flowed up through his body, made his muscles clench. Lyris gave a soft gasp and her eyes widened, and he knew that it was this magic that made her kneel and draw her mouth down his belly to his groin. He stared at the beautiful, impossible, golden wings fused to her back and also knew that if she touched him with her mouth it would be over in an instant, one blinding spill of heat that might stop his heart.

She knew it, too. He could tell that a part of her—the hunter that the magic aroused—wanted this. But Lyris was still in partial control, and she chose not to let the encounter end this way.

Her body was lean and strong as she moved back up his flesh, rubbing skin on skin until they stood with bellies pressed together. Then she reached up and wrapped herself around him, arms first and then legs. Magic enfolded them both and sqeezed them tightly. Some internal barrier came down and the two beasts that were inside them, the pooka and the sylph, rubbed up against one another for the first time.

Roman stared at Lyris, his breathing harsh and

his heart pounding. He wanted her and she wanted him, and part of him was still afraid of that wanting—afraid that it was prompted by outside magic. Or was he more afraid that it wasn't?

"Oh, Roman . . . what big eyes you have," Lyris said in a singsong voice. She pressed close, skin calling to skin.

"All the better to see you with, my dear," he answered.

She laughed softly, and suddenly his nervousness was gone, replaced by a conviction that this was something important he was meant to do.

She slid down over him, and Roman half expected her to continue teasing. Instead, she guided him to her and pressed—gasping as he entered her and arching her back in a sort of sensual shock. He understood, because she had taken his breath, too, with her sudden impalement.

He pulled her closer, carefully at first since he felt like he could probably bench-press a car and breaking Lyris would be so easy. But then he looked into her eyes and saw the wildness there. He brought their lips together. She kissed him earnestly. It pained him to even stop, but eventually they needed air.

Her expression oscillated as he began to move inside her: arousal, shock, disbelief, mischief, then pleasure. But not fear, not hesitation, not regret. He watched her eyes, loving the way they widened as he glided into and then out of her flesh. Her reactions made him feel as if he had just invented sex.

And then he realized that she saw all this with whatever it was she used to look deeply into people—and he loved it.

His body warned him that it could stand no more. He forced Lyris back against the plaster for a last time and her back arched as she screamed. In that moment he went blind with pleasure, and she was there inside him, watching, seeing everything he felt but could not put words to—for either her or himself.

"Oh, goddess," he cried at last. He dropped to his knees on the floor and then onto his back, being careful to shield Lyris in the fall. She collapsed, boneless, across his chest and they both lay there while the magical fireworks faded from their bodies.

The moon shifted, and eventually Roman's eyes cracked open. He took in the profile of the exotic creature using him as a pillow. As he came briefly back to himself he thought, *She looks the way a woman should after sex: flushed, exhausted, and just a little bit smug*. Then he chuckled softly because he realized they were still caught up in whatever magic had just happened and that he was only seeing himself in her.

"I wonder what *you* see," he said into her hair. "I can't read you the way you do me."

Lyris stirred, raising herself up and slightly away even as she pressed herself more firmly into his hips. Unbelievably, the movement aroused him. Fresh heat and magic danced over his skin, and for a moment Roman could see what Lyris did when she looked at him: his nipples had darkened and he was sheened with sweat. The scars on his legs were more vivid. His expression was stark, his eyes a little wild. And because she was also still connected to the part of her that was animal, this aroused her.

"What do I see? I see freedom from old prejudices. I see a partner." She looked down for a moment at where their bodies joined and shivered. "And I see chains. But that's all for later, if we survive. Roman, do you really want to . . . ? I mean, can you really . . . ?"

Chains? He didn't like that word, but he did sense some bond had formed between them. He pushed that thought away, too, for later examination. Thinking would only spoil the moment—the second moment. To which he was about to attend.

"Yes. Goddess, yes!" he answered, giving in to the magic. His hands went around Lyris's waist, and he closed his eyes because he found he didn't need them to see what she saw, to feel what she felt. "I *do* want."

Chapter Ten

Roman watched her carefully. There was no reason for him to be vigilant. It was high noon and the building was warded against the usual evil beasties. It was just that he found that he liked looking at Lyris as she rested. She seemed peaceful, as contented as a cat. She lay on his blanket, long legs slightly bent, face turned up to the sky with an arm angled across her forehead, half hiding her face from the hazy sun.

Looking at her, he couldn't believe that she was the same woman who had shared his bed last night. Making love to her had been like downing a fifth of nitroglycerin and then playing with matches. And he'd voluntarily—well, sort of voluntarily—chosen this woman for his partner. Why, he couldn't imagine. Why he had agreed to such a deliberate strip search of the psyche? Why had he chosen a women who could see so much and cared even more?

It was easy: Just looking at her made his eyes want to climax. Was there such a thing as retinal orgasms? It felt like there was.

She was an enigma. How could she be so calm today? His own nervous system was a hodgepodge of emotions: lust, curiosity, a strange form of anxiety, an even stranger form of excitement that teased the neurons of the skin and muscles until he twitched and tingled and wanted to run through the streets shouting. This reaction was aberrational. He hadn't planned on this level of attraction in his life—ever. He wished that he were again cradled in her arms in the state of brainlessness that followed the intense euphoria brought on by climax. It was so much better than thinking and wondering. And worrying.

Of course, that didn't mean that he wasn't enjoying her skills in a perverse way. He was. Immensely. He had never been with a woman who saw his flaws and frailties so clearly and didn't get anxious or judgmental when dealing with them. He understood now why Jack said she was a good reporter. Lyris was a committed voyeur, curious about everything, intelligent, alert, and able to see the underlying truth of people and situations. Yet she didn't seem to organize her discoveries into moral verdicts. Indeed, last night, she had not just accepted his differences; she had celebrated them. Theirs had been a drama—or maybe a comedy—in three acts. With two intermissions but no standing ovation. They had both been too exhausted to stand at the end, he thought with a fleeting smile. No, she hadn't been worried then about confronting his differences. Or about him discovering hers.

Of course, this lack of inner turmoil was what set her apart from her human counterparts more than any physical anomalies. She seemed undriven by human neurosis, as though she had stripped away that fundamentally human part.

Roman smiled suddenly. Her only obsession seemed to be Quede—and really, a goblin king was probably more easily dealt with than a morbid fear of aging or the irrational conviction that many women had about their bodies being fat or ugly or otherwise flawed. Quede could be stopped—killed even, if they had no other choice—but the female fear of body fat seemed to be forever.

Not that Roman was anxious to have anything else to do with Quede. The more he knew about the situation, the less he liked it. But it was fun watching Lyris's brain go on its speculative binges and come up with treasures of insights, Quede vulnerabilities, and other enemy exploitables. She made everything seem possible, even plausible. At some moments, she even made him feel as if he were some kind of modern-day Jack the Giant Killer. It was quite a change from his days as a Conscientious

Neglector when he deliberately stayed away from all things fey and otherworldly.

There was a slight rustle from Roman's left, a sound no stronger than a straying breeze wandering down a hollow pipe, but he knew the herald well. It wasn't the wind playing in the downspout, but rather the resident roof imp appearing on schedule, ready as always for his noonday meal.

Roman knew that the imps were pests, damaging to the plaster where they made their burrows and often chewing up the wiring in the walls, but he had gotten into the habit of sharing his lunch with the old, leathery beast whenever he had rooftop picnics, and now he and the old outcast were friends of sorts. Usually, it was just the two of them dining alfresco, but today the critter was going to encounter something new.

Roman watched with interest as the creature warily approached the foreign blanket, sneaking up slowly while favoring its lamed leg. It waited at the blanket's edge, searching for some sign of life from the strange occupant. After a few seconds of immobility, the imp's nose twitched and it began a confident exploration, first of the strange acrylic fringe of the blanket and then of the empty dishes. His expression was hopeful as he rummaged for food.

The only thing it found of interest was Lyris herself. A gust of crisp wind reversed itself and suddenly blew her scent his way, carrying her strange perfume right up his long nose and bathing him in it until he quivered with delight.

Roman almost laughed. *Sylph*: the universal and ancient aphrodisiac. It was a new smell for the imp, though—and apparently an intriguing one. The wind died, but the imp remained frozen in place, nose twitching violently. Finally he gathered his wits and crept up purposefully on her curls. He took a few deep breaths, trying to identify the foreign scent and perhaps determine if it was edible. Not content with just sniffing at her hair, he snaked his long tongue out once and tasted her tresses. Finding them to his liking, he reached out with his tongue again, taking up a shining lock. Slowly, he reeled his prize back in. As he sat with her lock draped through his mouth, leathery arms folded across his chest, he looked like a miniature *bandito* wearing gun belts and a mustache.

Lyris stopped breathing. "Roman?" she asked, feeling the gentle tug on her hair.

At her words, the imp dropped his hair snack and stared in consternation. Food wasn't supposed to talk!

"It's okay, honey. Just a curious visitor. The resident imp is checking out your hair."

Lyris let her arm fall back behind her and turned her head slowly until she faced the tiny interloper. Almost nose to nose, they stared into each other's eyes.

The imp blinked first. Finally encouraged by

Lyris's prolonged silence and relative stillness, the imp resumed his exploration of her hair, poking his nose into the tresses and snuffling loudly.

"They don't have fleas, do they?" Lyris asked softly, making the imp's ears perk but not deterring him from his fascinated exploration.

"I don't think so. But they do have teeth, and I think he is considering taking your hair home as a trophy. . . . Come here, you old mooch," Roman called, breaking off part of his sandwich and tossing it over. "You'll like this better anyway."

Torn between competing smells, the imp hesitated. The battle was a fierce one, but hunger proved momentarily stronger than curiosity. The beast moved back to the edge of the blanket and began to feast, making happy little grunting noises as it gorged.

Lyris watched, bemused. "That's a really ugly creature. But he—if it's a *he*—is kind of cute, too. Like a baby ostrich or something."

"Yeah," Roman agreed. "I know I should put out a trap—he's living in the walls and probably making a mess of the wiring and insulation—but I kind of like having him around."

"You can't *trap* him. That would be cruel. He's practically a pet. And anyway, you share a toilet. You're bonded," Lyris said. Her eyes settled on the imp's twisted leg, but she made no comment on the deformity. It had probably driven him away from the other imps. "He's almost tame."

"Not exactly. He still spits and bites if you try to pet him. And no one would ever have an animal around that was that mean and ugly." Roman shrugged. "I like him anyway."

Lyris nodded and pushed her apple core in the imp's direction. "He eats like he's starving."

"He's not, believe me. He's just fond of his meals. I think maybe they were scarce for a long time."

The imp finished his sandwich and then plucked up an apple. He grinned at Lyris, showing small pointed teeth. He looked like a Tasmanian devil with leather ears.

"He's being friendly, right? That's a smile."

"I think so. With imps you really can't tell."

Not surprisingly, the sylph had left her hotel. It was probably for the best, since the hobgoblin was likely still following her. But it angered Quede to think that she was living with the pooka. He didn't want anything polluting her scent, which would happen if the pooka made love to her.

Quede paced, a tiger in a cage, annoyed and dangerous. He had Schiem's coat wadded in his hands.

He lied to others—constantly—but he never lied to himself. And this self-honesty compelled him to admit that he was feeling jealous. The possible reasons why he was experiencing the emotion were not attractive.

Was it actually possible that love could be born from a tender scent? That the heart could be redirected from its chosen course by a smell? He had both melancholic and passionate memories these days, all easily summoned by the ghosts of ancient aromas. And it was all because of this sylph—she was a scent absolute, a sledgehammer to his senses even when delivered secondhand on Schiem's clothing. She strengthened all other scents around her and gave them new life.

It made Quede wonder, with fear, would actually meeting her in the flesh be a dizzying blow from which he would not recover? Could he withstand the memories and emotions that haunted him if they were made more poignant by her enchanting perfume? Could he ever face her in Caitlin's old bedroom?

The thought of this vulnerability shook him out of his reverie.

Bah! He was making a mystery out of something explainable. There was nothing magical about her. Research had proven that the olfactory was the only one of the dozen cranial nerves that led straight to the cerebrum. Goblins, like humans, came hardwired for vivid scent memory, and that was before having had vampirism make his senses hyperacute. It was all very automatic. Smell excited the limbic area of the brain, making one think of nourishment, blood, and sex, and other forms of repletion. It bypassed the neocortex, unlike sight and sound, and forced a response from the places in the primitive brain that held emotion. If no emotion was there, it manufactured it. She was a drug, nothing more.

If he took the sylph into the lab, dissected her, distilled her, ran her through a chromatograph, there would be no more mystery. It was what he *should* do. What he *would* do. Eventually. Probably. After she had answered a few questions about who had sent her to New Orleans. And after he had had her, body and soul.

In the meanwhile, he had to get back to the critical matter of breeding orchids and goblins. He was determined that his neon *dendrobium* hybrid would glow bright enough to read by before the flower show in March. And he wanted his army of plague carriers ready to move by summer.

And if that wasn't enough, there was the issue of that meddlesome, disobedient priest. Lobineau had to die. The cleric had outlived his usefulness. Quede knew he was up to something. There wasn't any direct proof of his treason, but certainly it was Lobineau who had raised the hobgoblin. *Someone* was controlling the thing.

Of course, therein lay the rub and all the cause for delay. Magic had the most damnable rules. If Lobineau had raised the hobgoblin, then only Lobineau could continue to control it. And the thing had to be controlled. Quede couldn't have the vicious bogey running amok among the tourists. The hobgoblin's sole purpose was to slaughter. Once started, nothing short of death would deter him—and death was difficult to arrange for supernatural killers of such a type. One needed a magic sword—a silver one. A sword that Quede himself wouldn't be able to touch without being burned to the bone.

No, this situation had to be handled delicately. The last thing he needed was sudden human scrutiny of his city. Things were going very nicely just now. Everything was on schedule.

But it still made him very angry that he couldn't take the sylph for his own while using her as a lure.

Quede buried his face in the soft wool of the coat and inhaled deeply.

A drug! She was a drug—nothing more.

"You know that we're either going to have to go back to Lobineau, get into Quede's lair, or leave town. The choice is yours, Uber-sleuth. Call me an incurable romantic, but I'd vote for leaving. Together." Roman set a glass of iced tea on the small table before her.

"I really don't like Lobineau, and don't think we have anything more to learn from him right now, so that's out. At least, for the time being." Lyris took a long drink of the tea. "Anyway, I don't trust him not to lead us astray."

"And I don't see you rushing off to pack."

"No. So, I guess that leaves Quede's lair." Lyris frowned and added with a conspicuous lack of enthusiasm, "Talk about choosing between the devil and the deep blue sea."

"The deep blue sea would be nothing. I don't suppose that I can appeal to your wiser nature and suggest that you leave this to someone who has been trained in this sort of work. Jack is bound to have people he can send." Roman turned his chair around and sat straddling it.

"Sadly, I don't think I have a wiser nature. Not about this. And it isn't because I'm obsessed. Or, it isn't *only* because I'm obsessed." Lyris spread her hands and added earnestly, "I mean, please understand, I'm scared. But no one knows Quede better than I do—at least, no one on our side. And who else besides you knows the ins and outs of New Orleans? Maybe in time someone else could be brought up to speed, but if Lobineau is right and Quede is getting ready to start some sort of widespread nastiness, then what we don't have is time. Anyway, I think if Jack could have sent someone besides us, he would have. We can't have been his first choice—a conspiracy theorist and a conscientious neglector."

Roman nodded gloomily. "When you're right, you're right. It's just that not being in the autumn or winter of my life, I wasn't quite ready to be off for a better world this week—which we doubtless will be if we keep hanging around looking for Quede's lair. Luck being what it is," he added with raised eyebrows.

"You don't have a lot of faith in me," Lyris complained. "I really am very good at investigating things—and at getting out alive."

"I go on record as having faith in your powers of observation, Uber-sleuth. I'm just also fairly certain that Quede is the most powerful goblin that has ever lived. Not even Jack has gone up against someone like him. I don't think it would be overstating things to say that Quede's the meanest, nastiest goblin alive."

"Or not. I mean, if he's a vampire, technically he's dead," Lyris pointed out. She was attempting to make Roman smile. It didn't quite work. "And if this gives him strengths, it also gives him vulnerabilities."

"Not any that count," Roman complained. "He's vicious, venial, possibly insane—but not stupid or inactive. And he seems to be able to come out during the day. And let's not forget that we have others watching us, creatures that may or may not belong to Quede." He sighed and dismounted. "Let me check my e-mail. Maybe there'll be something useful from Jack. Like tips on killing zombie hobgoblins. Or a map to Quede's secret lair."

"Being a vampire, he would have one—a lair," Lyris agreed. "He wouldn't feel safe while resting, even in the hive. But Jack isn't going to know it. I'm afraid that we're going to have find it ourselves."

"We are, huh?"

"Yes." Lyris's eyes narrowed. "And I'm willing to bet that I know where one entrance is."

"The sado's love nest," Roman guessed.

"Makes sense, doesn't it? He'd have wanted to spend the night with Caitlin, not traveling to and from the city. He wouldn't have anything connected directly to the hive. His lair would be someplace remote, hidden. Probably not the cemetery, but someplace nearby."

"So, we go back to lovely Toujours Perdrix?" Roman jacked in his portable computer and lifted the lid.

"Yes, I'm afraid so."

"Tonight?" Roman asked. He knew the answer.

"He's more likely to be out and about at night."

"So are the other nasties."

"I know, but I'd really rather not visit when he's in residence. Call me a coward, but I'm not certain I could rifle his effects for clues with him sleeping nearby. And that's assuming he does sleep during the day. He might not. His being a goblin could change things."

"If that makes you a coward, then so am I," Roman agreed. He shuddered. "I don't think I could do that either. If Quede and I *never* meet, it will still be too soon." He looked at his laptop. "Well, there's nothing useful here from Jack. He says he's sending a care package . . . timed to arrive tomorrow at two P.M. at the UPS station. So, I guess we go in as is."

"Sorry."

"Don't be. This isn't your fault. We'll leave as soon as I finish my set at the club. If you're still tired, why don't you try and catch another nap while I'm gone?"

"I'm okay," Lyris said. Then she smiled. "Anyway, it's my turn to cook."

"You cook? Why didn't you say so before?" Roman laid a hand over his heart. He was careful to keep what he was really feeling out of his voice: "I've found the girl of my dreams at last!"

Lyris looked down quickly, perhaps sensing that he was telling her the truth and not knowing how to react. "Maybe you should reserve judgment until you've tasted things. I said I cooked, not that I cooked well."

"Darn. There's always a catch," Roman complained.

Chapter Eleven

The kudzu epidemic had gotten worse, perhaps because of all the rain, and poison sumac had also taken up residence in the cracks in the walls. Its triplets of leaves dripped with clear poison that stung when it touched the skin. Lyris could hear her grandmother saying, *"Leaves of three, let it be."* Somewhere in the world there was probably someone who would find this scene attractive, but he'd have to be a connoisseur of death, disintegration, and decay.

She and Roman didn't bother with the upstairs floors this time. Quede's lair would be underground. It took some effort to push through the vines, but they soon found what they were looking for.

The door to the basement was a tantalizing dare, old, huge, and heavy. Its old lock looked like it had rusted shut a decade ago, but someone had recently installed a new one. Fortunately, they had not installed new hinges at the same time, and the wood around the old hasps was rotten enough to dig through with a soupspoon.

"Goblin sloppiness triumphs again." Lyris began to draw back her leg, preparing to give the thing an experimental kick, when Roman interrupted.

"Please, allow me. I'm good at this," he said. Slashing out, he gave a brutal kick that would have made a mule proud.

The spongy door broke in half. A second kick had Lyris and Roman just outside the opening and staring down the dark, uneven stairs. Lyris kept her eyes open and tried not to think about spiders. Or Quede. Or that it was dark and tight and gravelike in there.

"What's wrong?" Roman asked.

"Did I mention that I'm just a little bit claustrophobic?"

"Uh, no. How claustrophobic?"

"Just a little. I'll be fine."

Lyris stepped through the broken door and started down the stairs, very aware that they were probably below sea level. The walls held most of the groundwater at bay, but cold fluid was everywhere, in pools on the floor, glittering on the rough walls that ran green with slime, bubbling out of tiny crevices, and rushing softly, slyly, in the distance beyond their flashlight.

"A subterranean river?"

"He's got to have some way to travel below-ground between here and the city. Why not a river? Goblins like the damp."

"I guess. It's just a little *Phantom of the Opera*-ish."

They stepped deeper into the room, and Lyris looked around. It took a moment for her to make out the gray lumps on the floor. There was no way to know when the gruesome slaughter—or slaughters—had taken place, but it was long enough ago that no vibration of the horror was left in the air and the ghosts had all departed.

"I wonder if they'll ever turn into mulch like a body should. They look like rubber or something."

"Messy eater," Roman commented. "But then, being goblin as well as vampire, Quede would want his pound of flesh. And bone," he joked.

"I know he's a vampire and a goblin . . . but how can he stand this? I mean, these are the deadest-looking people I've seen," Lyris whispered, eyes moving quickly about. "It's like more than their lives were sucked out of them. And this place is awful—worse than I expected. The very earth is dead and rotting. No wonder there are no goblins around. Only the lifeless could tolerate such a state of affairs."

"Well, you know what the real estate people say. Location, location, location. This is a perfect get-away for the undead." His voice changed to that of a broker: "With the beautiful stench of death, new owners are sure to thank King Quede of New Orleans for all the work he's put in on this unique fixer-upper." Roman's voice returned to normal. "At least, I'm doubtful these people left instructions in their wills to have their remains dumped here under this rotting mansion. They were brought."

"Whatever," Lyris said. "I'm not blaming the dead. Let's move on. There's nothing useful here. I don't think anyone has been in here for a long, long time. Let's do this and get out!" She turned and walked toward the low, arching tunnel on the far side of the room.

"Look, I wouldn't count on that. Just because these bones feel old, it doesn't mean that—" Roman began to lecture.

Suddenly, Lyris's way was blocked by a wall of flesh. The creature who stepped in front of her had almost no space between its eyebrow—and there appeared to be only one—and its hairline.

Lyris stared in shock at the shallow, ridged brainpan and tried to make hasty judgments about what to do. Normally, she would have offered to shake hands with a stranger, but this time she was not inclined to do that. She had always prided herself on being broad-minded and accepting of other species, but it was difficult to remain nonjudgmental when the thing opened its mouth and gave a whiff of its blood-clotted breath. The sudden appearance of an Uzi, which it pointed at her, pretty much decided Lyris that this wasn't one of the angels and it was okay not to want to be friends.

"Come now," it ordered.

"No." The word was a denial, not a refusal. Lyris knew she should move—run, lash out, do *something*—but the sight of the Uzi moving toward her chest paralyzed her. Trolls did not usually use guns. It was like having a horse or dog suddenly pull a knife. In other words, it was abnormal and her brain didn't know how to react.

It took Roman a commendably shorter period of time to reach this same unhappy conclusion, and he responded more appropriately. Less than three seconds after the gun appeared, Lyris was thrust aside and the villainous troll was dealt a deadly kick to the head. Its skull reshaped as its fat neck broke like a stalk of wet wood. Having fallen to the floor herself, Lyris had a plain view of the troll's remodeled head hanging at an odd angle as he crashed to the earth.

She stared for a moment, stupidly waiting for something to happen.

"Are you okay?" Roman asked.

"Yes," she said, even before she knew it was true. Then: "I think so."

After a blow to the head, basic consciousness returned first. If one hadn't been hit too hard, comprehension and competence soon followed. But none of these things would be happening for this troll. He was dead, dead, dead. And it was odd, but even in death, he didn't seem to possess a nonhostile muscular arrangement of his ugly features. A perpetual expression of rage had creased another deep ridge into his shallow brow. He was still frightening, and he probably would be even after his flesh had rotted away.

Lyris recalled her father saying that all trolls were walking blunt instruments, bludgeons looking for a place to be used. She understood now what he was getting at. This creature had been built for violence. And on top of that, someone had trained him to use a gun.

Roman had mentioned that he could curse in fourteen languages, and Lyris believed him. For this occasion, he chose old Gaelic, calling on the ancient gods and goddesses to infect Quede with virulent and incurable pox while having unnatural sex with diseased trolls.

Lyris left off her study of the dead troll and listened intently to the comprehensive excoriation. She tried not to let her eyes wander back to the corpse, no matter how they wanted to. She hadn't received any cranial blows herself, but there were still constellations revolving over her head and she wasn't thinking clearly. Probably it was some form of shock combined with claustrophobia.

"Wow! I didn't know trolls could do that. I'll have to remember that one," she said shakily as Roman paused to draw breath.

Roman stopped swearing and blinked at her. "You know old Gaelic?"

"Yes, my grandmother insisted."

"Well, just forget you heard that. It isn't something a lady should know," he said austerely, offering her a hand. "I'm sorry about knocking you down, but you were in the way. Hell, I thought for a minute that you were going to shake his hand. I haven't been this scared in . . . well, ever."

Not able to help herself, Lyris went off into whoops of laughter. It was one part amusement and one part hysteria. It was also horrifying to think the idea of shaking the creatures hand had for one moment crossed what these days passed for her mind.

Roman didn't share her laughter.

"You sound just like my grandma," she gasped. "*Shenmhar* was always saying stuff like that. Don't touch trolls, *nighean,* or you'll get warts. Of course, you can get warts from them!" The thought made her laugh harder. Hysteria was gaining ground.

"Your grandma! You knew your grandma?" Roman thought about this. After a moment, some of the tension disappeared from around his mouth as he regained his habitual good humor. "You know, I think you must come from a very odd family. That or you have the weirdest form of claustrophobia I've ever seen."

"Oh, yeah. My family? Be glad you'll never have to meet them." Lyris stopped laughing. The thought of her dead parents was always sobering. If they weren't deceased, they would have made a great fey country-western song—depressing but not exactly tragic.

She took Roman's hand and allowed him to haul her to her feet, then hung on for a moment because her knees seemed less than resolute about keeping her upright. Holding her up was no problem for Roman. He didn't even need two hands. Once again, she was made aware of how very strong he was.

"Well, this just tarnishes our golden evening out," he said, disgusted. "And once again, amateur bungling somehow saves the day. I gotta give my guardian angel a raise. An Uzi! Goddess protect us!"

"You know what question is running through my head right now?" Lyris asked. She rubbed her hands on her jeans, trying in vain to wipe off the black mud. The sight of the slime made her feel a little queasy; there was no knowing what was in it.

Roman stared at her a moment and then said: "If it's about whether Quede had a dental insurance program for his thugs, I think the answer is no."

"You're close, actually. I *was* thinking about employers and their benefits," she answered, staring down at the troll-goblin crossbreed. He was still hideous and quite dead, but she was getting used to him. "What I was really wondering is whether he belongs to Quede at all. Mr. Muscles here just doesn't fit the profile. Quede's men are all very well groomed, remember? And either they're goblins, or goblin-human crosses. Quede doesn't do trolls. Or hobgoblins. He never has. Maybe because they are too hard to mind-control. They're awfully stupid and violent."

"But if not Quede, then who?" Roman's eyes narrowed. He quickly followed her thoughts. "You think this one may belong to our father with the elastic morals and selectively applied Christianity? Mouth breathers are more his style, but what would Lobineau's goon be doing down here?"

"Spying on Quede? Hunting for a snack?"

"But . . . why risk it? Lobineau has to know it would piss Quede off if the thug was caught. And Lobineau didn't sound real ready to be taking on Quede *mano a mano*."

Lyris shrugged. "We may never know why. But I think we can safely assume that Lobineau's flexible morality extends to double-crossing his boss if he thinks he can get away with it. He would see spying, et cetera, as using the devil's tools to fight the devil, and he might really believe that God would protect him on this crusade."

Roman shook his head. "A man on a divine mission? I'm still not convinced he'd take the risk. He seemed sullen and resentful, but too cowardly to actually act. I mean, why else would he try and recruit us to do his dirty work for him?"

Lyris shrugged. "I don't know. But look at this thing's chest. There's a tattoo. It's a cross, isn't it? That's not standard troll body art." She shivered with a mixture of renewed revulsion and cold. Her breath appeared in little puffs that looked like white smoke. "And now that I've considered it a bit, I'd say he was probably here looking for us in particular, as opposed to just generally looking."

Roman looked up, his face oddly flat. "With an Uzi? That's a little hostile. I'm pretty sure it isn't recommended in the *How to Win Friends and Influence People* manual. Besides, Lobineau wants us alive."

"Maybe. This guy definitely wasn't looking for us for friendly purposes. And Lobineau would know an unarmed troll cross couldn't take both of us. Is the Uzi loaded?"

Roman checked the gun. It was carrying a full load, and the safety was off. He grunted unhappily and pulled the thug's shirt open. Lyris was proved right. The gap revealed a particularly colorful rendition of the crucifixion that showed way too much blood. His voice was gloomy as he said: "So, he is Lobineau's. As my mother used to chant, 'Every day, in every way, things just get better and better.' "

"That about sums it up. What do we do with the body?" Lyris's voice was stronger, and her legs were finally cooperating. She was feeling better now that the revolving stars were gone. She was also growing accustomed to being around the dead.

"Well, I don't know about you, but I don't particularly want to take it home." Roman stood. "I mean, just imagine getting pulled over by the cops with *that* in the car. It'll be daylight soon, too. I'd say give it to the gators, but they won't eat troll. Anyway, he's heavy."

"So, we leave it here?"

"There are so many other bodies, maybe Quede won't notice one more."

"Maybe," she answered, but they both knew he would. Even a blind man would notice the troll if he came this way. It smelled ferociously both from its natural stink and some sort of aftershave that reminded Lyris of bug spray. "I think the more interesting question is, what will he do about it when he finds it?"

"Probably nothing. Cleanup doesn't seem to be his forte." There were both aware that wasn't what Lyris meant.

She sighed. "Maybe we'll get lucky and he'll blame Lobineau. I mean, why even suspect us?"

Roman nodded. "It would suit me fine. Those two bastards can take each other out."

"Lobineau is almost certainly going to try." Lyris looked at Roman and added gently, "The question is whether we are going to let him use us as tools. He's getting desperate, you know, to try something like this. If he did try this." She sighed and rubbed her forehead. "I just don't have the bandwidth for this kind of thinking. I'm more up on basic human duplicity."

Roman laughed. "Well, it was kind of him to think of us for the job, thanks but no, thanks. He can find his sword of retribution elsewhere. I don't like the idea of getting between those two he-bastards when they start beating on one another."

"I hear you. Still, keep your eye out for bright shiny swords. I suspect that we're going to need one. A silver sword covered in magic runes would be best."

"Silver?" Roman looked at her. "I thought vampires could only be killed with wood."

"Not for Quede. For the hobgoblin."

"The hobgoblin?"

"Lobineau—probably—sent a troll cross to fetch us this time, and it didn't work. What do you think he'll send next time?" she asked softly, unhappily. "And the hobgoblin won't give up like he did that first night."

"The first night?" Roman looked confused. "Oh, you mean the creature that attacked you in the alley. You think the other guy was Lobineau?" Then he nodded. "Of course it was. He was muffled up to hide his scars. You know, I seem to spend a lot of my time thinking one step behind you. It's kind of annoying."

"You've been busy fighting the minions of evil," Lyris pointed out. She smiled grimly. "And I've been thinking about Lobineau and the hobgoblin."

"A hobgoblin. Well, hell and damnation."

"I hope not." Lyris attempted a better smile. "We can cope with a hobgoblin. Maybe. But not the devil."

Roman looked surprised. "Is that a possibility, do you suppose?"

Lyris shrugged again and spread her hands. "If Lobineau knows how to raise a demon, I wouldn't be surprised if he does it eventually. The good news is, very few people know how." She paused. "Of course, he did raise an undead hobgoblin."

Roman stared at her for a long moment; then he again took up swearing in old Gaelic.

"I know," Lyris interrupted. "But we better get going. I don't want to round out the night by meeting up with Quede or any of his servants. It's scary to think, but Quede is probably a lot more dangerous than anything Lobineau can raise. Lobineau can hurt us physically, but there is no telling what Quede can do to our minds."

"I'm really wishing that wizards guild hadn't packed up and left town."

"They have?"

"Oh, yeah. About a month ago. They suddenly decided to spend the winter in Florida. They were pretty smart."

Quede poled his raft through the sluggish stream, feeling the ever-growing pangs of frustration. He worked relentlessly at looking unthreatening when he dealt with the human world. It was second nature for him to keep the robes of glamour pulled over his features. He had known from the start that the constant effort was draining but necessary. Old goblins looked as hideous as spawning salmon—and vampirism hadn't stopped this transformation wreaked by age. It was by will and magic alone that he appeared youthful, handsome . . . human.

It had been years since he had allowed anyone to photograph him. Film was not susceptible to glamours the way the human mind was, and photographs showed his true nature—celluloid and digital portraits of Dorian Gray. This wasn't acceptable. Humans, for all their talk of equality, preferred to deal with beautiful people. And Quede had lived among them long enough that he had come to adopt their standards of attractiveness even while despising them. Being thought handsome by his enemies had become something vital to him—like a heart or kidney. Though, that was perhaps an inexact analogy because he wasn't sure that he actually needed either of those organs anymore. He . . .

Quede lifted his head and inhaled. *Sylph, pooka, troll—and a hobgoblin!* All four had been in his mansion again. Damn them! How dare they invade his home! Was it a conspiracy?

Anger flared, and Quede's vision went red. His leniency had made them think that he was something with which they could toy. Well, he wouldn't tolerate it—not anymore! He should have killed the priest the moment he suspected him of trafficking with magic!

Galvanic rage filled his head, putting pressure on the bony plate that encased his brain and making

Quede almost certain that this time his skull would split in two.

He sent his message out into the air. He told people that he didn't like getting angry—but he knew it was a lie. Sometimes he enjoyed it. Sometimes he loved anger and its consequences more than anything, even life.

Chapter Twelve

"Danger makes one clear-headed, stiffens the sinews, gets one's muscles primed and ready to work, puts the senses on high alert—"

"And sometimes causes unwanted bowel movements," Roman joked. Then his head jerked up. "Damn it!"

Lyris felt it, too. It was electricity, like a billion ants boiling over her body.

"It's lightning. Run!" she cried.

A vicious flash followed by a vociferous roar drowned out her words. And, after that first explosion, the storm was an unbroken threnody of dazzling light and deafening thunder that chased their fleeing heels. It didn't require a great deal of imagination to guess that Quede's temper was behind the phenomenon.

"I guess he found the body," Roman shouted.

Lyris nodded as they ran. She saved her breath. Her muscles were burning oxygen at a terrific pace, and there didn't seem to be enough air to replace it.

Roman asked, "You think maybe the troll wasn't Lobineau's after all? Maybe Quede's pissed because we broke his toy."

"I can't think with all this noise!" she gasped. A sense of inescapable danger had broken over her like a sonic boom. It tore through the atmosphere, more dangerous than the lightning around them.

The rain fell on them like a shower of gravel, hard in a way that no normal water could be. Sudden cold clamped a vise around her temples.

"Ow! What's in this stuff?" Lyris's breath was white as she spoke.

Lightning, growing closer, answered before Roman could.

"I don't know," he said when the thunder quieted, "but it isn't normal. And the sooner we're out of it the better."

"I wish we hadn't been cautious and left the car so far away," Lyris complained, picking up speed, trying to match Roman's long, elastic stride. He didn't answer. They had already discussed this. Ancient red Jags were not ubiquitous and therefore not the sort of anonymous vehicle they needed. Probably he was grateful that his treasure was safely away from the punishing rain and hail.

"We won't make it to the car. Head into the woods. It's the only shelter!"

As they pushed through the narrow woodland, the mixed autumn trees' few remaining leaves fluttered overhead like frantic birds attempting a hopeless flight from danger. They would be shredded if they didn't soon escape the force of Quede's wrathful wind.

Not trying to speak anymore, they simply ran, leaping over barricades as they came to them, not slowing or detouring for streams, snares, or boggy ground. Still the lightning chased them, and all around the world turned white with frost.

"Here!" Roman gasped, grabbing her arm.

The night was in its last few fearful minutes, and Lyris on her last legs, when they finally stumbled into a stone ruin that might have once been a smokehouse but now housed a still.

"H-h-hallelujah!" Lyris muttered, stuttering with cold and a lack of air. In spite of their exertions, she was trembling with frostbite, and dizziness floated through her head, veiling it with mental cobwebs.

"Amen," Roman added, slipping off his backpack. He was also breathing hard, every exhalation a large white puff of frozen pant. "Hang on, honey, and catch your breath. Let me start a fire."

"Do we dare stop? It's still dark. He might come after us," she said. A vicious bolt of lighting struck outside, splitting a sapling in two. The thunder's reverberation seemed to shake the very foundations of the tiny building. Golf-ball-sized hailstones began to fall.

"I don't think we have a choice. We can't outrun the lightning anymore. Somehow Quede seems to be able to send it after us no matter which way we turn. And this storm is much bigger than last time." Roman's voice was hoarse.

Lyris had a sudden picture of them leaving an invisible but scentable trail behind that Quede could follow like spoor. She shivered and pushed the undermining thought away. Dawn, it was almost dawn. The storm couldn't go on much longer.

Old leaves and twigs blown in by the wind accumulated in a large pile, and it was the work of a moment for Roman to set the tinder alight.

"Come here," he said. "You've got to get out of those wet clothes."

Reluctantly, Lyris turned away from the door.

It took only a moment to get out of their wet clothing, and squatting on their makeshift hearth, they set about getting warm. Cuddles first, but once Lyris had stopped shaking, Roman began rummaging in his backpack, liberating the sandwiches and thermos of coffee he had insisted on bringing with them.

He pulled the stone top off of the still and took a whiff of whatever was brewing inside. "Whoooee! I don't know what the hell this is—maybe lighter fluid. But it's bound to warm us up."

"I don't know if I should."

"I'll carry you if he comes and you are too blotto to walk," Roman promised. She sipped cautiously at their coffee, so he said, "Come on, honey. It will take the chill away."

"If it doesn't make us blind."

"I'll take the risk. Finish that coffee. Your lips are blue and that just is *not* your best color."

"Thanks a lot." But already, her shivering was abating.

They dined on sandwiches, oddly content, and watched in silence as their clothes steamed dry, the delicate vapors from the wet cloth and the fire's wild shadows dancing across the old stone walls in a bizarre tango.

Slowly the gloom lifted and night ungraciously surrendered to Aurora's pale chariot. Dawn broke over the horizon—and over their minds. As soon as the sun found a fingerhold on the sky, the hail ceased and the cruel clouds fled. So abrupt was the storm's departure that there could be no doubt of its supernatural origins.

"Quede's gone nighty-night. Hell, he was so busy spitting at us, he must have dropped in his tracks when the sun came over the hill. It's probably too much to hope he was standing on his porch when it happened. I'd love to hear that he'd been crispy-crittered." Roman's voice was still a bit raspy. There was only so much that hot coffee and moonshine could do.

"But has Lobineau called it a night, too? I doubt

we're so lucky," Lyris guessed, thinking of how close they were to the Goblin Christian Community Center.

"Okay, *don't* look on the bright side." Roman sounded exasperated.

"I'm looking everywhere, but not seeing my way clearly anymore." Lyris stared full into Roman's fatigued eyes. The dawn light was harsh and unromantic, but even in that moment, she spared a thought for how lovely he looked. His hair was parted in the middle and unconfined so that it fell about his angular face like that of one of Raphael's angels. Of course, nothing else about him was even remotely angelic, but he still appealed to her. "Roman, what are we doing here? This is crazy."

"You're asking me?" His voice turned incredulous. "I thought this was your party."

Lyris half smiled at his returning energy. She shook her head. "You're the reality check, remember? I have wild ideas and you're supposed to shoot them down."

"I am?" He seemed amused. "Wow. I've never been anybody's reality check before. I guess I haven't done a great job so far."

"We're alive," she comforted. "That means we're winning."

"Do you ever get the feeling that we are being scripted into a bad horror movie by some perverse godlike being?" His tone had returned to normal.

"All the time. I think his name is Jack."

"You may be right."

Lyris reached out suddenly. This time, when she touched him, there was a sudden flash of magic and that dormant attraction between them sprang to life.

"Roman?"

"This is nuts," he said. But he knelt down beside her and laced a hand through her hair.

"I know, but . . ." She leaned toward him, breathing in his scent, allowing him to see the hunger in her eyes.

With a soft growl, he rolled onto the floor, pulling her astride him to make mad, passionate love.

Roman stood up, and Lyris noticed the soot marks on his bottom and shoulder blades as he turned away to search for his clothes. She'd probably have a matching set from sitting on the dirty floor. Soon he said briskly: "Up and at 'em, honey. We'd better dress and get back to my place. I think we need to have a word or two with Jack about hurrying up his gift, whatever it is. And then maybe it would be wise if we went to ground somewhere for the rest of the day."

"You think he knows about us, then?"

"Quede? Yeah. That storm felt kind of personal, and it followed us all the way from the plantation. We can't ignore it—much as I'd like to believe that everything is really okay." Roman pulled on his semidamp jeans.

"Of course. But I meant Lobineau. Does he know

what we're doing and why? I wish we knew for sure. He's the joker in the deck, and I just can't figure him." Lyris stood and began dressing. Her clothes were drier but still unpleasantly clammy.

"Well, he—or someone—knew enough to send that troll to Quede's place to find us. And Lobineau's bound to suspect something bad has happened when Mr. Muscles doesn't come back with our bodies tucked under his arms. Maybe he'll blame Quede for the disappearance, but we can't depend on it. I think we better count Lobineau as being in the camp with those who are pissed at us."

"That would be just about everyone, wouldn't it?"

"Yeah, especially when I don't show up at the club tonight. Well, I was tired of stripping anyway." Roman looked out the door, using his eyes but also inhaling carefully.

Lyris could smell nothing but charred wood and battered, bleeding leaves. She tilted her head, listening, but there came nothing but the same old metronome in her head, counting off the hours and minutes that remained before Doomsday.

"Come on. I think we're clear," Roman called, picking up his backpack and stepping outside. "We are lucky not to be bothered by daylight. A lot of feys are."

"You know what frustrates me? Our visit to Toujours Perdrix was for nothing. We didn't learn a damn thing and we lost another night." Lyris stepped out into the light and blinked her eyes.

"And now we have to go into hiding and come up with another plan. Damn Lobineau, anyway. I bet there was a lot more stuff he could have told us."

"I have no doubt that he is damned, no matter what his religion," Roman answered, starting toward the road. He added: "Of course, that isn't completely true, you know. I mean, that we learned nothing. Last night was actually fairly instructive."

"Instructive?"

"Yes."

"I see. Are you convinced we know everything we need to know?" she asked as she fell in behind him.

"No, but I'm convinced we know enough," Roman answered.

"Enough to what?"

Roman waved a hand in a gesture that could have meant anything. "Enough to know what we need to do."

"Stop Quede before he drowns or fries us?" Lyris asked. Then she nodded to herself. Her tone was calm as she added; "But we can't send for help, can we? Last night means Quede is definitely on to us. He has probably mobilized what passes for the law around here. And we are on our own."

"I don't think there'd be time to send out for help anyway. And there's no guarantee anyone could get into the city now." Roman's voice was equally calm. "Quede won't shut down the borders with walls and guards, but you can bet he's screening everyone who goes in or out. He's probably also adopted a shoot-on-sight policy where any fey is concerned. He may even be rounding up those that work in the nightclubs—another reason not to go into work."

"So, we can't leave either." She nodded again, though Roman couldn't see her. His broad back was comforting. Most people ran away from facts that threatened their comfort. But not Roman. He had seemingly reached a place where thinking the unthinkable was an everyday event. He could do it over breakfast. He apparently even did it in his sleep. Maybe there was more benefit to being a pooka than she had ever suspected.

"Not unless you know some way to get past that psychic miasma around this territory without being detected. I don't have that kind of magic. And I don't want Baby to end up with bullet holes in her if we run for the border." Roman's head turned slowly as he scanned the woods for enemies. "I guess we could try escaping into the swamp on foot. They probably don't have guards out there."

Lyris shook her head at his back, sure he knew what she was thinking even if he wasn't looking at her. On her own, she might have been able to cloak her mind and manage an escape, but she couldn't hide her mind and Roman's as well. "The swamp? No, thanks."

"Well, then what?"

"Then, I guess we don't have any choice. We have to find some way to stop Quede from doing whatever it is he's doing." Lyris half smiled, and it showed up in her voice. "However, what do you want to bet that we can't wander into the local hardware store and buy wooden garden stakes without attracting attention?"

Roman lauged. "Not much. However, that isn't a problem." He leaned over and picked up a broken limb, which he passed back to her over his shoulder. "One thing we are not lacking in is wood."

"True." Lyris brightened and she accepted the stick. "And we may not have to kill him, anyway. You can bet that's what the hobgoblin is for."

Roman stopped so abruptly, Lyris almost ran into him. His voice was distant when he spoke again. "Yeah, I'm sure it is. The only problem is that I think we're going to have to take the hobgoblin out too. Immediately."

"Why? I mean, if he doesn't come after us until Quede is gone, and Lobineau keeps him under control . . ."

Roman carefully stepped aside and gestured to the clearing before them. There were many unattractive things about the clearing, including a giant stand of poison sumac, but it wasn't that three-leaved nasty that grabbed Lyris's attention. Laid out like the hours on a watch face were twelve bodies, all gutted and missing their heads. They had obviously been partially eaten. Some trick of the breeze—or magic—kept the smell contained, but Lyris knew the stench would be horrible if the circle were broken by a corporeal being.

"You see, I don't think Lobineau *can* control him anymore."

"Oh, goddess!" Lyris breathed as she sensed something. "He's doing ritual magic. I can't feel what kind, but—"

"I can. The ground is trembling beneath my feet, dying. It's been picked clean of power. Look at the plants. They're all dead—except that red stuff. He's gorged himself with their life and power."

She understood what Roman meant. The turf beneath the twelve bodies was no longer a confederacy of growing things. It was a graveyard made up of a billion individual leaves of dead grass. The trees were wrinkling, too. Lyris turned her head and her eyes met Roman's, both of their gazes stricken.

"So, I guess we'll be paying a visit on the father today after all. He'll have to be convinced to lend us his magic sword." Roman's face was unnaturally grim.

"You think he has one?" Then: "Yes, he must. They would have buried the creature with one jammed through his heart."

"It's traditional."

"But, will Lobineau give it to us?"

"I think, if we promise to get rid of Quede, he will. Having his monster running amok, killing tourists and good little Christian goblins can't be part of his grand master plan."

"Even so—"

"He'll give us the sword, or we'll take it." Roman's voice was flat and his expression the most serious he had ever worn. He looked toward the sunset side of the clearing. "One way or another, we are getting that weapon today. We can't let this creature get any stronger. Another feeding like this and he'll be unstoppable. If he isn't already."

Lyris nodded her head, but each nod seemed to add weight to her bowed neck.

"But, first . . ." Roman tucked a hand under her chin and lifted her head.

"Breakfast?" she guessed, glad there were still some absolutes in her universe—even if this particular certainty made her stomach rebel.

"Absolutely. And we'll find someplace with Internet access so I can let Jack know what's going on—for all the good it will do us."

"Maybe he'll know how to kill a hobgoblin," Lyris said hopefully.

"Maybe. If anyone does, Jack will." Roman cocked his head and looked at her as she winced. "What is it? What do you hear? You've been listening all morning."

"Nothing," Lyris answered, not wanting to tell Roman that the ticking in her head had just gotten louder. "I'm just thinking that maybe this slaughter is a sort of good news, bad news thing."

"Yeah? How so."

"It could be that Quede wasn't after us last night. Maybe he was after the hobgoblin instead."

Roman shook his head. "It's a nice thought, but I wouldn't put any money on that. If we guess wrong, we'll be dead."

Chapter Thirteen

Lyris offered the manager at the cheap motel a bribe to forget the formalities of signing the guest book, and he made it clear that while he wasn't bored with the sight of her money, it would take more to make him excited about helping. But when she offered more, and he suggested that she might like to throw herself in with the bargain, she reached across the desk and gave him a hard punch in the jaw.

The man slumped without a sound, falling onto his side and half exposing his wide rear end as he draped over the chair's broad arm. It had a five o'clock shadow. Hairy butts she had seen, but not one sporting stubble.

"I don't want to know," Lyris muttered as she looked away from the whiskered derriere and down at her bruised hand. This was getting to be a bad habit. Was some latent tendency to violence beginning to erupt in her? Was her sylph side taking over? That lent credence to Roman's suggestion that she had a lot of repressed emotion.

Annoyed at this loss of control, she reached across the desk and tucked money under the manager's greasy plate, then plucked up the room key.

"I'm glad you don't get cranky real often," Roman said, as he pushed through the office door and looked down at the toppled manager. There was amusement in his voice, but no condemnation.

Lyris said, "Come on. Let's get the stuff out of the car. Do you think he'll report us when he wakes up?"

"Nope. I just implanted him with a suggestion that he forget all about us. If you'd held off ten more seconds, the love tap wouldn't have been necessary."

"You can do that? That's cool." But Lyris was not. She was actually quite hot with anger. She swallowed hard, though that probably wouldn't help.

"There's probably a lot about Pookas that you don't know."

"Probably."

"It only works on drunks," Roman added as he kindly pulled the manager upright and then followed Lyris outside. "Why are you grouchy? It was a solid right cross. I know a lot of guys who couldn't have done that as neatly."

"I'm glad something works—besides my right cross, which I am not actually thrilled to be developing."

"Oh, I don't know. I think that right cross might actually be a good thing."

Outside, imps scattered before Lyris like dry leaves before a hard wind. Roman was surprised that the cracked asphalt didn't show scorch marks from her angry passage. She muttered: "I hate losing my temper. It makes me so . . . *angry*. I am *not* my father's daughter. I don't hurt things."

"Yes, I can see that you are pissed." Roman's voice now contained actual laughter. "And I'm willing to go out on a limb here and say that you don't look anything like your dad, either. Unless he was a particularly attractive cross-dresser."

"I don't like being angry, and I don't like being afraid. I spend my entire life avoiding those two things. And just for the record, my father was many strange things, but not a cross-dresser." Lyris sighed. It took a hard effort, but she let go of some of the tension that had been riding her since they found the hobgoblin's slaughter. "And I'm tired and need a shower. That's what made me grouchy."

Roman nodded. "If you ask nice, I'll give you a rubdown after."

"And if I don't ask nice?" She glanced up at him. The look might have been playful, but with the blush of anger still burning her cheeks, it was difficult to tell.

He responded. "Well, if you ask naughty, I'll give you something else."

Her mouth relaxed slightly. "Hmmm. Let me think about it."

"You should have eaten a bigger breakfast."

Lyris wrinkled her nose.

Making love took away her last bit of anger, and Lyris's strength. But the sleep that followed was uneasy and plagued with disturbing images that faded in and out of a thick gray mist: watches without hands that spun in the air, cloaked figures who hid their face when she came near, tombstones pierced with silvered swords. Then, abruptly, the vapor parted and Lyris had a sudden, clear picture of a young Quede in a tuxedo waltzing around the rotting ballroom of Toujours Perdrix, all four arms wrapped around his dead partner's ice-white body as he kissed her dead lips. Hundreds of other bodies, both human and goblin, were propped up against the walls, their lifeless eyes looking on as the couple danced. Somewhere a gramophone played, filling the air with a scratchy voice that sang, "Dream a Little Dream of Me."

One of the pale guests turned its desiccated head. Its rouged lips crackled when they parted, and the guest said to Lyris in a dry, papery voice full of moths: "Our host finds the thought of power more invigorating than a good night's sleep."

A second corpse turned its head and joined the

conversation. The dusty voice sounded contemptuous as it said to the other: "Look at her. Silly creature. She is a piece that won't realize it is part of a puzzle until it is locked in place on all sides. She's been blinded by her emotions. She's *in love*."

Lyris knew that it spoke of her and not the corpse in Quede's arms, but she couldn't find her voice to protest the accusation. She never allowed herself to be blinded by emotions, but a part of her believed the condemnation anyway.

Quede himself finally looked at her. He lifted his head from his partner's face, where Lyris saw that he had been chewing, not kissing. His mouth leaked black fluid from both corners when it opened. "Come in, *ma chérie,* I've been expecting you. These *les belle morts* are tough as leathered mummies under all this perfume and dead social chatter. But they are perfect for my plague army, don't you think? They'll go forth and multiply when I command them. And the hour is nigh."

Lyris stepped back from his outstretched hand, and Quede began to laugh as a giant grandfather clock rolled onto the floor. It had no hands on its revolving face, but the roulette wheel finally stilled with the moon in the upright position and it started to chime the midnight hour.

"Don't run away now, pretty sylph. I so love the way you smell. I'd like to rub you all over my body—inside and out."

* * *

"Wake up, honey," Roman's voice said, and someone began smoothing Lyris's hair back from her face. "It's just a dream. Let it go. Come on now. Let me see those pretty green eyes. Show me that you're with me. Let it go."

It took a great effort to shake off the cloying mist of sleep and horror, but when she opened her eyes, Lyris found only Roman at the side of the bed. He was standing over her with a strange rifle in his left hand. It was not the sight she had been expecting, and it took a moment to locate her vocal cords.

"You look entirely too cheerful for a man holding a gun," she rasped. "Is that from our charismatic fey friend?"

"Yep. I went and collected our care package from Jack. Take a look. This isn't just a gun. It's a Hampton carbine. It's a sniper's rifle, nearly silent and works with a standard .45-caliber bullet you would use in a Colt pistol. Of course, Jack didn't send standard ammo." Roman reached into his pocket and pulled out a small cardboard box. He rattled it. "These babies are made of hardened hawthorn—a fertility wood, but good for hunting bogeymen or other things that go bump in the night. I'm hoping Jack laid some evil juju on them, too."

"UPS is certainly broad-minded about what they carry these days." Lyris sat up. She didn't care for the smell of gun oil that clung to the magicked weapon, but she didn't complain. Her dream had disturbed her, and she was not about to turn away any tool that Jack Frost thought would be useful. When a death fey crafted bullets, they surely delivered a fatal punch even to magical beasties.

"So, it's already time to see Lobineau?"

"How time flies, but yes. You want a shower first? It might help you wake up."

"No, thanks. But let's stop for coffee."

"And beignets," Roman added enthusiastically. "Good idea. There's nothing like fresh beignets to start the day."

Though it was afternoon, Lyris's stomach rolled over and for one moment she thought it would heave. A few deep breaths calmed the unhappy organ, however, and she was able to pretend some enthusiasm for eating.

"Did Jack say anything about what Thomas found?" she asked, standing slowly. It took a moment for the last of the dizziness to pass.

"Yep, and the fact that there isn't much to find has Thomas miffed. There doesn't seem to be anything helpful in any of the computer systems he can hack into. Lots of stuff about orchids, but that's it. Quede either keeps his private stuff off the Net, or else he doesn't use computers at all." Roman stepped back and laid the rifle on the desk. He also removed his pistol from his jacket pocket.

Instantly, Lyris felt better. "I find that hard to believe. You can't run an empire without keeping records. And there has to be some way to relay information."

"That's what Thomas says. He's still looking." Roman looked at her. "So, you wanna tell me what you were dreaming about?"

Lyris shivered. "Yes, but not yet. This isn't something to be faced before coffee."

"Okay." Roman looked at her strangely. "Also, I've thought it over, and I think maybe we better change hotels again. We'll just keep moving—changing cars and hotels. That way, no one can leave any nasty surprises for us while we're gone."

"That sounds wise to me."

"Better late than never," he muttered.

"What's wrong?"

"I had a little tour after I picked up the rifle, checking out some things that Jack warned me about."

"And?"

"And I think his H.U.G. contact is right. Their psychics can't see into the city anymore. There's some sort of psychic blackout that begins just outside and encompasses Toujours Perdrix. I didn't want to get close enough to set off any alarms, but I could feel a sort of barrier there, a psychic flypaper."

"Do you think we can make it to see Lobineau?"

"Yeah, that way isn't blocked. Which is cause for nervousness in and of itself."

"I know," Lyris answered. She pictured cattle being herded down a chute.

Chapter Fourteen

Roman and Lyris stood beside a tilled field that looked as if it had been disturbed by a giant's erratic harrow. The old chestnut trees flanking the crooked furrows and mounds were filled with birds, exotic and mundane alike, but who did not venture into the violated soil where one would expect them to be plucking worms and grubs.

"It looks like a crop circle done by an insane plow horse."

"No, not a horse," Roman answered.

The two of them sniffed the air. The absence of the subtle reek of goblin that pervaded the city should have seemed the greatest luxury, but the odor of decaying earth was thick in the air and somehow unnaturally sleep-inducing. Especially now that the wind had shifted directions. Even as Lyris felt the scent clogging her brain, sucking out her will, the tiny hairs on the nape of her neck were erecting themselves.

Lyris and Roman both fell back a step.

"Magic?"

"Yes, and of the darkest kind. It will go on expanding, eating energy as it goes until the hobgoblin is dead."

They looked over the contaminated ground one last time and then turned toward the Goblin Christian Community Center.

"He's here, then."

"Or very close by."

"It's the amount of money you can't see that is astronomical," the goblin lectured.

Roman thought about asking Lobineau how astronomical, because the daily cash flow he had witnessed flowing through Quede's empire rivaled the G.N.P. of most third-world countries.

Lobineau went on, "One would think that this was about avarice run mad, but it isn't. It's all about power and fear. All this wealth is about protecting one life. And it is such a waste! What work could be done with this money if he were gone."

The argument would have resonated more with Roman if he didn't have a pretty good idea what Lobineau would consider good works.

"And there is plenty for everyone," Lobineau added in a sudden fit of imagined cunning. "Even for you. If you cooperate."

Roman shook his head, too amazed at the goblin's shortsighted stupidity to be affronted at being bribed. "You've been out in the sun too long."

"Don't pretend to be above such things," Lobineau answered. "I know what you do for a living."

"I doubt that very much." Roman wouldn't have taken the money even if he'd been in need, but he certainly was not hurting. By all capitalistic standards, he was a success. And he had learned long ago that money couldn't fill the hollow place inside. Blood money especially. Anyway, though he might currently be a stripper, he wasn't a whore. It was stupid of the goblin not to make the distinction.

"Do you read Shakespeare?" Lobineau asked. "He is one of the few humans worth studying. He said in *Measure For Measure*: 'Our natures do pursue, like rats that ravin down their proper bane.' "

" 'A thirsty evil; and when we drink, we die,' " Roman finished the quotation. "But as you have pointed out, I'm not human. And I won't drink this bane or any other, however attractive it may appear."

"I love the Bard as much as anyone, but it's getting late. Literary discussions will have to wait," Lyris said. Her voice was neutral but shading toward cold. She had been very controlled and flat-voiced since leaving the dying field with the bodies. "We had best get down to business while it's still light."

"You've decided to take on Quede, then?" Lobineau asked, his voice a bit breathy. His words were slightly rushed, betraying his excitement. He moved about, restlessly but silently, and Roman found himself wondering if Lobineau had ever been a cat burglar. Or an assassin.

"We will *probably* take on Quede. But there is something else that must be dealt with first. Something more immediately dangerous." Lyris's voice remained calm and cool, but Roman could see a pulse beating in her throat and wondered what she was sensing. Something about Lobineau, probably—and it couldn't be good.

"Nothing is more dangerous than Quede!" the morally questionable cleric instantly insisted. "Don't you see that he's about to loose one of the riders of the apocalypse on your precious human world? Haven't you sensed it?"

"Let's be plain. I'm tired of games. Do you mean that he's about to loose a viral plague?" Lyris stiffened even as she asked the question, and Roman knew she was thinking of her dream: Quede dancing with a corpse while hundreds of other dead looked on. Her description of the vision had chilled him even despite a cup of steaming coffee in his hands.

"Of course." The answer was probably not meant to be a slap in the face, but it functioned as one. Lobineau looked at them as if they were stupid.

"But how could he infect everyone? We haven't seen or heard anything about him doing medical research. The hospital files are clean," Roman insisted when Lyris didn't speak. He looked from Lobineau to the pulse in her throat. She was definitely sensing something that alarmed her. "As far as I can tell, all he's doing is cloning miniature goblins—and making them sexless. That's unnatural and cruel, but not threatening to humans."

"Haven't you heard anything?" Lobineau asked. He practically spat the words, mocking. "But you wouldn't know where to look and listen, would you, pooka? You've spent all your time wandering around Toujours Perdrix, killing innocent Christian trolls. You've never been in Quede's greenhouses or in the hive. Not that an uneducated person like you would understand anything you saw there." His tone moderated. "You must understand that these days Quede thinks globally. He doesn't need hospitals anymore. His laboratory is the world."

"Fine. I'll buy that. But what do you mean, exactly? Give us details."

"Do I have to spell it out? Think! He's had his own society to practice infection on. And why should he go to all the trouble of using high-tech human systems and means when more traditional methods of infection work better?"

"Like what? Rats as plague carriers?" Roman guessed.

"Or imps," Lyris suggested.

Lobineau shook his head. "You are so sightless, so unimaginative. What has he got in vast, even limitless numbers? What can he control absolutely? Worker goblins."

"The worker goblins? But—"

"Yes, the workers. Think about it. They are perfect, the ultimate cheap method of delivering indiscriminate slaughter. He can clone them in vast numbers. Being small and sexless, they mature very quickly."

"But that doesn't make sense. What could he give them that wouldn't kill them, too? Goblins die of the major human diseases, too. What—"

"He's a *vampire*." Lobineau talked over her again. "He doesn't need to invent a new toxin, or discover a new disease. He *is* one. And his obedient little army is the ideal carrier. After all, isn't the world always howling for good help? Nannies, maids, gardeners, chauffeurs, clerks, crop pickers—Quede will supply them all. Those workers are waiting to go into the world as we speak, thousands of simple, sweet, obedient, sexless lutins all bred to be scentless, small, and appealing in their features. Have you actually seen them? They look like little green children. Having one will be the new status symbol. He could probably even market them as pets. That would save him from printing up work permits," Lobineau added with a frown.

"Can this be true?" Lyris whispered, looking over at Roman. She wasn't asking about Quede arranging work permits.

"Of course it can," Lobineau answered. "Haven't

you learned anything? Quede's bite poisons everything—even secondhand, it kills humans. His little goblins can fight their blood cravings for a while, but eventually they will need food . . . and then they'll take it anywhere they can find it. Man, woman, or child, they won't care when the blood lust is on them. Sure, the humans will probably fight back—even kill them—once they know what's happening. But it will be too late. The infection will be in the population and spreading faster than any disease you have ever known. Everyone will die."

"Die? This infection kills? The infected don't just turn into vampires?" Lyris asked. Not that it made a huge difference.

"Eventually, all who are infected die. Stop thinking about the movies. Quede isn't a normal vampire. He's a super infection. There'll be no human survivors except his selected breeding stock. That's the beauty of it, at least from Quede's point of view. He'll be unstoppable. And I assure you that he hasn't been developing antibodies for a vaccine in case he changes his mind. Quede never has second thoughts. The insane never do."

Roman fought the childish urge to say something like "Takes one to know one."

"The worker goblins? The early infected. What's happened to them?" Lyris asked.

Lobineau's face softened slightly at her question, but his voice remained bitter. "Yes, I've seen the early experiments. Victims are stunted from the moment of infection and became even more allergic to the sun. Most die within a year, a mass of unhealing sores and completely mad. Those few that survive—they're hideous and who knows what will happen to them later? Maybe they'll become vampires. Quede won't care so long as they go out into the world and do his bidding."

"If this is true, why haven't you told anyone?" Lyris asked. "Why didn't you tell us the first time we met? We could have gotten help then. Quede has shut the city off and now no one can get in."

"It was too good a bargaining chip." Lobineau shrugged. "If I'd told you earlier, you would simply have gone to your authorities, said your piece, and then left town. And they would do *nothing*. Quede would win. And we would lose everything I've worked for. Everything we've *suffered* for."

Lyris glanced at Roman, her expression troubled. She clearly believed what Lobineau was saying. And since she had the gift of knowing truth when she saw or heard it, that meant her nightmare was probably real.

"Okay, we get the picture, and we'll talk about Quede in a moment," Roman interjected when Lobineau drew another breath. "But we have another problem. A bigger one. And this one is all of your making."

"*Aaahhh*. You are referring to my secret weapon?" Lobineau asked, an unpleasant smile stretching across his lips. He turned from Lyris to Roman.

"He's not very secret, Lobineau. Step out your back door and have a look around. He has a bad habit of leaving large numbers of corpses out in the open. He is also sucking up magic at a phenomenal rate. He's got to be put down before he eats any more power. As it is, this area looks like a wasteland."

"But I have no wish to put him down. I'm sorry about the dead trees, but he is very useful to me. Yesterday he ate a quintet of Quede's watchers."

"I'm sure he *is* useful to you. But he needs to be put down anyway. Today. So why don't you go and fetch the magic sword and we'll be on our way?" Roman kept his voice polite and reasonable, but it took an effort. He really didn't like this goblin, and the feeling was mutual.

"You want my sword?" Lobineau's smile was truly nasty, and it showed double rows of jagged teeth. "Well, boys and girls, it's a seller's market and I have the monopoly. Are you ready to hear my price for the weapon?"

Roman sighed. "Don't push your luck, lutin."

"Lobineau." Lyris had suddenly rediscovered her voice. It wasn't much like her own, being deep and harsh, but it certainly captured the goblin's attention. Both men turned to look at her.

Lyris was discovering that her yardstick of irrational behavior had begun to expand. It was now the size of the largest tape measure she'd ever seen and it was getting longer and more flexible all the time. Yet Lobineau's revelation had left her temporarily unable to cope with the dimensions of the problem. She had to break it down into smaller components.

In her current circumstances, it seemed acceptable to either agree to Lobineau's terms—though he would probably ask them to murder Quede as well as the hobgoblin in some ritualistic manner that would bring him Quede's power—or else to simply take the sword away by force, killing Lobineau if necessary. Perhaps even if not. She turned her head and looked at Roman, leaving the decision up to him.

The action made Lobineau's smile falter and his expression suddenly became very nervous. Somewhere along the way—probably when the priest had admitted to making no effort to save New Orleans's humans, or even its goblins, because it wasn't convenient for him to lose his hold over them—Lyris had lost her impulse to be pleasant to this lutin because of what he had suffered. She was getting angry again. And annoyance at feeling her temper slipping away was carrying her back into a spiral where she was overcome by violent impulses.

"I think you better get that sword," Roman said to Lobineau, looking Lyris over and correctly weighing her expression. "Or my girlfriend will beat you up."

Lyris turned back to the goblin priest. She had kept her emotions locked away for years, but it was time to open doors and let them free. She looked into Lobineau's eyes and let her growing rage shine through.

"Here's the deal. And there will be no negotiation for terms," She said. She made very sure that her voice did not betray the sickness she felt inside. Fury helped her project the right tone, which was a full octave lower than any she had ever used. "You will give us the sword, and after we have dealt with the hobgoblin, we will take care of Quede. If you do not give us the sword—now—or if you make any attempt to call the hobgoblin, we will kill you and then take what we need. I'm a hunter. Rest assured that I can find the sword wherever it is."

"But you can't kill me. I'm the only one who can control him," Lobineau argued, obviously shocked. "Who will guide the goblins here when Quede is gone? You need me to help you."

"I doubt that," Roman answered even as he looked at Lyris with question in his eyes. She wanted to reassure him that she meant what she said, but Lyris didn't let her expression change by even a degree. Roman added, speaking both to her and Lobineau: "No one can really control him now. In any event, we'll take our chances. We have to. So, what's it going to be, Lobineau? Are you going to live to fight another day, to lead the goblins of a free New Orleans? Or do we make the world a better place for mankind and break your neck right now?"

Eyes red with venom, Lobineau answered. "I'll give you the sword, for all the good it will do you. I just hope the hobgoblin doesn't eat you before you kill Quede."

Lyris really hoped not, too.

"Good choice," Roman answered. "Now, let's go get that magical silver blade and we'll be on our way."

Chapter Fifteen

"So, your granny knew the old arts?" Roman asked Lyris as he unwrapped Lobineau's sword. The weapon was not a thing of beauty, but it certainly had about it an impressive aura of power and menace.

"Yes, she called it practical magic," Lyris answered. "The quick-and-dirty, help-around-the-home stuff." She leaned against his Jag. The engine was still warm and she found the heat oddly comforting. Though the dying day was far from cold, she still had a chill on her skin. Lobineau's evil had laid a frost over her nerves.

"And you can remember some of her spells? Maybe something that would protect us while we use this? Or put an unbluntable edge on the thing." Roman tested the sword's blade with a gingerly touch. Even with his exercise in care, Lyris had to bite her tongue to keep from warning him to be careful.

"Yes," she answered once Roman's thumb was away from the sword's wicked blade. "At least, I think I do. Hopefully it's like riding a bike."

"Then this might be a good moment to see if you have any—and if you can get by without training wheels."

"Okay. Lay it down here." She indicated the ground at her feet. She didn't want to touch the thing. Silver didn't usually bother her, but this blade was something more than just jewelry or a chafing dish.

Roman obediently laid the sword lengthwise at her feet, the hilt facing east in proper magical alignment. Feeling silly and more than a little nervous, Lyris nevertheless spread out her hands as her grandmother had done and recited a spell over it. The charm was something her grandmother had used to make household utensils stronger and more useful.

Spell complete, she looked up at Roman and muttered, "I don't really believe this casual mumbo jumbo works. Magic is supposed to be more ritualized. We should kill a chicken or something."

"Maybe, but go ahead and mumble some more jumbo, will you? I can feel something moving in the air around you."

"Okay." She swallowed. "You better hand me the rifle, too."

"It works on guns?" Roman asked, going to the trunk and getting out his keys.

"I don't know that it works at all. But it can't hurt, can it?"

"Good point. Just don't get in the way of anything Jack has done to the gun. You don't want to brush up against his death magic."

"I don't want to brush up against any magic. The sword and the gun are both packed with enough deadly intent to start a world war."

"Yet it just doesn't feel like it's enough, does it?"

Once they turned their senses to it, Lyris and Roman didn't take long to discover the hobgoblin's trail. His spoor was not visible to the naked eye, but their noses had no trouble discerning his scent, especially when it was mixed with the smell of new blood.

The hobgoblin had retreated deep into the swamp, perhaps to avoid the sunlight, perhaps to escape being hunted. Roman was certain that Lobineau had somehow managed to warn his creation that they were coming to put an end to his power orgy.

The good news was that it was avoiding Quede's barriers, so they were unlikely to stumble over any psychic trip-lines. And that was good because there were plenty of other things to trip over. The bayou was always a place of shadows and trembling earth, but this afternoon it was also filled with a sense of foreboding that silenced the residents' usual eerie songs.

Roman and Lyris ran along a stagnant watercourse that bubbled unpleasantly, staying as dry as possible, which wasn't very, since all the plants dripped and drooled.

Roman carried the sword, and Lyris had his backpack. They had decided against bringing the gun or pistol since wooden bullets, even magicked ones, weren't going to be of much use against a zombie hobgoblin. And there was always the danger of losing the rifle in the swamp. It stayed in the Jag.

"Keep an eye out for fireflies. They are supposed to lead to Jean Lafitte's hidden treasure," Roman said softly. His wind was excellent, and he didn't feel tired even though they had been running for nearly twenty minutes and leaping over anything that looked suspiciously damp or slippery.

"I'm keeping an eye out for spiders. I wish I'd brought that pistol after all," Lyris answered, dodging a giant web whose strands gleamed with silver stickiness. Her voice was not as steady and Roman slowed down a little. It was important they find the hobgoblin before dark, but he didn't want to exhaust Lyris before the confrontation.

"The bacteria is probably more dangerous. Though feys don't often get infections," he said encouragingly. "Besides, it's hard to be sneaking when you're blasting away at things."

"That may be true. But I don't like spiders. Their

bites hurt. And some creatures just need killing. You're from Texas. You should know this."

Roman grunted. "I reckon they do. You've been bit before?"

"Yeah. Trust me. They hurt."

"Speaking of things that hurt, you know what we are going to have to do after this, don't you?"

"Go to the hospital and maybe Quede's greenhouse?" Lyris guessed. There was a distinct lack of enthusiasm in her guess.

"Yeah. If we can get past security. Lobineau is probably telling the truth this time, but I'd feel better if we had some specific idea of just how many goblins may be infected, and what with, and where they are. If Thomas can't crack any computer files, we'll have to go."

"I really am hoping that Quede hasn't started infecting goblins yet, that we'll stop him in time. I'm no fan of lutins in general, but I feel sorry for those poor sons-of-bitch clones. No one cares about them."

"I feel sorry for them, too. But if we're too late to stop Quede from infecting them . . ." he warned.

"I know. They'll have to be destroyed." Lyris tried to keep dejection from her voice, but it was there.

"I'm sorry. I know this is hard for you," Roman said, knowing he sounded serious and regretting it. This wasn't the moment to have Lyris doubting her ability to hide her emotions, or to have her start thinking that he was coming to understand her in a way that no one else ever had—even though it was true. Something told him that though she was used to having long, clear looks into other people's souls, she wasn't accustomed to having her own self examined.

Fortunately, there was no resentment or shyness in her voice when she answered him. Once again, truth prevailed for her over comfort. "I know. Me too. But we'll do whatever we have to."

Roman stopped at the edge of a small grove filled with grave-sized hummocks and damp ground that looked suspiciously like a bog. He took a deep breath.

Lyris also stopped dead in her tracks, slowly inhaling until something unpleasant tickled her nose. "He's close," she whispered.

"So, I'm going to climb up into this tree and start following you from up there. Just stick to the hummocks and you'll be fine." His voice was as soft as the sly wind inching along the black waterway.

"Following me?" Lyris asked. "You're going to wait in the trees, while I make like a tethered goat?"

"Sort of. You aren't tethered, though. You're trolling." He grinned.

"Like fishing? So I'm a worm? I'd rather be a goat, but—"

"Be whatever you like, so long as it's cautious."

She glanced at the glade and then nodded. "Roman?"

"Yes?"

"How do we know that the hobgoblin isn't already up in one of those trees?"

"Good point." He thought for a moment. "I've never heard of hobgoblins climbing trees, have you?"

"No. But you will be very careful, right? Don't get bit by a snake or anything."

"Oh, yeah. Don't worry. And I'll be closer than your shadow and just as inseparable."

"I just hope you're more useful," she answered, watching him scramble up the tree. He was proud of the fact that he managed the job silently. It wasn't easy with a giant sword strapped to his back.

"Okay, I'm off," she whispered from below, grabbing the pack's straps and jumping out onto the first of the mounds. Then she let out with a soft "*Baaaa*."

Roman snorted once in surprise, then contained his laughter. He had to admit that she sounded a lot like a goat.

The hobgoblin was on her with barely an instant's warning. He came at her from downwind, surging up out of the black water like an orca after a seal, and clutched at her arms with all four hands.

But Roman was true to his word. Faster than Lyris's own shadow, he fell down out of the sky. The silver sword shot over her ear leaving a trail of kinetic energy. Lyris had a moment to consider the belief that you aren't supposed to hear the bullet that kills you, but that it seems more than likely you would hear the air being cut by the sword in the moment before it lops off your head. Then she stopped thinking. Cold, black blood spattered her hair, chest and arms. As soon as the cruel talons around her loosened, she rolled away from the dying hobgoblin.

"The heart!" she gasped, the surrounding air having turned unimaginably foul, and the hobgoblin making a sort of nonstop gurgling that suggested its voice box was a steel engine and not located in its throat.

"Got it," Roman answered. Plunging the suddenly tarnished silver blade into the creatures chest, he then leaned on it as a gardener might a pitchfork stuck in a particularly stubborn patch of ground. The hobgoblin screamed in a tone so high that she and Roman could barely hear it with their ears, and yet it somehow managed to shove needles into their brains. Roman bore down until the sword was up to the hilt.

"Are you all right?" he asked Lyris, when the beast finally stopped shrieking and its ghastly face imploded like a shriveled apple. Rot seemed to set in immediately.

"Yeah. Mostly. I'm developing a real persecution complex, though. Next time you can be the goat."

She forced herself to stop rubbing her arms and to look at the hobgoblin. The creature looked and smelled dead. Of course, it had smelled dead before. She wiped the blood from her face with an unsteady hand. "Is it really gone? Just like that?"

"I hope so. It just seems easy today." Roman let go of the sword and stepped back. She watched him swallow hastily and understood. The bile was rising in the back of her throat as well. The nose wasn't able to accustom itself to the stench because the stench kept changing—and always for the worse.

"Did you bring the flares?" he asked.

"Yes." Lyris turned and reached for Roman's dropped backpack. She had declined to tuck them in her cargo pants pocket. The bushes nearby began to rustle, and she took it as a good sign that the forest imps that had scattered when the hobgoblin approached were now creeping back, their noses twitching.

She waited until Roman removed the sword, then dragged the body farther up the mound and handed him a half dozen flares.

"I hate to deprive them of a meal," she said, looking at the colorful imps who waited in the shrubbery.

"If they want him, they'll have to eat him flambé." Roman struck the first flare and dropped it onto the hobgoblins body. Surprisingly, the thing burned like pitch, making the flames blue and green. "I don't like the look of this. You better keep back. He might explode."

"I guess so," Lyris agreed, not wanting to watch and yet unable to look away. The unnatural flames burned brighter. "That looks like foxfire. It's probably good that we're surrounded by water."

"Get some wood," Roman said. "Leaves, sticks—anything that will burn. We want to be thorough about this. I have a feeling that Father Lobineau hasn't really learned anything from this experience, and he might well decide to try and resurrect this creature if we leave it even slightly intact."

Lyris nodded.

"You did a great job with those spells," Roman told her as he started to unbutton his shirt. "Or maybe the sword carried one hell of an enchantment already. Anyhow, while the first blow was at an awkward angle, it still nearly took his head off."

Lyris nodded again, dragging over several branches with dead leaves attached. The air was improving as the goblin disappeared, but she didn't relish the idea of having the stink in her mouth. She kept silent until she could get upwind of the pyre.

"I don't like it when you're quiet," Roman commented. "What nasty thing are you thinking about?"

"It isn't nasty, just a little harsh."

"And it would be?"

She tried to explain. "We feys exist by nature's consent. The goddess's. And so do the goblins. But what about this thing? I know we had to kill it, but . . . well, what was it? What gods did he belong to? What sort of power might we have unbalanced by ending him this way? We didn't put him down with incantations and magic, but I still felt something pass out of him and go into the earth."

"You've been reading too much Lovecraft. I don't think we need to be worrying about ancient evils from beyond."

"Ha! Just tell me this thing was natural!"

"I can't. Nothing will ever convince me that this creature had Mother Nature's blessing. It was an abomination—not even alive in any sense of the word as you or I would use it. But that doesn't mean he was claimed by anything divine. Freaks do just happen."

"No, it wasn't divine. Yet. But I think it was trying. To be immortal." She swiped at her face again. "Or maybe it just wanted away from Lobineau."

"Maybe, but it doesn't matter what it wanted, or why it wanted it. What matters is what it did, and what it would have done. We stopped it because we had to—and before you bring it up, it wasn't murder. Don't even go there. These are monsters we're fighting. You can't waste time arguing moral postures. They aren't human. They aren't fey. They don't play fair. And we can't either. We don't have time for an attack of the guilts."

Lyris snorted. But then she added, "And Quede?" She asked softly, "What of him?"

"I don't know," Roman answered truthfully. He sounded a bit harassed. "I've never really bought the notion that contracting vampirism could mean your soul was forfeit, any more than being fey does. And yet, if what Lobineau said was true—if Quede is a killer vampire who is planning the destruction of the world, then he can't be considered a natural creature of evolution. He's just a genetic accident, a horrible one that has gone morally askew and wants to kill us all. The need to survive, to protect others must overcome kindness and even charity." Roman looked at her.

"So, he's to be executed."

"However we define the act, he has to die. Better to see it as self-defense. Even world defense. Every living creature has a natural right to protect itself and its kind. That's what we're doing. And we'll never be safe again while he's alive. No one will."

Lyris nodded and laid a hand over her abdomen. There, the smallest of butterflies was shivering. Yes, for many reasons, Quede had to die.

"Are you okay?" Roman asked, apparently already letting go of the tension and horror of the moments just past. He threw his head back and sniffed the air the way a stallion might.

"Yes." She dropped her hand. This didn't seem the instant to mention the child she suspected she now carried. Instead, she watched a relaxed Roman strip off his shirt and hold it over the burning corpse.

The heat of the fire made it billow, and the shirt reminded her inappropriately of a hot air balloon.

She wished that she could be like Roman and just put all ugliness aside. Idly, she asked, "I love the fact that you'll never have an ulcer or tension headaches, but you aren't going to start acting like Ferdinand the Bull, are you?"

"Ferdinand the Bull? From the children's book?" Roman grinned suddenly, once again completing the transformation into a mischievous spirit. "You mean, am I flinging off my garments so I can roll naked in the pansies—or, in this case, poison sumac? It's a thought, you know. We should celebrate somehow. I mean, this was epic. We just won a battle with a legend, and he didn't get in a single blow."

"Thank the goddess!"

"Mostly I was just thinking I should burn my clothes. They have blood on them and reek to high heaven. I don't want to get anything nasty on Baby. She wouldn't like it."

She. The Jag. Lyris wondered if she would eventually develop a jealousy of her metallic rival.

"And you are going to have to burn yours, too," he added. "And wash your hair. And everything else, too," He grimaced as he looked at her face and matted tresses. "Geez! He skunked you good. There's hobgoblin all over you."

"Wash? Here . . . in the swamp? With *that* water?" Lyris looked around at the spiky shrubs full of disappointed imps and then down at the bubbling goo that moved sluggishly beyond the edge of the small mound. "Absolutely not."

"Don't worry. The smell will keep the alligators away," Roman assured her with cheerful heartlessness. "And the mosquitoes don't seem at all interested in you."

"Roman, I'm not washing in that water. It's filthy and full of mud bugs and things that pinch. *Baby* will just have to tough it out. I'll take my clothes off when we get to the car."

"Now, honey, don't be scared. It's just water and some itty-bitty critters smaller than you," he reasoned, coming toward her with hands outstretched. "A little mud won't hurt you."

Correctly interpreting the gleam in his eyes, she leaped away from him. But Roman was faster and caught her on the fly.

"If you throw me in that stream, you're a dead man," she warned him, twisting in his arms. His strength both thrilled and alarmed her.

"What a thing to say! I would never throw you anywhere," he assured her. But he shifted her onto his shoulder. He gave a small paean of triumph, then jumped in cold blood right into the black river.

"Damn it!" Lyris gasped before the water closed over their heads.

In less than a moment, they bobbed to the surface. Roman gave her a quick kiss, which she grandly rejected. Roman tried to look wounded by the rebuff but she just glared.

"Come on, Lyris. It isn't that bad. You'll be happier when you're clean."

She didn't answer and held herself rigid in his grasp. A moment later the slightly chastised Roman set her free, and she quickly moved to the shore feeling like an affronted cat. Roman effortlessly kept pace beside her, swimming with a grace she didn't have. Lyris didn't look into his face; but she was pretty sure that he was still smiling.

"Your relationship with that car is unnatural," she said coldly.

"You're not jealous of her, are you?" he asked, sounding amazed. And amused.

"Ha! As if! But you could have drowned me! What if I couldn't swim? Did that even cross your mind? Some people are afraid of the water," Lyris snarled once she was back on land and wringing out her dripping hair. Something wriggled in her pocket and she quickly flicked the small shrimp away. The water hadn't been all that horrid, but she didn't feel like forgiving Roman for the dunking—especially since she was still uncomfortably aromatic as well as miserably wet and coated in a layer of slime.

Roman bent to retrieve the shrimp, tossing it back into the water. Then he straightened and stared at her for a long moment, making Lyris feel that she had said something ridiculous. Finally he shrugged, rubbed his cheek—a smooth one that never seemed to need shaving—and said without smiling: "Don't be silly, honey. I'm a river horse. No one drowns unless I want them to. Hurry up now. I'm hungry. We need to eat before we go to the hospital. A little coffee will fix you up. Caffeine withdrawal is probably making you crabby."

And with that, Roman picked up his backpack and the sword and started briskly for his car. He completely ignored the smoking remains of the hobgoblin in the middle of the clearing.

Reminded once again of what Roman really was, a suddenly speechless Lyris also straightened and sloshed after him.

Chapter Sixteen

Lyris and Roman sniffed carefully at the conditioned air, not certain that they could smell an ambush, in the unlikely event that one was laid on, but hoping that they would recognize the scent of danger if it lurked inside the gray hospital building.

Lutin Memorial was an upscale hospital that didn't look like it did a great deal of charity work with the underprivileged. It had lots of thick woven wool from exotic species on the floor of the lobby for people to wipe their Gucci and Prada on, and it was chock-full of heavy furniture made of real wood from old-growth forests, worked by hand by skilled, underpaid craftsmen centuries before. There wasn't anything plastic in the place, discounting the computers and the patients.

All the help seemed to shop at fashionable boutiques and, male or female, looked like they could make every teenager's sex fantasy come true. Which was what they were supposed to do. This was a place devoted to beautification of the outer person. Each employee was a living testimonial to the hospital's efficacy.

There were also security cameras everywhere, including those hiding near the floor beside giant urns of orchids, which served no purpose that Lyris could see other than looking up women's dresses. Fortunately, there was no sign of thermal scanners.

Of course there were the expected guards near the doors, but those guards were too busy posing and flexing their implanted biceps to notice anything much going on around them. They also proved that the new lutin dentist in town was a genius. They had smiles bright enough to sunburn anyone not wearing sunscreen.

"Sloppy security," Roman said. "Lucky for us."

"Very sloppy. Too sloppy. It makes me nervous," Lyris complained.

"Good. This wouldn't be a great moment for either of us to get cocky."

"I just want to know, where is H.U.G. when you need them?"

"Probably not at the donut shop. Unless it's one outside the city. I don't see Quede opening the borders, even if the hobgoblin is dead."

"Ungrateful bastard."

Roman nodded.

Lyris took another look around. This laxity on the

guards' part was probably due to the fact that the biggest danger they had ever faced was some hysteric with a maxed-out credit card being denied a nose job, but she had to wonder if somewhere in the building there lurked a true goon squad. There had to be some serious security somewhere, since this massive structure had to be a main entrance to the hive.

"Okay, I only see the four guards and regular cameras. I think we're a go. Ready?" she asked.

"See you in twenty minutes. I don't care if you discover the lost tribes of Israel, don't be late getting back here. We're looking for clues, not *beyond-all-shadow-of-a-doubt* proof." Roman didn't look at her as he spoke; his eyes were moving slowly over the crowd, still evaluating. His seriousness reassured Lyris.

"I won't be late," she promised. "This place gives me the willies."

"Get ready. Here comes cover."

"I see them."

Fortunately, the hospital was crowded with patients who provided ample camouflage for their movements. Most goblin surgeons preferred to work at night, and so did many of their clients, particularly those who chose to lead a fashionably vampiric lifestyle made popular by the great novelists who resided in New Orleans. Given the hordes of people and the general noise level, it wasn't any great trick for Lyris and Roman to split up, lose themselves in a passing gaggle of nurses, and begin a search of the facilities. Even with Roman's height, all he needed to do was move slowly enough that his physical assurance and grace didn't show on the security cameras.

They had studied a layout of the hospital provided by Roman's mysterious hacker friend, Thomas Marrowbone. Lyris's objective was the atomic medicine lab located in the basement. It was one of the two places in which Thomas was interested. It seemed an unlikely thing for a hospital that specialized in plastic surgery to have, and the name suggested a nefarious purpose to her, especially since its computers were not hooked into the lutin empire network like almost everything else in the hospital.

Roman, accustomed to following Quede's paper trail, had selected the research wing's record office, located on the sixth floor. It also was a hopeful location because it was listed on no public map, either, like the atomic medicine lab. Such goblin trickery had his hackles rising.

Lyris broke away from the nurses and walked boldly to the service elevator. She pressed the down button and was pleased that her hands didn't shake. She tried hard to look like Dr. Clwyd, whose badge she wore. Among Roman's other skills was an ability to pick pockets, and he had suffered no difficulty in liberating a couple of badges from the day shift as the docs had headed to their automobiles.

Her hands were slightly damp and her heart was beating too quickly, but Lyris wasn't in any danger of giving herself away. Not as long as she didn't get any more nervous. She knew that blending was a talent she had. She had used it for years to cloak both her sylph and siren natures from her human companions, but she had never tried hiding her identity in a goblin stronghold before and wasn't certain she could do it for long periods of time.

The elevator doors slid open and out gushed a gasp of chemical-smelling air. But that was all that confronted her; Lyris had the car to herself. There weren't even any security cameras that she could see.

She punched another button, then watched in consternation as the floor numbers clicked by in both Lutin and Roman numerals. Small things like this confused her and made her worry. There were so many things about the goblins—possibly dangerous ones—that she didn't understand. Why put both Lutin and Roman numerals in an elevator? Was this significant? The worry made her aware of the clock again ticking in her head.

The elevator dumped her in a long corridor that was empty of all life and even sound. Lyris looked about uneasily, not caring for the heavy shielding she could sense in the walls around her. Just as she had expected, the second basement's atomic medicine department wasn't a popular destination. There wasn't even a nurse manning the lobby desk.

That made things at once easier and more difficult. More people meant more eyes to fool. Fewer people meant she had to deal with eluding the electronic eyes tracking up and down the corridors.

She forced herself out of the elevator, making her steps as silent as possible so as not to disturb the utter quiet of the hall. Her senses were on full alert, looking for any psychic trip lines Roman had mentioned.

She had already decided that she didn't like this hospital. Not that any hospital was a vacation spot, but she could sense all around her the desperation and neuroses of people who equated the loss of their youth with the loss of life. Lyris had always assumed that she was as vain as the next woman, but she couldn't understand making being beautiful her life's work. Yet, however much she might dislike them, at least there were real human people upstairs. Down here in the basement, there was nothing but look-alike doors of reinforced metal, fluorescent lights, and giant stands of disquieting orchids that came in shapes and colors she had never seen in the world. Some of the more spidery flowers even glowed like they were transfused with neon. Bits of sticky drool dripped off some of them, reminding her of the nasty plants in Toujours Perdrix. She carefully avoided those as she paced down the hallway.

Finally, she ran out of corridor. All that was left beyond the atomic medicine department was the morgue, and she didn't want to go there. A quick peek along the bisecting hallway told her that she was also in between security cameras whose sweep was slightly mistimed. If she moved now, they wouldn't know what room she entered. It was time to take a look behind door number 17 and see if she won the big prize.

Roman pushed open the door to the records room and eased into the space, peering intently at the creature behind the desk even as he readied his excuses for his intrusion. He hoped it wouldn't turn into a sudden-death situation, but his muscles were ready for that, too. Odds were against his having been spotted and someone ordering that he be met by a squad of goons wearing guns or baseball bats, but this investigation had taught him that Quede had long arms and an even longer, vindictive memory. It paid to be cautious.

But the creature behind the desk was a surprise: small, sexless, cute in a kittenish way. She—he—whatever it was—had the feeble gaze and vacant smile of a human goblin-fruit addict. But Roman knew that lutins usually weren't addicted to their fruit. Something else was going on here, and he was pretty sure that he knew what it was. Lobineau had been telling the truth. Quede's new tame worker goblins could be sold as pets or adopted as children.

"Hello," Roman said, keeping his voice easy as he captured the creature's gaze and ordered it to take a short nap.

The little lutin gave a half nod and then slumped back in his chair with a tiny sigh. Appalled, and a little sickened at how easy the thing's mind had been to overshadow, Roman righted the lutin gently and set about tossing the office.

Ignoring the computer for the time being, he started on the shelves of files where thousands of patients' records were stored. He knew that these couldn't be all the records for the hospital, since the institution had been around for some eighty years, but they seemed far too numerous for a simple experimental laboratory. It also made him nervous that most of the folders bore goblin names.

He had opened his third file and was reading about severe patient photophobic reactions when the first hint of alarm ghosted down the nerve endings of his neck. It was specific in its warning.

"Lyris!" He jammed the file back on the shelf and headed for the door.

Quede was in a bad mood. The sylph and the pooka had disappeared, and his incompetent staff couldn't find them. If only he could walk outside! He would go hunt them himself. But even at night the sun hurt him, its light bouncing off the giant full moon. It hurt his eyes, hurt his head. And it was too much bother to call a storm just to veil the baleful orb.

Soon, very soon, his foes would come to him. The hobgoblin was dead. They had obligingly killed it. There was nothing else for them to do except leave or confront him—and he was quite certain they would not try to leave. He just had to be patient and wait. And maybe kill a few of his staff as an incentive for the rest to find the sylph.

As though sensing his master's thoughts, Schiem insinuated himself into the room.

"Good news?"

"They found her. She's at the hospital. In the atomic medicine lab."

Yes! Quede almost laughed, his headache forgotten. He had hoped she would take the bait, and he had ordered that floor cleared of personnel.

"What would you like the guards to do?" Schiem's voice was colorless.

"Send the trolls. They can hurt her if they must, but I want her alive . . . and uneaten."

"And if the pooka is there?"

"Bring him. Or kill him. I don't care. And, Schiem . . ." Quede paused. "Make sure the troll master is clear about keeping a low profile. I don't want any seen in the hospital. If there's an incident, I'll feed him to his trolls myself."

Schiem nodded, but Quede knew he didn't approve. Like all his part-human servants, Schiem didn't like the man-eating trolls.

Tough.

She found what she was looking for at http://www.lutinempire.com/hive/index.html.

Welcome to the hive. Events for the night include briefing on the autumnal production schedule posted at www.lutinempire.com. Troll Masters should pay special attention to the new intruder protocols at the atomic medicine lab . . .

"This doesn't sound good," she said to herself.

In answer, the door opened with a small hiss and then slammed against the wall. Lyris looked up from the computer screen to unhappily see the creature who had just entered the room. He had the sort of chest development that could only be found on freaks who took steroids and lived at the gym. Or on trolls. This, unfortunately, was one of the latter. Worse, he had a hospital badge on his uniform.

Lyris had gotten to the troll master security memo just a little too late.

"Hello," she said. Her muscles tensed, readying themselves to either flee or fight, but she managed to ask with creditable calm, "May I help you?"

The troll grinned at her and stepped into the room. His long nose pointed at her like a gun, and he obviously hadn't taken advantage of the company's cosmetic dental plan. His teeth were still saber-sharp.

"Oh, yeah, I think you can," he chortled.

Lyris didn't wait for him to take a second step. She feinted right, and as soon as the troll was off balance she jumped left, clearing the desk with room to spare.

Eyes angry, the troll spun about and reached for her with his upper right hand. Borrowing from Roman's style of fighting, Lyris swung her leg in a fantail kick and connected with the point of the troll's right elbow. Apparently the funny bone was the same in both troll and human physiology, because the troll's long arm dropped lame, and he clutched at it with his second right hand.

He swiped at her with his longer left arm. But Lyris was ready for it and quickly dropped under his clublike limb. Again, using Roman's style of kickboxing, she lashed viciously at the troll's left buttock, aiming for where the human sciatic nerve was located. She followed up with a faster, shorter kick that dislocated the monster's knee. It was a dirty sort of street fighting, but she had no hesitation about abandoning fair play when battling something four times her weight that would cheerfully eat her.

The combination of kicks worked. When the troll dropped to his uninjured knee and began to bellow, she was tempted to finish him off with another kick to the head. But he was flailing about with his uninjured arms and might get in a lucky grab. Rapid retreat seemed the smartest thing to do. She couldn't know if reinforcements were coming, and what she wanted to avoid at all costs was a fight in close quarters with two or more trolls.

As if to encourage her choice, she heard distant voices shouting. Warned, she turned and leapt for the door, leaving the bellowing troll behind.

There was no time to play cat-and-mouse games with the security cameras. Not bothering with trying to hide her inhuman speed, she raced flat out for the elevator at the end of the corridor. Thomas's map said it was the only way out.

Behind her, the doors to the morgue crashed open and two more troll voices joined the hue and cry.

Lyris didn't bother looking back. She had only a small lead, but that might be enough if she didn't stumble. Mercifully, the elevator was already coming.

As the soft *ding* announced the car's arrival, Lyris thought it would be too bad for her if there were more trolls inside. She launched herself at the opening doors, arms drawn back for a strike, just in case.

The doors opened on a flying Lyris. Her posture was one of attack, so Roman wisely got out of her way. He didn't need her warning to hit close and jam his finger into the ground-floor button. Angry trolls had started shrieking and were lumbering toward them.

"There may be more in the lobby if I tripped an alarm on the computer," Lyris gasped as she thudded against the far wall, denting its thin metal panel. She spun around and faced the doors.

"I don't think so," Roman answered, watching the doors close and numbers flick by. "There'll be those four goblin guards, but even if they've been alerted, I doubt they'll want a public scene."

"And if they do?" Lyris flexed her foot, which had begun to throb.

"Then, they'll be sorry." He looked over at her. His voice was calm but his eyes were not. "How many were there?"

"Three trolls." Roman's eyebrows shot up. "I only fought one. Running away seemed wisest when the others showed."

"I agree." His voice was grim, and he didn't say anything else. "Okay, here's the plan—we try walking out nice and calm and humanlike. If anything looks the least bit suspicious, or anyone draws a gun, flatten whoever is in your way and run for the exit like a pack of gargoyles are after you. If they lock the doors, go through them. The glass will hurt like hell, but you'll heal."

"You had to mention gargoyles," Lyris growled. The elevator slowed.

"Ready?"

Lyris smoothed her hair. "Yes."

The doors opened and they stepped out. Her nerves were screaming, her muscles were tensed and ready for battle, but nothing happened. The same mob of well-dressed beauty queens was milling around the lobby. The same guards were still admiring their own pectorals and biceps and smiling their heads off.

"Okay, it looks like we're clear." Roman took her arm. Across the lobby, the bank of elevators lit up like a Christmas tree.

"You spoke too soon."

"Damn. Okay, we're leaving now. Smile pretty until we get outside, then run for the shrubs along the drive. I don't want to give them an easy target if they actually use guns."

"Got it." Lyris forced her lips into a smile and tried to look as if she weren't troubled by anything more than a painful liposuction.

Schiem's second intrusion into Quede's dark study was even more hesitant than his first.

"I sincerely hope you aren't about to tell me the sylph got away."

"She hurt one of the trolls. Broke his elbow and knee. The other two couldn't catch her." Schiem swallowed nervously. "She's very fast."

"Who was wounded?"

"Glabor."

"Have him killed. Slowly."

"Yes." Schiem hesitated, waiting to be dismissed. When Quede said nothing more he asked, "Will there be anything else? The guards are out looking for them."

"Just one more thing. I think we need better watchdogs at the estate. Open the mausoleum and turn the worms loose in the tunnels. Not in the hive, of course, but let them roam everywhere else. Pass the word that no one is to go near the plantation or my greenhouse. Unless they want to be eaten."

Schiem clearly wanted to argue, but he didn't dare. He was still marginally more afraid of Quede than he was those first, failed genetic experiments.

"At once."

"Thank you," Quede said, watching Schiem blink nervously at the courtesy. He sometimes enjoyed being nice to his servant just to see the confusion. Uncertainty was the spice of life.

Roman opened the door to their "borrowed" van. His breathing was still slightly uneven when he said, "I've had a moment of inspiration."

"Being chased by trolls will do that," Lyris muttered. "What's your epiphany?"

"Before we do anything else, I want to see if we can find someplace that has supplies for mineral collectors. They should have UV flashlights. The suckers eat batteries like crazy and the bulbs don't last long, but they might be a help in the underground. If we can't manage that, I think we can pick something up at a pet shop and rig a battery pack."

"A pet shop?" Lyris pulled a handful of dead leaves from her hair. The shrubbery they'd dived through had been dense and filled with withered leaves.

"They use UV heat lamps for snakes, but that is definitely a second choice. I want something portable."

"You think that UV light may be something we can use against Quede?" Lyris asked. Her breath was still far from regular. Trolls on top of the hobgoblin were proving to be a bit much.

Roman spread his hands. "It's a shot in the dark. But so is everything else. I know Jack's rifle should do the trick, but . . ."

Lyris nodded. Even if she had been inclined, she was too tired to argue.

"You can nap on the way," Roman suggested as he helped her into the car. "You look beat."

"No. I'm not sleepy." And she wasn't. Not yet. But the need for rest was coming. She hoped that she wouldn't dream of Quede again, but feared she might. Some nightmares were like man-eating sharks: Once they got the taste of blood, they would stalk you until you were dead or you made it to a safe shore.

"We'll stop and eat, then. You need to get some food in your body. Sylphs cannot live on nerves alone."

"Wanna bet?" she mumbled to herself. Her stomach rolled over.

Chapter Seventeen

Lyris liked the way Roman drove: smooth and aggressive, but without the suicidal air of many devil-may-care taxi drivers or tour bus operators. It was also convenient that he could hot-wire an engine.

They headed toward the suburbs where the houses grew farther apart and more weathered. The smell of rotting leaves drifted through the open windows, and Lyris wondered if she would ever be able to think of autumn and not remember New Orleans. They were headed to Quede's greenhouse.

No dome light appeared when they opened the van doors. Roman had popped out the bulb earlier, both to spare their night vision and also to prevent them being easily targeted if watchers were out. Goblins had very sensitive eyes. So did vampires.

The greenhouse was a shock, a frivolous Victorian affair made up of iron gingerbread painted flat black and filled with giant panes of frosted glass whose surface suggested refined sugar but cut like a million tiny razor blades. Ancient wisteria, now bare of both blossoms and leaves, covered much of the translucent walls, though it kept a respectful few inches away from the panes of glass. It was surprising that Quede had allowed the plant to remain, since its tiny tendrils were working their way into the joints and slowly pulling the construction to pieces. The building's double wooden doors, having shrunk over the years, were also a less-than-perfect fit, leaving nearly an inch gap at the base, which Lyris and Roman could peer under if they stretched out flat.

What was not so quaint and Victorian was the grid of lights arrayed around the door, which showed up plainly when the UV flashlight was trained on them. This *Mission: Impossible* team couldn't get through. There didn't seem to be an external way to turn the grid off, either—probably because Quede never disarmed it. He would most likely come and go through an underground entrance. If Roman and Lyris wanted into the greenhouse, they'd have to find a way from inside the hive.

Dawn exploded suddenly around them, a painful sheet of pink fire reflecting off the glass and bouncing crazily off the water that filled the ornamental pond just outside. Yet even with the natural light in full play, it was easy to make out the less usual illumination of the specimens that resided in the greenhouse. On the other side of the glass, they seemed not only to glow but to sway and shiver with some gentle breeze that shouldn't exist indoors. Especially not when all the fans looked still.

"Seems kind of out in the open for a goblin as security conscious as the king." Roman got to his feet. "What's to stop someone from putting a bat through the glass and climbing in someplace away from the alarm? Not to mention the fact that Quede would think himself in a toaster oven if he wandered in here midday."

"I bet you anything that this glass is stuffed full of UV filters, and it's probably bulletproof. I am also betting there isn't anyplace that isn't wired."

"So, we aren't going to be able to make like a sniper and take him out from a distance while he's pottering around the workbench."

"No." Lyris, still flat on her belly, watched intently as the stranger flowers continued their dance.

Roman turned and looked at the ground around them. Much of the area was covered in crushed oyster shell that wouldn't take a footprint, but the few patches of lawn were pristine, their delicate blades uncrushed. It didn't look like the truant goblin came trysting here. The place wasn't dead, but it was utterly deserted.

"What is this place called again?"

Lyris answered absently. "It means *peaceful* in lutin. The peaceful greenhouse."

"Peaceful it is, in a creepy sort of way. You're

pretty good with lutin. I've never gotten the hang of juggling those goblin sibilants."

"They aren't easy to do without spitting. Our tongues aren't long enough."

"I haven't heard you complaining."

"Roman!"

"What? My timing is perfect," he said.

Lyris sighed.

"So, were you thinking of taking a nap?" he asked when she didn't get up.

"Hand me your flashlight." She reached up a hand.

"What is it?" In an instant, he was beside her. "Do you see a way in?"

"No, but watch this." It was difficult in the confined space, but she was able to play the light over a few nearby orchids. At the beam's touch the buds gave a small quiver, and each slowly started shifting away.

"Well, I'll be damned. They're acting like goblins. I bet if you keep the light on them long enough, they'll pull their little roots out of their pots and crawl away."

"Goblins, or vampires? But why breed plants with either thing?"

Roman looked amused—and disgusted. "Because he's perverse? Maybe his mommy didn't let him have a chemistry set when he was younger and it warped him."

"Maybe. Or maybe his flowers are another way

of spreading his disease. Orchids can grow anywhere, in any climate. Of course, people don't eat them. . . ." Lyris sighed again and got to her feet. "It's damned strange, but I don't know if it helps us. We still don't have a way inside."

"I'm pretty sure there's an entrance from the hospital basement, but I don't think that we dare go back. They must have thermal scanners somewhere in the building—that's how they caught us. Probably in the basement levels, or they would have come after me as well."

"No." She shuddered. "Goddess, no! Let's not go back. I wasn't expecting to run into trolls. I didn't think Quede used them."

"Well, what next? There are those riverboats. They go somewhere. Or we could allow ourselves to be taken prisoner. You can bet our wanted posters are all over the place down in the hive. All we'd have to do is show our faces somewhere public and every goblin in town would make a citizen's arrest."

"And risk getting eaten by troll enforcers en route to Quede? Bad plan. Besides, we can't throw ourselves on Quede's mercy and appeal to his better nature. It is highly likely that he doesn't have one."

"Then I guess we are left with further exploration of Toujours Perdrix. There has to be an entrance to the hive someplace on its grounds. If not in the house, then maybe in the cemetery."

"The mansion makes more sense, being built up

on that mound. But . . ." Lyris said a bad troll word. The profanity made Roman smile.

"Yeah, I know. It has to be done, though. However, I want breakfast first."

"Okay, we'll stop and eat." Food sounded repellant as usual to her, but Lyris had learned there was no fighting Roman's appetite. She wondered what it would be like to live in such joyful expectation of her own next meal. For her, food was fuel, a necessary evil that one had to make time for; but maybe she would eventually learn to enjoy it. If she and Roman stayed together.

"What do you say to bacon and eggs with a mountain of toast and gallons of coffee?" Roman clipped his flashlight onto his belt. "You must be hungry by now."

"I say let's start with the coffee and see what happens."

Chapter Eighteen

Toujours Perdrix's basement hadn't improved since their last visit. If anything, it seemed worse to Lyris. The dark and dank underground, festooned with ancient cobwebs, rather reminded her of every horrid monster movie she had seen as a teenager. There were strange mummylike shapes projecting out of the bulwarks, covered in thick blankets of lichen and web. Cracks in the walls and ceiling leaked thick water, and there was one large dent in the south sidewall that looked like it had been formed by a barrel-sized mallet. Or a troll.

Roman and Lyris hadn't found any secret tunnels yet, but she figured they were there—all haunted castles and mansions had them. With masterpieces of cinematic horror firmly in mind, she declined Roman's suggestion that they investigate what was beneath some fungus cocoons or pry out several battered stones to see what was bricked up behind them. She didn't really want to discover that there were gargoyles or mummies sharing the underground. The cast-off bones they had to walk over and the strange acoustics of the room were bad enough.

"Do you hear it, that hissing?" she finally asked.

"Yeah, but I don't think it's a snake. And did you notice? Lobineau's troll's body is gone." Roman played his flashlight around the room. The UV flashlight gave everything a funny blue cast.

"I noticed. It doesn't smell as bad. But still, this feels . . ." She stopped again, listening. "This noise is really weird. It isn't a voice exactly."

The stone of the walls seemed to have woken up, and it whispered. Sometimes the sound was mournful, sometimes confused, often angry—and Lyris had the increasing uncomfortable but certain conviction that they were reaching the *genus loci*: the devil's home.

"Want to go back?" she asked Roman. "We could try again tomorrow."

He shone the light at her. "Of course I want to go back. But the answers are this way. Quede is this way. And I have a feeling that time is running out."

"Unfortunately." Lyris's internal clock said the same thing. She jerked her head toward the end of the room, and Roman's light followed. "There's another door over there."

"And it's locked with a brand-new lock. That's promising."

They approached the door cautiously, trying to avoid the larger drifts of barren bones and some oily-looking puddles. Almost, Lyris wished for some rats or insects or anything alive. Almost.

"That's a serious lock." She shone her regular flashlight on the hasp. They had only been able to find one UV lantern.

"I'd worry, but it's putrid wood." Roman jerked the industrial-size lock from its rotting mounts and threw it aside. He forced open the narrow wood door. It took some effort and a great deal of noise because someone had piled a lot of lumber against the door in a careless or hurried barricade. But two hard shoves cleared the path and Lyris and Roman found themselves staring into a sort of hallway, or a wooden tunnel.

The whispering stopped.

"Ladies first?"

"Only if you insist."

Roman shrugged Jack's rifle back into place on his shoulder and went through, flashlight first. He said encouragingly, "No spiders in here. Not even any webs."

"But a wood floor?"

"Wood everything."

Their tentative footsteps echoed hollowly, though they tried to step quietly. The air smelled of damaged timber and something else that neither of them could identify.

"You know, I was thinking that this whole underground was designed as a crypt—a spacious crypt, but still basically a mass grave where Quede could leave his scraps. It makes sense, doesn't it? It's even practical. I mean, the mound might have been designed for something else originally, but I'm talking about the building. Whoever heard of a first floor without windows? However, this tunnel is just plain weird." Lyris shook her head.

"I don't like it," she continued. "Goblins don't use wood. It doesn't stand up in the damp. And look at the construction. It's just cobbled together, boards nailed every which way and then strung together with rope or something. Like someone was trying to keep out a sudden storm and didn't have time to go to the hardware store."

"Yeah. I know." Roman stomped on the floor for a couple of steps, making it sway slightly.

"I'm getting vertigo. That or the room moved. Could we actually be suspended from ropes or something?"

"This is almost like one of those covered bridges they have in New England. After it's started falling down."

"Only it's shorter, without openings, and is hung on ropes or chains. You know, it's more like a really big coffin being lowered into the ground."

"Don't even go there."

"Yeah." Their footsteps slowed as they approached a jumble of lumber that blocked their path at the other end. "Another barricade? This is turning into an Agatha Christie locked-room mystery."

"What a cheerful thought." Roman stared at her. "Are you feeling something? I mean, something specific that I should be worried about?"

"No, sorry. I'm just being morbid. But if it is some sort of bridge, then what's it built over? I don't hear any water, do you?"

"No. But who knows what's inside this mound? There could be canyons or fissures."

"Maybe. But everything else in the building is made of stone. Why would he build this . . . this giant crate?"

Roman shook his head again. "I don't know. Actually, now that I've thought about it, you know what this reminds me of more than anything? A cattle chute. They use them—"

"Look out!"

A trio of creatures flew at them out of the darkness overhead, two of them winged nightmares that were all teeth and claws. There was no time for Lyris's mind to translate her eyes' horrified messages into words of identification, and no time for Roman to aim the gun before they were overcome.

Lyris felt her stomach muscles contract as she braced herself for a blow. The rest of her body moved without thinking, dropping her flashlight and grabbing the nearest taloned wrist with bone-snapping strength. She used the thing's own momentum to fling it into the wall with skull-crushing force, breaking both its carapaced body and the flimsy wood it hurtled into. A shower of silvered scales burst like fireworks, but before they settled on the floor Lyris spun about, looking for the next threat.

Roman grabbed the second creature by its head and, also using the hurtling body's own momentum, he let it reach the end of its tether before efficiently snapping its neck. He swung about in a short circle and threw the dead creature into the path of the third mass of fangs and claws dropping down. The sound of crunching bones was loud as the monsters collided, but it was soon replaced with an even more disturbing high-pitched hiss.

Unfortunately, the leprous skin of the second monster's face clung to Roman's hand, having peeled off the creature's skull like a surgeon's latex glove.

Roman made a sound of disgust and, striding over to the third monster snarling at its broken arms, gave it a tremendous kick in the head.

"Okay, no more locked-room mystery." His voice was rough.

"I guess we know what was making that noise now. What are they? Harpies?" Lyris asked, glancing nervously at the three bodies, then up at the void overhead. Nothing moved, but she wasn't reassured. She felt in her jacket pocket for Roman's handgun.

"I don't know." He knelt and looked closely at the single set of arms on the creature he'd just killed. "They might be goblins. This one looks a little different, though. Only one set of arms and longer hair."

Lyris knelt. "Could they be some of Quede's experiments?"

"Sounds like a reasonable guess. This would be as good a place to hide out as any if you needed to stay clear of the sun."

Lyris caught the glint of something bright in the creature's gray wattle. "Wait. Shine your light over here. Look at this. This one's wearing a necklace."

Roman reached out and pulled the jewelry out of the folds of withered flesh. He turned the pendant over. He shown his light over it and read slowly: "C-S-B."

"Oh, goddess." Lyris touched the creature's hair. It had a few patches of blond clinging to its angular skull. It didn't look human, but Lyris's intuition rose up suddenly and supplied her with an identity. She pushed the flashlight away. It was beginning to make the creature's dead skin blister. "This is human hair. Roman, I think this might have been Caitlin St. Barth."

Roman stood up fast and pulled Lyris to her feet. "Caitlin St. Barth?" He suddenly paled. "I killed Caitlin St. Barth?"

"Stop it! You didn't kill a woman. Look at this creature. It isn't human anymore. Caitlin has been gone for a long, long time." Lyris's voice was deliberately sharp. "And they attacked us. We were just defending ourselves."

"But—"

"Would you rather one of us was lying there?"

"Of course not." Roman swallowed. "You're right. I know you're right. Sorry. I've just never hurt a female before."

"I know." She touched his arm and let her voice soften. "This isn't what I'm used to either. But we have to stay calm. We have to think. I'm starting to get a bad feeling."

"Oh, great. You and your bad feelings."

"Roman, what if this place is some kind of a barricade? What if Quede wasn't trying to keep something in? What if these poor creatures were trying to keep something out?"

He looked around. "Maybe the hobgoblin?"

"Maybe, but . . ."

"I don't like the sound of that *but*. Come on—we're getting out of here. Now." Roman reached for her arm and began towing Lyris back toward the door. "You're right. The hobgoblin is dead. What would they be keeping out? Quede?"

"I don't know. Maybe, but—" she began again.

There was a low growl that shook the frail floor, and then the wall beside them exploded into giant splinters. Roman turned fast and shoved Lyris behind him, away from the wooden missiles and the many-armed things that came boiling through the fractured wood.

"Roman!" Lyris screamed, as he aimed the rifle into the mass of pale bodies, but she had no time for more. The flimsy wood beneath her cracked and Lyris fell.

Chapter Nineteen

Whiffs of blood-fragrant breath stole over her. She'd never smelled anything quite like it before, not while awake—though she had breathed the scent once in a dream. Still, she knew it instantly, recognized the danger as it slipped down her throat and into her lungs. *Quede*.

Alarm forced her back to consciousness. She opened her eyes to almost complete darkness and pain. It took a few moments for understanding to return, but when memory arrived, it came in a horrifying rush. Quede's creatures—things for which she had no name, except that one had been Caitlin St. Barth—had attacked them, and then something else had broken through the wall. Roman had tried to push her out of the gray monsters' path. There had been a bright explosion from Jack's gun, but before she could see if the beasts were hit, the rotted floor had given out beneath the sudden weight of her falling body and she hadn't been able to save herself from tumbling down . . . *here*. She'd been knocked out, had a bad dream.

But if she was awake now, why could she still smell him, still practically taste him?

Lyris shifted her weight carefully, turning in a circle, staring in disbelief at the highway-sized tunnel that stretched beyond the range of her dazed eyes. She could smell him because this was what they had been searching for. This was how Quede traveled between New Orleans and the plantation. It was the goblin king's private roadway.

So where was Quede? Where were the goblins? His bodyguards? Still half dazed, she listened hard but there was no sound. Nothing.

The creatures were gone, either taking Roman with them or frightened off by—

"Roman! Oh, goddess!" She spun about, trying to balance in the shattered wreckage as full awareness returned to her. She had to move! Now! Quede would be coming. He'd come as soon as . . .

As soon as he had dealt with Roman. And Lyris had no doubt that the king had Roman, or would have him shortly. There was no way that Roman would have voluntarily left her down in this hole, and her nose told her that he was gone.

"Noooooo," she whimpered, and then, horrified at the weak mewling, she said again: "No! You won't kill him. I won't let you. Quede! You leave him alone!"

Her eyes quickly adapted to the darkness, using what little light spilled in from the hole overhead. She was in a gallery of some sort, a natural cavern that resembled a train station but that echoed eerily with the sound of dripping water. It took an effort to keep the claustrophobia at bay. Searching for Roman's pistol helped, though the small weapon was nowhere to be found and would be useless against Quede.

Tick, tick, tick.

Knowing that she risked injury, Lyris nevertheless began running, searching for some path, stair, or tunnel that would take her back up to the floor above. She would only take the highway to New Orleans as a last resort. And only if something had happened to Roman.

There were several openings in the roof overhead, but many were too small for her and all were way beyond reach. She tried to take comfort from the idea that if she couldn't get up through one of these holes, Quede's monsters probably couldn't—or wouldn't—get down through them, so she didn't need to worry about something larger than a spider dropping on her head.

She ran on, but soon began to feel like a rat in a maze. Or some lost soul caught in a labyrinth. It was hard not to fear the Minotaur. Slowing down, she tried to be methodical. Lyris selected a hole overhead and then walked in a straight line to the nearest wall. She began following the rough edge, fighting off cold and increasing dizziness. The air was bad.

She came to a crosscut that opened on the right, a hole that was an even blacker shade of darkness where her eyes peered and peered, but she could see nothing. It was the black of deepest space, of the grave.

I can't go in there. It's daaarrrrrk and smaallll and tiiiight, the voice in Lyris's head pleaded.

"Shut up. You don't need your eyes and we'll stop if it gets too tight."

Someone whimpered, but Lyris ignored it, knowing it was herself.

She listened carefully, sniffing at the air. It was dead, utterly lifeless. Nevertheless, the path seemed to angle upward, so moving carefully into the crack, she started feeling her way along the ever-shrinking tunnel. She let herself worry about spiders because it was better than thinking about what Quede or monsters might be doing to Roman.

Soon physical distress intruded on her mental discomfort. She suddenly realized that it was cold, horribly cold, and getting worse. Even her panicked exertions were not enough to prevent her hands and feet from slowly going numb. Her breath was freezing in place as soon as it left her body. She didn't know how it could be possible, but she felt the solidified vapor falling down on her chest like a light snow.

Quede was playing with the weather again.

The tunnel angled suddenly downward and in only a dozen steps she was up to her ankles in ooze, an underground river filled with thick slime. Repulsed at the odor she had stirred up, and by the vague sensation of movement in the thick brew, she quickly retreated back up the dark passage.

Quede wouldn't be down there. Goblins don't like cold. Neither do vampires. I don't need to go down there. Please, I really don't.

She retreated as quickly as she dared.

Lyris next tried going in the opposite direction. There was some slight light in the other passage, for which she was grateful. But the floor of the gallery began to slope downward and was soon coated in a gray webbing that smelled faintly but fearfully of rotting things. It was marginally warmer, making her digits tingle painfully as the foul breeze ghosted over them, but the path was too rank, even for a goblin. Her hackles raised as she knelt to look at the tangled mess on the floor. Whatever the ropy stuff was, it all but glued her shoes to the ground. It would peel the flesh off a goblin's bare feet. It was too much like a funnel spider's lair for her taste. No one would go down there.

Again she retreated, circling over to the left wall and searching for another opening. She was moving faster again, beginning to perspire in spite of the cold.

There was no other opening for a long, despairing while, and then the sound of gushing water began to fill her ears. Rushing toward it as she would a beacon, Lyris soon came across another narrow breach in the cavern's rough wall.

"Wait." She was frantic to get to Roman, but also reluctant to go anywhere near Quede's underground river when she couldn't see. Lyris shuddered. It was too easy to imagine being caught in an icy torrent and swept into the very bowels of the earth, pinned against bone-fracturing rocks until she drowned. This was worse than her usual claustrophobic visions and made her double over.

"Stop it." Her voice was harsh as she reprimanded her imagination. "Use your brain."

She straightened slowly and then reached out with her foot. She slid it along the ground as far as she could without actually stepping into the crack. The passage seemed to head upward in a fairly tight spiral that suggested it was not natural in origin. Who would bother to build a path into danger? Perhaps it was simply some weird trick of sound that made her hear water. Surely no one had ever climbed *up* to get to a river. And if there was water nearby, there would be some scent of it in the air. There wasn't. She was having an auditory hallucination.

"I can do this." Taking a deep breath for courage,

Lyris rested a numbed hand on the rough wall and began feeling her way through the darkness. The roof began to descend on the curved passage, and soon she was walking nearly doubled over, trying to breathe only shallowly of the stagnant air.

She hit her head on a protruding rock and cursed softly, borrowing from Roman's collection of obscene troll. Annoyed and sore, she dropped onto hands and knees, and crawled on until she came to an intersection. She didn't think about what sorts of things might be making those faint cracking noises beneath her hands as she rested them on the floor.

Right or left? She had to choose. Slowly, she turned her head and sniffed at both passages, trying to ignore her aching eyes that screamed at her because, for the first time ever, they were in a place where they couldn't see—but they still knew that things were closing in, getting tighter, going to crush her. She was going to die in here, alone and . . .

"Stop it!"

Nothing. No light, no sound, no odor, just the echo of her frightened voice. But as she had already discovered, the absence of smell did not mean an absence of danger. She closed her useless eyes and listened harder, trying to hear beyond the pounding of her heart and the crashing of the surf in her ears as her panicked blood rushed by. But even when she opened herself up, trying to tap into that inner sense she had of what was true and what was not, she could not find anything to guide her. She might as well have been deaf as well as blind.

There was nothing to choose between the passages.

"So flip a coin. Just keep going and don't get lost. If that happens, you're done for, so pay attention." Yeah, she had to be methodical.

Lyris went right.

The passage sloped gently upward and was dry. And it was warmer. Almost, she began to believe that she had found a way out. But the tunnel ended abruptly in a rockfall. The roof had caved in, blocking the way with a nasty pile of shattered timber and stone that cut at her hands with wicked splinters when she tried to explore it.

Cursing, and finally beginning to feel the tickles of true, mindless panic that were welling up from her subconscious, she backed down the tunnel until she reached the junction.

The left passage, even more silent and gravelike, waited for her. Though she repeated her actions to herself—*left wall, left fork, left passage*—she had a feeling that the verbal map didn't serve. A creature of vision, she was beginning to lose her sense of direction down here in this cold, lightless maze. And she wouldn't be able to hold fear back forever.

"So go on. Now." The left fork began by curving downward, but it quickly regained its lost altitude and started climbing upward again in a series of ledges that resembled stairs.

"See? I'm fine." Lyris sighed and let go of some of her anxiety. Once more, she could push back the fear that she would be lost in these passages forever. Or until Quede or his monsters found her in some horrible oubliette.

The tunnel narrowed gradually until it was only about two feet wide and barely taller. Once again, she was forced to hands and knees, and then finally to her belly. But always the passage headed upward, so she kept on, even when the claustrophobia set in and started telling her that the roof above was cracking, about to crush her alive.

After fifty or so yards, the tunnel again enlarged to the point where she could crawl. Lyris picked up speed then, ignoring the bite of small stones in her palms and knees. At least she wasn't crawling on bones or web.

Then, suddenly, her bruised hand met nothing. Overbalanced, she screamed, and her ears and other senses told her blind, helpless eyes that she was falling.

Her stomach muscles contracted convulsively. Rearing back hard enough to hit her head a second time, she saved herself from tumbling into the void by clutching at the cracks in the tunnel's narrow, rough walls.

It was only then, her heart pounding so hard that she was sure her throat would burst, that she remembered she was carrying a lighter. Cursing herself for an idiot, she pulled the lighter out of her pocket, turned up the wick, and struck a flame.

Almost instantly, she regretted it. The gap before her was a deep one, apparently bottomless, but not wide—probably no more than a dozen feet. If she were able to make a running start, she could jump it. But on hands and knees, the space might as well be the Grand Canyon.

She said more bad things about trolls and threw in some goblin obscenities for good measure. For once, she was grateful that she couldn't shed tears. Had she been in the habit, she probably would have curled up in a ball and sobbed forever.

The lighter was getting hot, so she let the flame go out, trying hard to clear out the mental cobwebs and decide what she should do. Retreat seemed the only option. But she was afraid to try. Though she had not wandered far, perhaps because of the blows to her head, or maybe because of being below-ground and far from her element, her sense of direction was badly confused and she feared that she might not be able to find this tunnel again if no other took her back upstairs.

Then, as she sat regaining her breath, a soft, stealthy sound floated up the passage behind her, a noise so faint that it might only have been the wind. But she knew that there was no wind in the underground. And she'd heard the sound before. It had followed her and Roman through the basement just before they were attacked.

Breathing hard, she used the lighter again, looking back fearfully at the passage behind her, and then taking a second look at the gap, trying to find some way across. After a moment of peering, she could see that at one time there had been a sort of platform over the break. Supports had been driven into the walls to hold up the planks. The wood stubs that remained looked green and more than a little rotted, but they were spaced just close enough together that she could make the climb over the gap.

If they held together.

Lyris didn't like trusting her weight to those rotting stumps, especially not after having similar supports give out underneath her once already. But even less did she like the furtive slithering that was growing steadily louder. There was no way that she could fight off a creature in this confined space.

Letting the lighter go out a second time was even harder. But she couldn't make the climb with it clutched in her hands or mouth. She would need every bit of strength and concentration for the climb. She'd have to do it in complete blackness and with both hands free.

Saying the sort of prayer she had not uttered since childhood, Lyris reached out over the bottomless pit and grasped the first piece of spongy wood. She swung her legs over the edge, moving as silently as possible. It took her a moment to find a toehold, but once her foot was secure, she went across the horrible gap as quickly as she could, clutching desperately at rotting wood, her belly pressed against the wall as she repeated her litany of petitions for divine aid.

Finally on the other side, she collapsed on the cold floor, breathing hard.

"Never again! Goddess, never again. Let this passage be the way out because I can't do that again."

Growing aware of a sound, louder than her own gasping, Lyris reached in her pocket and quickly flicked the lighter. She had only an instant to take in the horror staring at her across the great gap—an eyeless thing of leprous skin and gigantic tusklike teeth—when a white, whiplike arm reached out from a crevice and grabbed her wrist. The lighter fell to the floor and darkness came down on her again.

"There you are, pretty sylph," Quede said, his grip cruelly tight. His voice was the same as the one in her dreams.

Lyris turned her head slowly. Terror made the tendons in her neck so tight they popped as she looked over her shoulder at the vaguely luminescent form who had taken hold of her.

Staring back from the crack in the wall was a creature that had teeth equally as long and sharp as those of the thing on the other side of divide. Its incisors had actually pierced his lower lip and left a pair of ragged yet bloodless holes. But unlike the other monster, Quede had slightly radiant skin and intelligent eyes, evil black things that reached into her skull and tried to suck out her will. Lyris retreated instantly behind mental barriers and prayed that Quede wouldn't come looking for her.

"Come along now," the king said gently. "You don't want me to leave you to *the Mouth*, do you? He's terribly hungry. And there are others down here."

"No," Lyris breathed. But she couldn't have said whether she was agreeing with Quede, or just denying the nightmare. Unable to help herself, she asked: "Where's Roman?"

The black eyes flicked over her face, pausing at her forehead, and Lyris realized that she was bleeding. She also realized what she would have to do. Her mind and heart screamed at her to flee, but she couldn't. And she couldn't let Quede know what she was thinking. She had to cooperate with him, at least until she was out of the tunnels.

"Upstairs," the voice said soothingly. It might have worked at calming her if she hadn't been able to see so clearly what had her by the arm. Truly, she wished that she couldn't see him as he licked his lips in anticipation. But that had always been her gift—and her curse—the ability to see truth, to know what lay beneath the surface. "Come along. I'll take you to him."

"All right," she said, pretending that he had stolen her will and successfully hidden his true nature. There was no point in letting him know what her strengths were and how hideous she found him.

Quede's vanity was his weak point. He'd probably kill her out of hand if he suspected that she had seen through the spell of beauty he cast over himself. She added, making her voice weak, "I'm dizzy. I think I hit my head."

"Did you?" the voice cooed, and a second bony hand reached for her face. It dabbed at the blood on her forehead and then quickly retreated toward Quede's mouth. He all but moaned with pleasure as he licked the stickiness from his fingers. Lyris looked at the scattering of small holes in his body and realized that Roman must have shot him several times. She hoped the wounds hurt. Certainly, they were not healing as they might.

The hateful voice went on. "Well, you won't have to worry about that for long."

Lyris couldn't help it. She began to shiver.

"Cold, pretty sylph?"

"Very."

She tried to take comfort from the thought that the sun was overhead, and that it would kill Quede if they could disgorge this creature from his place beneath the earth. But that light was a long way off through a mountain of stone, and Lyris felt very small and alone with only her vision of truth to guide and protect her.

Chapter Twenty

A shocked Lyris actually heard Quede thinking: *What a pity she believes in vampirism already. The surprise would have been exquisite.*

Terrified that he might be able to hear her own thoughts as easily, she clamped down even harder on her feelings of revulsion and made herself picture a blank white wall.

Quede guided her through a maze of ever-lightening tunnels and finally to a heavy plank door, which he thrust open casually with a clawed hand.

With a surprising gesture of Old World courtesy, Quede stood aside and let her enter the room ahead of him. "After you, my dear."

Feeling more than ever like Alice down a cobra's hole, a slightly dizzy Lyris muttered the clearly expected short thank-you.

Unfortunately, a further exchange of courtesies

was aborted when she saw a battered Roman hanging in chains from some sort of a giant metal frame. He was breathing but unconscious.

Her eyes reluctantly looked away from his bruised body, trying to assess the immediate danger. There was a thick power cable that ran from the rack to a portable generator that sat in a shallow puddle of water. The yellow cord terminated in a strange, three-pronged plug. There was also a can of gasoline sitting on the floor. The device in no way resembled anything she had ever seen, but her brain still insisted on identifying it with two ominous words: electric chair.

Her horrified eyes went back to the manacles that bound Roman's wrists and ankles. The skin around them was scorched black. Suddenly, Lyris's dizziness left her and her wits were working again. Rage like she had never known began pouring from her brain and into her body. For several minutes—perhaps even hours—they had been nearly immobilized by panic and fear of the dark and unknown. But now she knew exactly what she was facing and what she had to do. If she had ever had any doubts about her ability to kill coldly, to take a life in something other than immediate self-defense, they were ended. She would snuff out Quede's life without a moment of hesitation if he gave her the opportunity.

"I used to bring Caitlin here," he said softly. He nudged Roman's rifle aside with a frown of annoyance and then touched an iron flail resting on the same table. It had fresh blood on it. Lyris didn't try and see where Roman was marked. "I come back here when I want to remember her the way she was."

Thinking of the poor creature Roman had killed, Lyris felt a fresh flood of hot revulsion rising behind her teeth and she pressed her lips together, hoping to stop the emotional spate before it poured itself into Quede's unstable ears. If she had had Jack's power to kill, she would have let fly, but she knew her gifts didn't work that way.

She turned to stare at Quede. He stood, eyes unfocused, looking almost wistful. What kind of heart would mint such terrible memories of its lover and then treasure them? Who would leave the person they claimed to love in such a hideous state? A monster. That was the only answer—and she already knew this about him, so there was no reason to be shocked into immobility.

Yes, she had known he was a monster, but a newly awakened part of her wanted to hit Quede, to hurt him, maybe even kill him slowly and painfully because he deserved it. Because he had hurt Roman. Because he had hurt Caitlin. And because he frightened her when she was lost in the dark.

She averted her face. She reminded herself that reparation could not be made to the dead, and hurting Quede wouldn't make him any less cruel, any less monstrous, any less of a threat to her or the captive Roman. Punishment was for those who could learn from the experience. Quede was mad, his soul destroyed, completely given over to evil. The same could not be said of her. She still had something left to lose. Torture, cruel killing in cold blood—even in these circumstances—was a line that she had not yet crossed, and would not cross now. Not if she had any choice. *Take this temptation away, O Goddess, for I could so easily become a monster too.*

At her thought, Roman's eyes slitted open and slowly focused on her. Alarm rose in them.

"This is wrong . . . and pointless. Let Roman go." Lyris turned and faced her captor. She could feel Roman's gaze resting on her back. He was only barely conscious, and she prayed that he remained still and didn't draw Quede's attention. "After all, you have me now."

"Let him go? Why ever should I? I can't think of any reason why I should." The king's head cocked. "My dear sylph! Do you actually think that you love him? Is that it? But you can't possibly. Don't be ridiculous."

"Why not? We have a lot in common. He's amusing and helpful. And we're friends." She kept her voice soft, reasonable.

"But you are better than he is. Sylphs mate for life. You couldn't throw yourself away on a pooka. Don't be ridiculous. Your life wouldn't be worth living inside of six months. He couldn't be faithful if he wanted to. And you know as well as I that he'll never want to be. I'll be doing you a favor by getting rid of him. I'm saving you from the eventual disenchantment that is one of life's surest cruelties. It's all chemistry. I know this because I'm older." He added with a terrible smile, apparently unable to see the irony of what he was saying: "But if you want, I'll have him first—then you can share blood with me. That way you can keep a part of him forever. At least, for as long as you live. I have high hopes about this, though. Sylphs are strong. You may not be affected like the others."

Quede moved purposefully toward Roman and Lyris rushed into speech.

"You know, I can't help feeling that it's a matter of perspective," she said, ignoring his suggestion that they could share Roman's blood. She added bluntly: "From where I sit, your life doesn't seem worth living. True, your body will never dwindle and die. Age will not come for you as it eventually will for the rest of humanity. But you cannot love."

Quede paused. "True, but I cannot lose either. Love! I've put all such emotional stupidity aside. You will, too. In time. This I promise."

"I don't think so. You'll feel no pangs of parting from those near you, but that is because you have no memories worth cherishing. You've never allowed yourself to create them—not even with Caitlin. I don't want that. Emotional death is as terrible as the physical one." She added softly, seriously,

"You know, I didn't think it possible, but I pity you."

Quede's face tightened and went white—quite a trick when he was already deathly pale. "You are very rash to speak to me that way. I can break you so easily."

Lyris looked him full in the eyes. It took an effort, because no sight on earth had ever frightened her the way those black pits did.

"I'm not that rash. I just don't believe that you'll hurt me." She added, "That isn't what you want to do, is it? Because you don't want to lose me like you did Caitlin."

"No. I won't do that to you." Quede looked once at the iron whip on the table. He added, with sudden rage in his voice, "But I definitely want to hurt *him.*"

Spinning, he leapt on Roman, making Lyris's lover sag in the chains that bound his wrists for a moment before one manacle broke under the added weight. Lyris saw Quede's lips peel back and his long, curved fangs jut down out of the roof of his mouth much as a viper's before its strike. He struck.

"No!" Even as she screamed, she picked up the flail. Reversing it in her hands, she jammed it through Quede's back, angling upward so it would pierce his heart. Legend said vampires had to be killed with wood, but goblins didn't like things made of iron. Not stuffed through their bodies.

Quede gasped and dropped away from Roman's

unconscious form. He rolled over, staring down at the inch of iron protruding from the front of his chest.

"You'd kill me?" he whispered, incredulous that she had somehow broken his mind control and used violence against him. He touched the spike projecting from his ribs. "But I read your mind. You were calm. You didn't want to do this."

"No, I didn't want to. But I'll do what I have to in order to save Roman." She sidled back, feeling for Roman's rifle. She didn't dare take her eyes off the goblin king.

Quede began to laugh. The sound was awful, a gurgle filled with black blood.

"You're too late," he wheezed and then started to rise. "Your pooka can't be saved. I've already bitten him."

"I think he can be. One way or another." Lyris found the rifle and dragged it toward her. She had no way of knowing if there were any bullets, but she aimed it directly as Quede's head.

The vampire heaved himself off the floor in a blur of speed almost too fast for her eyes to see. But almost wasn't fast enough, and Lyris pulled the trigger.

A soft *whup* and a splash of black blood and brain on the wall told her the gun was loaded.

A part of her made note of the fact that a wooden bullet through the cranium seemed to work as well as a stake through the heart. With the top of his head gone, the prone Quede suddenly seemed very dead.

Her brain said that she could stop shooting now, but her hands went on pulling the trigger until Quede's fanged head was gone and her gun was empty.

Carefully, she put the rifle aside and turned to face Roman, terrified to see up close what Quede had done.

Chapter Twenty-one

"Lyris, I've been bitten by the vampire," Roman said, grim and patient as she pried the manacles off of his ankles. For a moment his frustration seemed to give way to satisfaction. "I knew nothing good would come of this adventure, and I told Jack so."

"I know you were bitten. I was here. If you recall, I'm the one that stuck a stake through Quede's heart to get him off you." She stood up and reached for the piece of torn shirt she had laid over the wound in his shoulder, not bringing up the matter of the gun and her success at turning Quede into Swiss cheese.

"I recall. It isn't something I am likely to forget." His lips flattened but not, she suspected, because of the physical pain. It might have been, though, because he winced as she pulled the compress away from his neck and shoulder to look at the bite. "I'm just saying that we don't know how this will affect me. I'm saying that you should leave me. Now. Before nightfall. In case I turn. Control was never my strong suit."

His horror finally showed through the bravado like tender flesh through a chink in armor, and he turned his face away and averted his eyes. The small gesture tore at Lyris. For the first time, Roman was truly frightened and vulnerable. The sight made her feel stupidly tearful and quite uselessly frightened, so she forced herself to say briskly: "Roman, I know you're half horse, but try not to act like the ass end of the beast, okay? Look, you said it yourself. We *don't* know the effect of vampirism on feys. It may not be the same as it is in humans. After all, we aren't affected by virus or bacteria. But if it is . . . well, whatever comes, we will deal with it. Anyway, get real. You'd never hurt me. Never." Lyris threw the bloodied bandage aside. The wound was already healing. That sight made her more cheerful. "You can stand up now. You look very romantic and pale, but I think I've had enough gothic drama for one day."

His head turned back and there was—thankfully—the distinct gleam of nascent amusement in his eyes. It was small but still beginning to push past the mental torment that had darkened the terrifying moments when he was in Quede's power. "You have a lousy bedside manner."

"I know. I'll get kinder when you get better. I'm

too frightened to be sympathetic. Thank heavens you've stopped bleeding. You'd make a mess of Baby otherwise."

"Is that how it works?" he asked, lifting his freed hand to her nape, where he fondled a wisp of her wild hair. "You get nice when I get better?"

"Unfortunately for you." It was her turn to avert her face. This was not the moment she wanted him to discover that she had finally allowed herself an emotion that was deep enough for her to die for, and that he was the recipient of those feelings.

"Okay, then. I guess I just have to get better. I've been wounded in the line of duty—and I am *by the goddess* going to get some TLC out of it. You just be ready." His voice was soft, and Lyris was afraid that maybe he had sensed her feelings after all.

"Stop bleeding totally and you've got a deal," she said gruffly, eyes still averted.

"Done." He added, "I really don't know why you decided to care about me. I like it, but it's nuts. Completely illogical."

"Like I had a choice here. Fate and Jack Frost were both working against me."

"But still. I just hope it lasts awhile—"

"Look, I don't know a great deal about it, but it seems to me that love is not an opinion, or a mood to be changed on a whim. It may not in every instance be immutable, but surely it is less changeable than that?"

"I wouldn't know." He sounded serious. "I've

never been in love before. I mean, before now. That sounds right, though. I can't imagine that my feelings for you will change."

"It's a new one for me, too," she admitted. "We'll just have to make it up as we go along—and maybe not ask too many questions that don't have easy answers."

"Okay. I can live with that for now." Roman closed his eyes. "Now, if you'll get me out of these damned chains, I'll be a happy man. The iron burns like a brand even with that damn machine turned off. Quede really was a sadistic bastard."

"Roman—I'm sorry! Damn it all!" she gasped and set about freeing him from the rest of his shackles. They both pretended not to notice that she was crying tears of blood.

Chapter Twenty-two

Quede didn't conveniently turn into dust or go up in flames when he was dead. As Lobineau had reminded them, this wasn't the movies. Destroying Quede's body took some time, eating away at the precious daylight hours, but the gasoline in the generator had made a good start. They doused Quede in it and set him ablaze with a book of matches that Roman had managed not to bleed on when his clothes were stripped away.

Not certain why she did it, Lyris stripped off the Shiva medallion that Quede had been wearing and shoved it in her pocket. Roman had raised an eyebrow, but she could only shrug. For some reason, she didn't want it to burn.

Quede's servant, Schiem, had come creeping down the tunnels when he smelled smoke and discovered them in the act of destroying the basements of Toujours Perdrix. Schiem didn't say a word or make any move to hinder them, so Roman and Lyris showed the same restraint toward him.

He disappeared briefly when they were busy committing a second act of arson on the bodies of Caitlin St. Barth and whoever the two other creatures were, but Schiem soon returned with clean clothes for Roman and a box of flares. After that, the torching ceremony went faster.

Though Roman was moving slowly and clearly in pain, he and Lyris took advantage of the sunlight and—this time with Schiem's cheerful help in disarming the alarm system—made a meticulous job of destroying Quede's special greenhouses. The quicklime the goblin king kept in the garden to destroy his hybrid failures ate up everything, even the bone pots he kept the hybridized plants in. Lyris didn't say anything, but she was certain that she could hear the plants screaming as they melted away.

As much as they wanted to be through with things before they left the city, neither Lyris nor Roman could come up with a plan for getting rid of the orchids at the hospital, nor making certain that none of Quede's worker goblins had yet been infected with the vampire supervirus. Schiem hastily assured them that the only infected creatures had been the monsters in the tunnels under the mansion, and that they were likely all dead now.

Because they were running out of daylight and strength, they chose to believe him.

They parted ways at sundown. Schiem told them that he was fairly sure that he could take care of the trolls before Lobineau got to their handlers, but that he would meet them in the morning with the latest news if they planned to stay the night.

Lyris looked at Roman's pinched face and said that they would be leaving the city, but that they would return the next morning to make sure everything was going smoothly.

Schiem nodded and walked briskly away. He seemed taller and certainly more confident than the creature he had been a few hours before. Perhaps the petty vandalism against his dead master had made him feel he was taking his life back.

"I can sympathize, really, but is that how a vampire servant is supposed to act when his master dies?" Lyris asked.

"Damned if I know. Everything about goblin worlds is weird," Roman answered. "Let's go get Baby and make some tracks north."

"You feeling okay?" Lyris asked, being careful not to sound anxious.

"Yeah, just hungry. I could eat about a dozen burgers. With chili fries. And a chocolate shake."

Lyris smiled a little at that. "You know, for once I'm hungry too."

* * *

They found a flannel-suited Schiem early the next morning standing in front of an old movie poster displayed in the theater's aging marquee. He looked almost wistful, staring at his younger more innocent self.

Lyris could understand. It wasn't every man who was privileged enough to have put his arms around Mary Pickford.

"She really was beautiful," Schiem said quietly, not turning his head. "Inside and out. I wanted to marry her, but Quede got there first. Of course, for her sake, I had to let her go."

"What will you do now?" Lyris asked after a moment's respectful silence.

"Move back to California and write my memoirs." He turned his head and half smiled. He didn't belong to Quede anymore because his master was dead, but there was still a bit of youthful deviltry in that grin. She wondered when he would begin aging. It would probably start soon, now that Quede was gone.

"You won't stay and work with Lobineau?" Roman asked.

"No, I think not. He's angry about the trolls getting killed and will soon discover that I ordered it done. And I've already seen one goblin-cleansing in my lifetime. There really isn't any need to witness another. Particularly not when I am apt to be one of the cleansed. I want to spend whatever time I have left someplace away from New Orleans." He cocked his head. "And what of you two?"

"We're not sticking around, either. Someone else can take over and see to the human interests here. We've passed the baton." They had e-mailed Jack last night, passing the word that someone else would need to come South and keep an eye on Lobineau. Though Lyris had been against it, Roman had also told Jack about being bitten. Jack had urged them to leave immediately for Cadalach where their healer could have a look at him.

Schiem nodded in approval. "I'm glad you survived. And I wouldn't worry too much about side effects from your encounter with Quede. The legends are right. Vampire contagions usually die when the host does."

"That's good to know. Feys almost never get sick, but we'll take any and all words of encouragement," Lyris answered.

"You are welcome to mine," Schiem answered formally. "You have done me—and the goblins of New Orleans—a tremendous service."

"In killing Quede?" Lyris asked. "That remains to be seen, doesn't it? I'm not sure that Lobineau is an ideal leader."

"No, he's not. But killing Quede was necessary, by far the lesser of the evils." Schiem added quietly, "I loved him, you know, but I also hated him. And I am a realist. He was quite mad at the end."

Lyris thought about what she had seen in Quede's

mind in the moments before she had killed him. She nodded back. "I know." Reaching into her pocket, she pulled out Quede's medallion. "I don't know if you want this . . ."

Schiem stared for a moment, then reached out a tentative hand. "I *would* like it." He swallowed. "Thank you."

"You're welcome." She stepped back. "Take care."

"And the goddess watch over you," Schiem answered, putting the medallion away. He turned abruptly and walked off.

Epilogue

Lyris looked over at Roman. He seemed completely at ease as he piloted his beloved car west. She had suggested flying, but he had been adamant about not leaving Baby behind. Since he was showing no signs of vampirism—in fact, he was enjoying the sun and food more than ever—she hadn't insisted on an emergency helicopter to evacuate them to Cadalach.

"You're speeding again." She tucked her hair back behind her ear. They had the windows down to let in the wind, and their hair was loose. There was a certain amount of dust in the air and they were both of them far from tidy after their days on the road.

Roman looked over at her and grinned. "Baby can't drive fifty-five. Anyway, there's nothing here in the desert to worry about. Not until Sin City. I hear they still haven't caught that dragon on the loose."

"Nothing to worry about except running out of gas, and the odd desert rat highway patrolman out to make a ticket quota," Lyris corrected. "Baby better pray that fuzz-buster is working. I have a feeling we are due to run across another one soon. They have at least one in every town."

"I never get caught," Roman said smugly.

"Hmph!"

"Come on, that isn't what you've been thinking for the past hour. What's on your mind?"

"Just . . . stuff." Lyris stroked her abdomen absently.

"Like?"

"Well, I was wondering if you'll miss dancing in that club."

"Who said anything about giving up dancing?" Roman's eyes began to twinkle, and for the first time in days, Lyris found herself laughing.

"No one. By all means, keep dancing if you like. Fortunately, you don't seem to be scarring. I've never seen anyone heal so fast or so cleanly." There was suddenly a small question in her voice.

"Oh, that was because the only thing that can really hurt me—aside from a broken neck or getting shot in the heart or head—is being whipped with hair plucked from my own mane," Roman assured her. "I don't think it has anything to do with turning into a vampire."

Lyris stopped smiling. "Are you serious? I mean, about the hair?"

"Oh, yeah. Brian Boru used the trick to get rid of the evil pookas that were terrorizing Ireland. Those scars on my legs? I picked them when the local bully managed to pull out my hair while I was in horse form. I should have drowned him that night, but settled for dumping him in the gulf and kicking him a few times. I didn't realize he still had my hair. Anyhow, he figured out how to lace my mane through a whip and caught me during the next full moon. He killed all our horses that same night. It's a good thing he managed to wipe himself out in a car accident, or I would have killed him the next time we met."

"You're lucky he didn't decide to garrote you," Lyris said, appalled.

"The thought occurred to me at the time. Anyhow, you can stop being nervous. I'm fine. And I don't let myself change at the full moon anymore, so it'll never happen again." He shot her a glance. "Smile, damn it. You're looking worried again, and it ruins my appetite."

"Sorry. I guess I'm just a little stressed out still."

Roman nodded. "I know. But I'll tell you if I feel anything changing. Now or at the full moon, okay?"

"Okay."

"So . . . when were you thinking about telling me that I'm going to be a father?"

Lyris stared at Roman in shock. "How did you—"

"I think some of your true sight rubs off on me when we make love. I'm getting better at reading you. You are pregnant, aren't you?"

"I suspect so. But I shouldn't be." Then with bafflement: "You know that feys don't conceive without magical intervention. It's why I've never bothered with the pill. Maybe I'm hallucinating. It's hysterical pregnancy. That could be it."

"But magic did intervene that first night, didn't it?"

"Yes. And the next night, and the next night."

Roman grinned. "It's great, isn't it? What a rush!"

It had been a rush, but Roman hadn't touched her since Quede had bitten him. And he wouldn't, not until after the full moon came and they saw if it changed him.

"I guess it's great." She threw up her hands and said a bit helplessly, "I never planned on having kids, though. What do I know about being a mom?"

"Hey, I didn't plan it either. Never planned on getting married for that matter. But I'm happy about this. And we'll figure it out somehow."

Lyris turned her eyes on him and looked for the truth. She saw some concern, a lot of happiness . . . but most importantly, love.

"You're still not real trusting, are you?" Roman asked. "I wouldn't lie to you."

"Sorry," she said again. "It's just habit. And we can stop in the next town and get some lunch."

"Wait! You can see when I'm hungry? You actually feel what I feel? I mean, when we're not making love?" He sounded awed.

Lyris shook her head. "Not everything is mystical, you know. It's just been four hours since your last meal. You must be starving."

"Oh." He sounded a little disappointed for a moment, but then added more cheerfully, "I bet we can get buffalo chili and fries out here."

"You do and you eat alone," Lyris warned him.

"Come on, honey. You gotta learn to try new things."

"Take it up with your son," she answered back. "He's the one being difficult about things."

"My son?" Roman smiled again.

"Yes, I'm pretty sure."

"Well, that's okay then. We'll have plenty of time to eat Tex-Mex later." Roman reached over and squeezed her thigh. He gave her another happy smile.

Lyris smiled back, and willing her words to be true, she said, "Yes, we have plenty of time. All the time in this world."

Who's Who In Goblin Town—the Good, the Bad and the Ugly

The Good:

Jack Frost—	death fey, the leader of the surviving magical peoples
Io Cyphre—	siren fey, Jack's wife
Thomas Marrowbone—	half-dragon, half-wizard; a computer hacker
Cyra Delphin—	half-selkie, half-kloka (conjurer elf); Thomas's wife
Zayn—	love-talker fey; former employee of Humans Under Ground
Chloe—	Zayn's wife; human; sister of the leader of H.U.G.

Romeo Hart—	half-pooka; a friend of Jack Frost's
Lyris Damsel—	half-sylph; JFK conspiracy-theorist

The Bad:

Horroban—	goblin king of Detroit hive
Lilith—	goblin queen of Las Vegas hive
King Quede—	vampiric goblin; king of New Orleans hive
Father Lobineau—	renegade goblin priest

The Ugly:

Goblins/lutins—	six-limbed creatures living in hives, sworn enemy of mankind
Trolls—	large stupid creatures used as hired muscle by goblins
Hobgoblins—	larger, fiercer, smarter goblins imprisoned deep in the earth or inside trees; whom even other goblins fear
Gargoyles—	monsters made of living stone that will eat any living thing

Imps— pests and gargoyle food, often mistaken for gremlins

Author's Note

As ever with this series, I must begin with an apology to the city I have populated with goblins. I adore New Orleans. It is unfortunate that the goblins love it too.

This cycle of goblin stories has been an adventure to write—fun, exciting, nightmare-inducing at times. I suspect that my publisher has had nightmares over these books too. I give credit to my editor for not blanching the first time he heard the words goblin and romance put together. He was, after all, the one who had to go to marketing and explain why this series was a good idea. If anyone else blanched at that meeting, I wasn't told about it, and everyone at Dorchester has been heroic about getting these books to market in very short order. I owe them bottles of champagne and millions of calories in chocolate.

I want to say thank you to my readers as well, both those who have taken the time to write and those who appreciated in silence but showed their support by following the series. The pleasure of your company on these adventures is always deeply appreciated. I am taking a short break from the goblins for another project, but please do come visit us at either *www.melaniejackson.com* or at *www.lutinempire.com* and let me know your thoughts. And for those who prefer dead tree mail, I can be reached at P.O. Box 4792, Sonora, CA 95370.

Merry we meet. Merry we part. Merry we meet again.

Melanie Jackson

AN INTERVIEW WITH MELANIE JACKSON BY CHRISTINE FEEHAN

MELANIE: Christine! Thanks for coming. Can I get you anything? Coffee, tea, lemon water?

CHRISTINE: *We'd better save the lemon water for later. We don't want this interview getting out of hand. You know the reputation I have for drinking that stuff!*

MELANIE: I've witnessed this phenomenon firsthand. Speaking of hands: You've been busy—about typed those fingers to the bone. Will we see some new Carpathians soon?

CHRISTINE: *Yes, I'm working on a new novel and I'm very excited about it, but I really wanted to talk about your world. It's such a crossover of horror and romance, very unique and intriguing. I can't get enough of it. Please tell me you've been working on another Goblin book?*

MELANIE: Yes, **STILL LIFE (with Goblins)**. It's definitely another crossover novel. In fact it *crosses* a bit more than usual.

CHRISTINE: *This is the fourth book in the series? By now do you know everything there is to know about your Goblin world or are you still surprised by what happens in your stories?*

MELANIE: The general outlines of the world are in place, since the project was conceived as a series with more details being revealed in each book. But there are always surprises. All one can do is be flexible and let the characters' true natures come through when and how they may.

CHRISTINE: *I love that about your books. I do the same with my Carpathian world. Are the Goblins really the bad guys in your world, or are they an oppressed minority with a legitimate axe to grind? In other words: Are the Goblins monsters, or are they simply a race with bad leadership?*

MELANIE: They are both good and evil, just like humans. The difference is that Goblin leaders are universally evil and cruel to their own people, while human tyrants are fortunately scarcer.

The Goblin citizens are another matter. They are—the good and the bad alike—an oppressed people. Their ancestors were kicked out of Europe and forced to migrate to the Americas. Once here, rather than being embraced and made part of our society, they were ghettoized and denied a chance to participate in human culture. As has happened with human minority groups, they developed coping mechanisms and found a way to survive. And once they had power and wealth, the Goblins were expelled from their new homes and driven into other less desirable places. Only the ruthless survived. It isn't surprising that they developed a regime of control that more closely resembles the Mafia than any representative government. Of course, some Goblins are pragmatic about this; some are bitter.

CHRISTINE: *I often incorporate today's issues in my books to make the paranormal elements seem more real and to heighten awareness of very important issues in today's society. George Orwell wrote* Animal Farm *as a commentary on the rise of communism in Russia. Are there elements of your stories like this? I ask because I see parallels with the current strife in the Middle East and race relations.*

MELANIE: That's very perceptive of you. Afghanistan and Iraq—and domestic terrorism—have rather been on my mind while writing these stories. And not just because of the Goblin villains. My heroes and heroines are also part fey, another minority that are only reluctantly given a place at the American table. They work hard to save their adopted country and are never thanked for it because the general population has no idea of their service and bravery.

CHRISTINE: *How does Goblin society integrate with human societies? What have been the significant Goblin contributions, and have these contributions been lauded and cherished by Man?*

MELANIE: They sure didn't integrate in France, and as the Goblin Wars got bigger, it ended up spilling over into the rest of Europe. Finally they were expelled in a series of pogroms. Someday, I would love to tell this story. I haven't mentioned doing a Goblin *War & Peace* to my editor yet. I might.

CHRISTINE: *My Carpathian world is very real to me. When you're creating a fantasy world, do you ever envision yourself living in that world? If so, what do you see as your place in it?*

MELANIE: Like you, I have to see myself there. I don't think that I would be able to write convincingly about any situation I couldn't place myself in mentally. And I get to be everyone—super-cool heroines, magically powerful heroes, black-hearted villains, and terrorized Lutins.

Christine: *What is life in a Goblin hive like? Are Goblins mindless drones or do they have dreams and ambitions? What do Goblins do for fun? What would be a typical day in the life of a lowly Goblin?*

Melanie: You can catch a glimpse of Goblin life at www.lutinempire.com if you are feeling intrepid. Goblins—some of them—*do* have dreams and ambitions. That is why Orel in **OUTSIDERS** so endeared himself to me. He was a Goblin, but he was also a teenage boy who loved motorcycles and was shy about introducing himself to a pretty human girl. However, not all Goblins are as fortunate as the ones who lived and worked in Sin City. Those of you who have just read **THE COURIER** will know that life was very hard for the genetically altered Lutins in New Orleans. And the Lutins in **TRAVELER** were forced into the life of a worker-drone in an insect hive.

Christine: *I have to say I think your Lutin website is one of the cleverest websites I've ever encountered. From the first time I knew of its existence, I was eager to go explore. But what about H.U.G.? How is Humans Under Ground structured? How do they get their recruits? Do they ever receive support from legitimate governments, or must they always function in secrecy?*

Melanie: Thank you. Much of the credit for this website goes to my husband the technical wizard. And we have discussed the possibility of H.U.G. setting up its own website so they can recruit readers to the cause.

In the beginning, H.U.G. worked a bit like Greenpeace—or maybe Earth First, or P.E.T.A. They started off content to spy on the enemy, try peaceful interventions and to raise public awareness. But their efforts were met with ridicule, and as the Goblins escalated in violence so, too, did H.U.G. become more draconian in its methods for dealing with the enemy. Frankly, I find some of the leaders of H.U.G. to be as terrifying as the Goblins.

Christine: *Many fantasy worlds are post-apocalyptic, painting an ominous picture of the future. Do you feel that your alternate reality, which includes Goblins, is a better world in which you'd like to live? Do you ever see the Goblins and Man living together in peace? What would need to happen for peace to be achieved?*

Melanie: As the saying goes: It's a swell place to visit but I wouldn't want to live there . . . This world—like most fantasy worlds—has the defects of its virtues and the other way around. I would love a world where the fey had survived and where magic could be used by the citizenry to right horrible wrongs. However, things look pretty grim for the humans right now—and will continue to be desperate until one of three things happen: the Goblins are wiped out, the humans are wiped out, or the two races make peace. I'm holding out for peace, but I don't know if the Goblins are going to be reasonable. The humans aren't doing their part either.

Christine: *The **WILDSIDE** books include romance, tight plotting, action, and adventure. How do you balance these elements in your stories to weave them all together? What are the most important story elements to you, the most fun to write, and what do you try to achieve with each element?*

Melanie: I think a great story needs all these elements, but the balance is different in each book. **TRAVELER** was a pretty even mix. **OUTSIDERS** was more of an emotional story, both because of the hero and heroine's inner quest, but also because it introduced the theme of Goblin humanity. **THE COURIER** is weighted slightly toward action and adventure.

Christine: *Your Goblin stories are quite unique; however, are there other authors who have influenced your ideas or writing style in this series?*

Melanie: Of course! And it's a mixed bag. The whole idea of the Goblin fruit being used to enslave people comes from Christina Rossetti's magnificent erotic poem "The Goblin Market." But the stories are also a blend of styles from the fast-paced adventure novels by authors like Alistair MacLean and Desmond Bagley. And, of course, I am grateful to writers like you and Laurell K. Hamilton who have opened the minds of romance readers to series that incorporate magic, action, and darker kinds of romance. You have prepared readers for books that cross genres.

Christine: *Who is your favorite character in your **WILDSIDE** series and why?*

Melanie: Well if you promise not to tell the others: Jack Frost. Jack is a unique mix of characteristics—a reluctant leader, compassionate yet still willing to do the hard thing, and his mind is still a bit of an enigma to me. I may spend the rest of my life trying to understand him. What about you? Do you have a favorite? I know that, of your Carpathians, Gregori is still my favorite.

CHRISTINE: *Hey! Who's getting interviewed here? All right, I'll admit I have a thing for Jack Frost myself. What is your favorite scene in your Goblin series and why?*

MELANIE: Now you're getting tough. I have a few. One of them has to be the fight at the end of **OUTSIDERS** where Thomas's dragon finally gets his own body and the hero and heroine have to confront what they have done by loosing this dragon on the world. I also like the moment in **THE COURIER** when Roman and Lyris meet the Christian Goblin leader, Father Lobineau.

CHRISTINE: *One of your Goblin books,* ***OUTSIDERS****, included a Selkie, a fantasy creature that was dominant in your book* ***THE SELKIE****. How much crossover is there between all your fantasy worlds—is it possible that all of your fantastical characters spring from a common pool of magic?*

MELANIE: All my creatures come out of the same mystical pool: the one the ancient Celts and Norse spent time gazing in. That is always the starting place for me—the "reality" I apply to my worlds. Obviously, the magical beasties get contemporized to our industrial world, but the rules of their powers and their universe are the ones that our ancestors knew, and I suspect that if I had the chance to travel back in time and take my place by the tribal fire, I could tell these stories and they would be understood.

CHRISTINE: *Our time has run out. I hope our readers enjoyed this brief glimpse into the world-building of the* ***WILDSIDE****, and I invite them to join us for a live tea as I grill—I mean interview—Melanie. The taped interview can be seen by visiting www.christinefeehan.com in my members-only section or by going to Melanie's website www.melaniejackson.com. Please also feel free to look around the Lutin website www.lutinempire.com—but be very careful; you never know what you'll find. I had a great time, Melanie. Thank you so much for all the information.*

MELANIE: You are welcome, and I am so glad that you could take the time to come for tea and grilling . . . Would you like that lemon water now?